DEATH
BY MURDER AT SEA

RAYMOND BELL

DEATH
BY MURDER AT SEA

READERSMAGNET, LLC

Death By Murder At Sea
Copyright © 2017 by Raymond Bell

Published in the United States of America
ISBN Paperback: 978-1-947765-43-6
ISBN eBook: 978-1-947765-44-3

All rights reserved. No part of this publication may be reproduced, stored in a retrieval system or transmitted in any way by any means, electronic, mechanical, photocopy, recording or otherwise without the prior permission of the author except as provided by USA copyright law.

No lines, parts and quotations was taken from other books or any previous publications.

The opinions expressed by the author are not necessarily those of ReadersMagnet, LLC.

ReadersMagnet, LLC
80 Broad Street, 5th & 6th Floors Finance District | New York City, NY 10004 USA
1.646. 880. 9760 | www.readersmagnet.com

Book design copyright © 2017 by ReadersMagnet, LLC. All rights reserved.
Cover design by Ericka Walker
Interior design by Shieldon Watson

Chapter One

I Found myself sitting in a booth near the back of one of my favorite watering holes; no not booze. I was drinking a Coca-Cola. There was a slice of pepperoni pizza on a plate in front of me. I put the glass of Coca-Cola down, picked up my paperback Louis L'Amour book, The Sackett brothers were meeting up after the Civil war. I had the book in my right hand my left hand had the book. Without thinking, I took a big bite out of the pepperoni pizza. My eyes water and I almost yelled a profanity as the extremely hot pizza burned my tongue and was burning my throat. I tried to spit it out, but it was too late. My mouth and my throat were on fire. Tears were running down my cheeks as I sucked the ice out of my glass. I had my head tilted as I tried to let the ice rest at the back of my mouth.

It had been over ten years since I'd been in the City by the Bay. I never thought I would be back, at least not in my old cracker Jack suit. They were two weeks old Navy Dress Blues. The blues were issued to me as I processed through the San Diego Recruit Center. I am not new to the Navy. I spent two weeks in San Diego processing and re-learning the military and, in particular, the Navy.

While my tongue and throat cooled, I looked up to watch some pimply faced girl spin pizza dough near the picture window in the front of the restaurant. Ten years it would have been some skinny teenage guy wearing the same white tomato stained apron and the same sweat-stained white paper hat. Most nights the kid in the window looked as if he needed to run a razor across the few whiskers trying to grow on his face.

While staring out the picture window in front the girl spinning the pizza dough, I noticed a dream with fiery red hair. She was wearing a cloth coat, with a fur collar. I could see a wrap around, green and yellow plaid skirt peeking out from under the jacket. The skirt barely reaches her knees. I couldn't see her shoes, but I bet that she was wearing flats.

I took another sip of my Coca-Cola and continued to read my paperback. I dared to pick up my slice of pizza and looked toward the window. It seems my fiery red-head had vanished. I sensed more than saw someone standing next to me. When I looked up, I saw the most stunning green eyes. Eyes that put me in mind of something painted by Keen.

What I hadn't noticed was a giant blond gorilla standing next to her. The gorilla's blond hair was cut short, the sides of the gorilla's unnaturally large head were all but shaved. The gorilla speaks, "Hey Morag, look at this kid dressed in a sailor suit."

Right, I am small, but I haven't considered myself a kid for quite some time now. The first time joining the Navy the recruiter made me eat ten pounds of bananas before he took me in for my physical.

The gorilla put both his hairy ham hocks on the table. With a growl more than a voice, the gorilla says, "OK, squid. You can get out of our booth."

I proceeded to scoot out of the booth, reaching to grab my peacoat when the gorilla reaches down and smacks the back of my head I saw stars. I reached for my coke and the slice of pizza when the gorilla grabs the front of my Navy jumper and pulls me out of the booth. This time he open hand smacks me in the face. I saw my glass of coke hit the floor. The glass shattered, and the coke splashed over my highly glossed shoes. The fiery red-head put her hand out to help me out of the booth when the gorilla backhanded her across her face.

I tried. I really did, but that was it. This was not the first time I had to put up with a bully. I really thought I could walk away. I mean there are only a few things that are worth fighting over. That last bite of pizza would not go down, my heart was pounding like it was about to beat out of my chest. There was a ringing in my ears that just seemed to be getting louder. Then suddenly, I felt calm. As I stood, I looked at that angelic face with a sprinkling of freckles across her small turned up nose and then a big purple handprint across her cheek.

I heard the woman scream, "Russel!"

He turned to her, then turned and glared at me. His eyes were blue, although I couldn't be sure because they were blood-shot. I did notice as he was glaring at me that the pupils of his eyes were dilated, or at least one of them was.

The woman yelled again, only louder. The gorilla telegraphed a move. It was just a split second, he closed his fist, and there was no doubt in my mind that he was going to hit the woman. I dropped to a squat, kicked out with my right leg and heard a squish. I intended to come up and kick him in the crotch. I missed the groin, and my foot landed right on his kneecap.

It looked to me like he was genuflecting as he went down on one knee. I think I really pissed him off. Coming off his knee, I could see that this man's ruddy complexion was turning purple. In less than a blink, and with all the strength I could muster I put my fist on his jaw. He swatted my fist away as if he were swatting at a mosquito. His head did not move.

He swung at me with a closed fist, I ducked. As I rose, I came up with an open hand and caught him under his nose. This time I could feel the cartilage in his nose crunch. Blood did not drip but gushed out of his nose. Although blood was coming over his chin, he did not seem to notice. Now he was mad. He came at me like a rabid dog. He was swinging wildly. He connected to my chin. I saw stars, then blackness. I blinked several times as I watched the floor coming up at me.

My head felt like a spinning top. Somehow, I managed to turn out of my fall, regain my balance if only briefly, but enough to come up and catch the gorilla once again under his nose. He did not go out. Wiping my eyes, I looked back to see him sitting cross-legged on the floor with a finger under his nose.

Fantastic, I was standing. I felt my heart drop, as I thought for sure that the cops had been called. Looking around the restaurant, I could see a few people looking my way. A dark-complexed skinny man with a protruding Adam's apple wearing a white shirt and a skinny tie was heading my way.

The red-headed woman grabbed my hand and reached down with a warm, soft hand, and without any sign of emotion stepped over the gorilla and led me towards the door. I could feel the sting of cold air as the woman pushed me through the door. A few doors down from the restaurant we stopped. I had trouble catching my breath. Every time I tried to take a deep breath it hurt. The redheaded woman was still holding my hand. I pulled my hand away put my hands on my knees and bent over. I felt I needed to cough, but when I did my chest felt as if someone had placed a sharp break inside my chest. I coughed up a little pinkish sputum.

Standing up the redheaded woman placed the back of her hand on my forehead and asked, "Do Ya want to go to the hospital?"

"No, I'm starting to feel better already. By the way, me name is Connor, Connor Fitzgerald."

With a smile, that should have stopped my heart. The redheaded girl said, "Aye, Connor and my name are Morag, Morag Frasier. I am so sorry. I've only known Russel for a few weeks, but he has always been a gentleman. He was not the man I met a few weeks ago."

The fog had turned to ice crystals, but I did not notice. All I saw was this angel in front of me.

Morag looked down at me with those large round green eyes, reminding me once again of the artist Keen, and said:

"Dè a t-ainm a th'ort?"

There for a few seconds, it felt as if I had cobwebs in my brain. The woman was speaking, but the words were gibberish. I stopped and stared at this woman, "What?" I looked down and then back into the restaurant, my peacoat was back in the restaurant. I grabbed Morag by her shoulder, and said, "My peacoat is missing, I left it in the booth." I started to head back into the restaurant.

The woman held up a small white clutch in her left hand. I then noticed that she had my peacoat draped over her right arm.

"You are a lifesaver. I thought there for a minute I'd have to go back in and retrieve my coat."

The woman just gave me a look. I don't know if she was going to ask my name again or was wondering if I would go back in the restaurant. Looking down at a torn jumper, and severely stained uniform trousers, I needed that coat just to get past the shore patrol. The first thing the Navy Cops would do is assume I had been fighting and escort me back to my ship. Which of course I had been, but I don't need something like a bar fight getting on my record. Even though it really wasn't a bar fight.

"Tha mi duilich! she said, "Sorry I told you my name, now what's your name? "Oh, besides your coat I also have your book."

For an Irishman, I was suddenly at a loss for words; the Irish always have some blarney. I also told you my name, "I'm Connor." I was having trouble, and couldn't stop staring at this woman; not only her fiery red hair. Even her cream-colored jacket, looking at her perfectly formed legs and down at her feet, and she was wearing flats.

I was thinking; I must have a concussion, I saw an apparition. I suppose I was staring at this woman with my mouth open. "Am I waking?" I struggled into my coat.

"Aye, that you are. And I just asked your name. I think that I slipped into Gallic."

With her hand in mine, she quick-stepped down the sidewalk. Still, a little out of breath I queried, more to myself than to Morag, "That guy just wouldn't go down. He was brushing my punches away like he was swatting mosquitoes."

Morag turned toward me and looked down. She stated bluntly, "Aye, Connor You're right. He was a real pig. His name is Russell. I'm not sure, but I think his last name is Cole. I met him a few weeks ago and believed he was the nicest man I'd met since coming to America. Like I said he was a real gentleman. I don't know what happened. It's like he's somebody else. Tha mi duilich! I said I'm so very sorry. By the way, thank you." The girl with the brogue looked down at me, "You're a mess, Connor Fitzgerald. Are you, all, right? If ya hadn't noticed I'm a Scot, and yes, we do speak English, but most the people in the small village I come from are not all that fond of the English."

She started to turn away, stopped, and turned back towards me. I replied, "Thank you for reminding me, but I think most of the damage is to my uniform. My head still hurts where he slapped me. Talk about being emasculated and with an opened hand slap to the back of my head? Believe me, my grandmother's slap was harder than that." My head was still spinning. "Can you get home, all, right? Need me to get you a cab?"

"It's only a couple of blocks." Morag turned back towards me, and with those green saucers opened wide, asked, "Connor, please don't be offended, but you are not all that big."

"Believe me. I look at myself in the mirror every day; sometimes more than once. I am aware that I am height challenged."

"How were you able to put him down?"

"Ya know I am a little guy. Well, this little guy got tired of being bullied." I started to turn away.

Morag stopped. "OK, Irish. Finish what you began to say?"

Now looking at my scuffed shoes, I replied. "Let's just say that I spent a lot of time learning how to take down big guys. The truth is, it is not the big guys that usually pick on me." Pointing back at the restaurant "What about our friend in there? Think he'll be mad enough to go to your place?"

"Never invited him up to my flat. So, he doesn't know where I live. Besides my neighbor is a cop."

"Could I get your phone number? You called me Irish. How did you know?"

"First, I have yet to see a Brit with a ruddy complexion, plus, your first name is a giveaway."

"I would give you my phone number if I had one, but I'm a nurse at San Francisco General. Just ask for Nurse Morag Frasier. Besides the fat lip and bruised face, does anything else hurt?"

"Fat lip? That's why I'm having trouble talking. I wish I could say yes. Then maybe you'd invite me up to your place?" I buttoned my peacoat, and replied, "Well, it was worth a try. Being a nurse and all why don't you have to have a phone?"

"My neighbor is a cop. Tom or his wife take those calls for me." once again she started up Eddie Street, and turned back toward me. "Sorry, but if you are hurt, I'll take you to the hospital. You gave me your name, and I'm sure there are not that many Connor Fitzgerald's in the Navy but are you on a ship, or at Hunters Point?"

"Yes, I'm on the Isaiah Dove. I was taught that aircraft carriers were named after battles, then I was told that aircraft carriers were named after states. Seems like now a politician can get his name on anything. We are at Hunter's point, but our home is Alameda."

I watched as she walked away. Even for a small girl, she might have been just slightly taller than me; she walked with confidence. The air was still, and the fog was thickening. What I saw was her turning up Eddie Street, the mist was dispersing. Most women bounce a little as they walk; Morag walked with no bounce. It was like she was walking on a cloud.

Shit! It is a good thing I am wearing my peacoat. Opening my coat and looking down at my Navy jumper I couldn't imagine a way I could patch, sew, or restore this jumper. The only thing I could do was to go the ship's store in the morning and buy a new set of dress blues. Of course, with me being height challenged, I'll have to have the storekeeper order my dress blues. In the meantime, I guess I'll be staying aboard.

OK, so I'm barely five-four, and on a good day I might weigh one-thirty, and the gorilla was, let's just say big, I should have at least caused some pain. I did draw blood, but this guy seemed to be numb to pain. Oh, hell, I gots to get back to the ship. Cole may not have felt pain, but I felt pain in places on my body that didn't know I had.

Even opening my eyes was painful. I might be able to understand this pain behind my eyes if I had been drinking, but I haven't had anything intoxicating in several years. My head itched, and my vision was blurred. As my vision cleared, I sat up and looked around. What I saw was crowded with pipes, valves, ventilation ducts, cable runs, electrical junction boxes, and rows of racks, civilians mighty refer to these shelves we sleep in as bunks. There was definitely no place to hang a favorite photograph whether a girlfriend a wife or both. If such an empty spot had existed, some naval engineer would undoubtedly have found a way to shoehorn in a fiber optic relay terminal or a casualty power transformer. I had to think, '*What day is this? Where am I?*

I'm aboard ship." I was finally able to focus, and looking at my watch it felt as if my heart stop. '*I'm late for formation.*' I am never late for muster. Call to Colors is at zero-eight-hundred hours The Division gathers in some semblance of order. Lining up one next to another and at the word Fall-in we come to attention. Most days the first-class petty officer shouts out, "All present and or accounted for."

I heard the Master at Arms banging on our ladderwell with his baton. Also, heard him call out grab your socks. I even listened to my shipmates getting dressed. I heard the last of my shipmates scrambling up the ladderwell. Silence, nothing but silence. I was out of my rack with my shirt on, and buttoned, I was on my butt on our Navy issue couch with one leg in the leg of my pants. Petty Officer Baily, my supervisor was standing over me.

"Fitzgerald, I had to report to the chief that Damage Controlman Second Class Connor Fitzgerald was not present for our little gathering." Baily was leaning against my personal locker. Looking down at the clipboard in his hand. "I have already given out the assignments for the day."

I was hopping around on one foot trying to get my boots on when Baily came up to about an inch in front of my face and told me I was to inspect all the fire extinguishers aboard ship.

I tried catching up with Baily. My muscles, every joint in my body, a few I didn't know I had, refused to allow me to run. Baily, was my supervisor, even though he was still scraping his knees on the playground when I was serving my first tour aboard ship. When I caught up with Baily at the ladderwell, the half staircase and half ladder. I yelled, which is not a way to impress a person's supervisor. When I caught up with Baily at the ladderwell, the half staircase and half ladder. I mentioned, "Baily!" He turned and stared at me.

I lowered my voice, "Baily, this ship is over 1,050 feet long, it displaces 80, 000 tons of water. We have over 6,000 men aboard, there are more compartments, and decks on this ship than the floors of the Sears Tower. All living spaces and workspaces are supposed to have a fire extinguisher. I can't check all the fire extinguishers by myself." I scratch the back of my neck. "Isn't that why we have people from every division on the ship to work with us. Can't they inspect their own fire extinguishers?

Ducking his head to avoid a wrapped steam line that crossed just above the stairwell into our living birthing area, turning, and staring at me, Baily commented, "What the hell happened to you? It looks to me like you got hit by a freight train."

Baily took a breath and let it out slowly. The sounds of the generators, the power tools on the hanger deck made it difficult for me to hear. Lighting one of his Camel cigarettes, Baily commented, "What is wrong with you? You know the Lieutenant, and you know the chief. I don't ever remember you being this late before. What did you get so drunk on your day off, and you forgot about coming back to the ship?"

"No, I did not get drunk. I was sitting at a table near the back of the restaurant when some marine, at least I think he was a sea-going bell hop picked a fight with me. I was aboard ship early, but I had a problem climbing out of my rack this morning."

Shaking his head, reminding me of my dog trying to get water out of his ears, "I don't know why, but get yourself down to sickbay. Make sure nothing broken. It looks like a handprint a large hand print on your left cheek, and that right eye. It's swollen. You know an excellent leadership sign is to delegate. You can use the people you trained. I don't care. What I do care about is having all that paperwork checked off and signed by close of business.

While you're getting yourself patched up, I'll put Chambers and Reynolds on the fire extinguishers. Report to me when you get back. I swear if it was anyone else... If the Doc lets you come back on duty, report to the CBR room. You can help me inventory chemical suits and masks today."

"Thanks, boss. Think I could stop by the ship's store. My dress blues are beyond repair "Don't push your luck.

Now get down to sickbay."

"Don't push it, Fitzgerald."

My job is so exciting that it gives me the opportunity of climbing up and down ladders. Tripping over coams, or the lips at the bottom of a watertight door, or hatch. I must not forget that even for a short guy like me that if I don't duck the lip at the top of that same watertight door will leave a mark on my forehead. I go from one frame to the next checking for damage. The bottom lip of the hatch was to prevent water from getting from one frame to the next It is also very convenient like I mentioned in damaging one's shins. I've often pondered how a bigger man avoids cracking his shins, or for that matter cracking his skull on the upper portion of the lip. We are also the ones that lead the firefighting parties. Hell, we even fight fires on the flight deck from the second deck, which is below the hangar deck.

A lot of people are under the impression that I am creative, and I build things. No, my job is to train people on how to patch things. Building with wood is for our ships carpenter. Fixing an electrical fixture, or changing a light bulb is for our Interior electricians, they also run the projector for our movies and make sure Skipper's speaker systems are working. We even have plumbers, but our plumbing system is simple it operates by gravity, except for the showers and toilets below the waterline. Now submariners have a problem, if they don't turn the right valve, the toilets will flush up instead of down. As Damage Controlmen we do everything in our power to make sure the ship floats.

It was still early. There was a line at sickbay, not long maybe six in front of me. The corpsman looked up from the roster and pointed than waved. I started to wave back. I dropped my hand when I realized that the corpsman was motioning me to advance to the podium. I got dirty looks from a few of the professional goldbrickers standing in line;

those men whose sole desire was to spend their Navy career in sickbay.

"You," said the corpsman. "What the hell happened to you?"

"Ah, would you believe I got jumped last night?"

Scratching his left ear, "Here aboard ship?"

"Naw. I was downtown San Francisco. At first, I thought I was run over by a truck until I saw this nine-foot gorilla walking away."

The corpsman looked at me and started feeling me up, touching everything, starting from my head to my feet when I said, "Think maybe an x-ray will answer your questions?" He nodded. "How about your head? you got a headache?"

"I just told you I am still looking for the truck that hit me. Yes, my head hurts, but no more than a hangover; that is when I used to get hangovers."

"You don't drink?"

"Nothing stronger than a Coca-Cola."

I saw the Doc. Doc just started feeling me up. Put his finger on my eyelid, pulled it up took out his dependable pen-light, shining the light in both eyes. A headache wasn't all that bad until he started shining his penlight in my eyes.

The verdict is; there are no broken ribs, I guess since I wasn't hallucinating the Doc decided that I did not have a concussion. The senior corpsman gave me an official-looking memo, or what is called a chit. So, I had the rest of the day off.

Ship Serviceman First Class Modesto has been behind the counter every time I've come down to our Small Store, (where we could buy clothing). I made a mistake the first time we met; I called him a Filipino. He corrected me, "No my little ruddy Irish friend; I am from Mindanao." The last I heard Mindanao was part of the Philippines. I guess He has accepted me. He shares some of the food that his wife sends.

A bony Filipino hand reached across the counter, and squeezed my hand, "OK my friend, more socks?"

"No, I need a set of dress blues."

Just then I sensed the heat of a body behind me. I turned, and my heart stopped. It was the blond gorilla. I didn't say a word. I felt those baby-blues boring into me, then after a few seconds, the Marine turned to Modesto. "Hey, Modesto you got my shoes in yet?" Not only was I height challenged, but so were my feet.

Modesto answered, "No my friend. I don't think they have been able to find enough elves to make them."

My heart stopped; who would believe that this blonde gorilla was a Marine aboard **my** ship. I stepped back, and looked down at his boots; I honestly don't think I have ever seen a foot that big.

The gorilla looked at me, and said, "I'm sorry. To be honest, I didn't see you."

Modesto looked up at me then at the Marine, then staring at me again and shrugging his shoulders. Commenting, "Ya know Fitzgerald, I think Cole here would be better off just wearing the boxes the shoes come in."

I noticed that my nemesis plopped down in the closest folding chair.

Modesto came around the counter putting his arm under Cole's armpits and helped him sit up in the folding metal chair. "Cole, What's, happening?"

"Ernie, I don't know. I woke this morning, and my nose was bleeding. Couldn't get it to stop."

Ernie Modesto looked over at me. "Fitzgerald, you still wearing 29, 29?"

I couldn't help staring at Cole. I left him at the restaurant; he was sitting on the floor with a nosebleed.

I looked up at Modesto, "Hey, Ernie, You're good. I think I did have a 29-inch waist the first time I came down here. Fraid I put on a couple of pounds, and I'm sure I grew an inch wider. Too bad I can't get that inch in height."

"Yes, sir. That's my job."

I looked up and then down. "You are still good." I looked back down at Cole. Cole's eyes closed his breathing was shallow. I looked again, and blood was flowing out of his nose.

Ernie had his back to me looking for something on the shelves. I yelled, "Ernie, there is something wrong with this Marine."

Modesto must have noticed too, "Cole, what's wrong with your nose?"

"Modesto, I don't know. There was blood on my pillow; not a little blood, but a lot. It feels like I have a whole roll of toilet paper up my nostrils. If I keep this wad up my nose, it won't flow."

"I was about to have you come around the counter and try these blues on, but I think we need to wake this Marine and get him to sickbay."

I thought this is the guy that beat the shit out of me, tore my perfectly serviceable uniform. I took a long look at him. This Marine was without color. His breathing was slow; I mean I didn't think he was breathing. I looked over at Modesto, and said, "Ernie, can you get the corpsmen down here. This man is in trouble."

"That would be great. How's that nose?"

I couldn't help but think that the only damage I did to this guy was to give him a bloody nose. Looking down at him, sitting on the deck with his legs sprawled out in front and his head resting on his chest I could see blisters on his lips, and under his profusely bleeding nose.

Cole started to move; leaning forward and putting his hands on the deck. Coles' knees seemed to wobble. He took a few steps, staggered as if he was about to fall. I was thinking, please don't fall there is no way I can't pick you up. What I said was, "Woo. Cole, are you, aw-right?"

Stopping, he turned and put his arm out. He grabbed my shoulder. It was like a repeat of the night before. Only this time there was no malice. "Listen, Fitzgerald. I don't know what's wrong. Suddenly I'm getting dizzy. I mean real shaky. Cole took a deep breath and removed his hand from my bruised shoulder.

Modesto came around the counter and said "I'm sorry bout that. There's like a sewing room off the extraction room. See Kalama. He's a Samoan. He is also a good tailor. The Samoan can patch your blues, even make them look new. You'll find him down in the laundry."

Cole stood, and turned to look at me, and his legs seemed to be turning to rubber. It appeared he was getting ready to do squats when he fell flat on his face. I turned just as the corpsmen arrived.

The noise down in the laundry was deafening. There were men in tee shirts pressing clothes on the big presses. There was something about those brass globes at the head of each of those steam presses. I just had to touch that large brass globe. I won't do that again. A couple of the laundrymen just stared at me as I pulled my hand back from the brass ball. I wanted to scream, but I took a deep breath and put my burnt hand down by my side like nothing happened.

Burnt flesh has a unique smell. Some people describe it as the smell of charred lamb.

The sewing machine appeared dwarfed by a sizeable tanned man looking more like a powerlifter than a tailor. I was licking my burned fingers when the big man turned the sewing machine off and turned to look at me. I assumed that the brief lull in the sound of the sewing machine was an appropriate time to introduce myself. I said, "I'm Damage Controlman Second Class Fitzgerald." He, the large, shaved head, Islander at the sewing machine just stared at me. The big man then pulled earplugs out of his ears.

Looking as if there were a big question mark on my face, he said, "Sorry were you talking to me?"

"Yeah, I'm Damage Controlman Second Class Fitzgerald. Ernie Modesto down in the ship's clothing store thought you might be able to help me." I took the folded dress blues that I had tucked under my arm, open the blouse and showed him my torn dress blue jumper."

"By the way, I'm Ship Serviceman Third Class Aleki Kalama. Everybody, including the old man, calls me Al., I can have this blouse looking like new. Be ready tomorrow morning." Al threw the shirt he was working on in the pile of shirts on is right. Turned the sewing machine back on, looking over his shoulder he said, "What's your first name, bruder?"

"It's Connor."

"OK, Connor come back down here after morning formation. See ya."

I looked up to see a Marine officer. Not the tallest of men, but he still possessed an *intimidating presence. On each shirt collar, he had a silver bar. Above his right pocket, there were two rows of ribbons; what I refer to as fruit salad.

He looked back at me and then at the large Islander. Pointing at me, he demanded "**Who** is this?" he did not take his stare away from me.

The Islander answered, "This is Petty Officer Fitzgerald."

The Lieutenant turned toward the Islander and reiterated, "Kalama, you flat-headed Samoan." Pointing with his index finger at me, "What is he doing here?"

With a little tremor to his voice, the big Samoan replied, "This is Damage Controlman, Connor Fitzgerald. I volunteered to patch his uniform."

The Marine Lieutenant responded, "Fitzgerald, Kalama, as you were. Kalama, I need you to find me in an hour." The Lieutenant turned abruptly and walked out.

Kalama got up from behind the sewing machine, walked to the entrance of his makeshift tailor shop, and looked up at the ladderwell. I assume he was watching the Lieutenant leave the laundry. The big Samoan looked at me, headed back to his sewing machine, and asked, "Fitzgerald, what can I do you for?"

Kalama had a glossy photo I one good looking Polynesian young woman taped to his sawing machine. I was having a tough time taking my eyes off the woman.

The Samoan turned and looked me right in the eyes, "She a fine looken woman. Her and I are gonna hitch after this cruise." He was sticking pins in my uniform. Out of the blue, he stated, "Ya know if I was to retire as a seaman, I could live like a king back of the island. Noe put that jumper on."

I reached out my hand and said, "Kalama? I'm Connor, Connor Fitzgerald. Ernie down at the ship's store told me you might be able to repair or restore" pointing to the dress blues that draped over my arm, "Modesto his sending off for a new set of dress blues for me. I was just wondering if you could" Pointing to my dress uniform draped across my arm, might be able to patch, repair, or just make them serviceable until the new blues come in?"

"Two things I know. Like why you come down to the laundry? Is the Laundry part of the tour? And second, Ernie called and told me you were coming. Ernie also said that your ass was too skinny for these blues he was going to have you try on. And by the way, my full name is Aleki Kalama, Ship Serviceman Third Class."

I handed my uniform to the Samoan, "It 'd be good if you could repair my jumper. I'm sure the pants are all right."

"No, we take in the ass."

Opening the blouse of my dress blues, sitting once again behind the sewing machine. The Samoan, while rubbing his large hands and thick fingers over the jumper he proceeded to make sounds like grunts and groans, clicking his tongue. Then looking at me, while operating the sewing machine. Then Kalama stopped sewing broke the stitch from the sewing machine, folded the khaki shirt he was working on, placed the folded khaki shirt on the pile of shirts to his left; all the while just staring at me. Rubbing his chin, he said, "Yes, I'm gonna have to do a little weave, I'll have this jumper good as new." Kalama taped a piece of paper on my jumper with my name on it. "I can have these ready for you by tomorrow. You take your pants back. You know Ernie, long?"

"Not really. Been making monthly visits to the ship's clothing store for a little over two months."

The Samoan wrote my name on a sticky put the sticky on my blues and threw into the pile of clothes on top of the khaki shirts on his right side. "Dat's OK bruder, Al will get it done."

I just stared at him and asked, "Who's Al?"

"Dat's me."

He said, "Bruder, you gonna associate with me you gotta look good. By the time, I get finished with those Navy issue dress blues you gonna look like you bought them and had them tailored at that fancy place in New York City."

"Am I gonna associate with you?"

"Dat's right bruder, the crew ain't even gonna know that they were even patched. you don't like me?"

At the sound of a someone clearing their throat, I turned just as Al was getting up from the sewing machine almost tripping over a pile of uniforms. I had not noticed the Marine Lieutenant return or sitting there all that time.

Kalama made an abrupt turn to his right. He was staring a pile of khakis. Then I heard the voice again. "Hey valea, where have you been?"

"Smart ass. Just cause dat Marine knows a few Samoan words."

Al was heading out of his little tailor shop just as the Marine Officer was leaving. He, the Marine, stuck his head back in the room. Al took a deep breath, and under his breath said, "It must be true. It hasn't been ten minutes." Glancing back at me, This Marine can't tell time; not unless you show him where the big hand is, and the little hand is."

"You need to be available when I need you." Said the Lieutenant.

"El Tee, I don't care that you some kind an officer, I don't appreciate being called stupid. What are you doing here? Besides, you said an hour. It has only been ten minutes."

The Marine Officer started to come back in, and it looked as if he was heading my way, he pointed at me and motioned for me to get up. Glaring, the Marine continued to badger Al, "I thought I told you that you needed to find me in an hour." Pointing to me, the Lieutenant declared, Get rid of him. We need to talk."

The Samoan walked over to the chair that the Lieutenant had been sitting on, and looking down at the empty chair, "I'm sorry El Tee, but last I checked you ain't my boss, at least not on this boat."

The Marine moved within an inch of the Samoan's chest and staring at the Samoan. "You need to reconsider how you talk to me. I may not be your supervisor, aboard, but if you do not change your disrespectful attitude, I will personally march your ass down to the brig. Now you can go to the commanding officer with that."

Replying in a belligerent voice, "Yes sir. But if I do wind up in the brig, just maybe Master Chief Benedetto might like to find out about your part in our side business."

Sucking in air, Lieutenant Reese replied in a much softer voice, "I'm sorry Al, it's just that we need to focus more on our other business."

Al reached out and lifted the Lieutenant by the throat, off the deck. With his sharply creased green trousers, his immaculately pressed khaki shirt and black shoes that looked like mirrors dangling two inches off the tile. It was funny, and it was all I could do not to crack a smile. Pulling the officer close, and in a whisper, he said, "Listen, sir, you can't even get me off the ship right now, the XO has requested that I finish altering," pointing to the pile on the deck, "these uniforms."

The Marine was looking a little sallow when he responded, "Well I guess that must do. Do you have a way we can get in touch with our clients?"

Al still sounded a little peeved when he answered, "Yes sir. Do you want me to call them?"

"No, I'll call them. I do not want anyone calling from the ship. It's not like the war will start without our merchandise. Just let those greasers throw rocks at each other as far as I'm concerned. We do **need** the product, though. We need it before we go to WESPAC."

I was sure I was listening to a conversation in code. Also, I have never seen or heard an enlisted person talk to an officer like that. Oh, I'm sure there is someone that talk backed to an officer, but a Marine officer. And that one enlisted person is still in the brig. Things have changed since the last time I was in the Navy.

Chow time. My headache is gone. My jaw hurts, and it feels like I got a sunburn on my cheek. Before heading for the chow line, I stopped in at sickbay to check on Cole. Sickbay was quiet; I guess being a shipboard hospital it should have been called a clinic, except this clinic, was as good if not better than most any hospital.

Tradition…The Navy thrives on tradition; no chewing gum aboard, no whistling, you had to act like you were at a funeral or in church while in sickbay. The First-Class Petty Officer at the desk told me that my friend's condition went from serious to critical. Corporal Cole had not improved, and he got a helicopter ride to Oak Knoll.

Standing in the chow line, I felt a tap on my shoulder. It was my boss, First Class Petty Officer Baily, who sarcastically stated, "I missed you this morning."

My reply was to pull out a small sheet of a memo pad with the corpsmen's name on it stating that I was not to perform any of my duties for that day. I handed the chit to Baily.

"Will you be able to join me this afternoon?"

"Yes, Baily. My uniform is now in the trash. I had to find someone to put the patches…"

"Stow, it! Just join me in the OBA locker after lunch."

I could have been in trouble for not keeping Baily informed of my whereabouts. I also should have told him about Corporal Cole.

"Fitzgerald! Fitzgerald, hurry up. You're taking some of the newbies over to Treasure Island. They get to sink USS Buttercup today." USS Buttercup was the only commissioned ship in the Navy that had never gone to sea, but least five times a week the ship would go down to meet Davy Jones.

"I spent almost two years on that ship."

"Yeah, I know. Just so happens I did read your Service Jacket. That's why I want you to teach these guys."

None of the twelve men I took over to Treasure Island kept the USS Buttercup from sinking. The odds were against them. No class has ever saved the USS Buttercup. Most of the sailors were fresh out of boot camp or some tech school. They impressed me, and I gave them all a passing grade. The grading system was easy. I had no choice as the course was either pass or no-pass the twelve newbies were motivated, and the truth told I'm sure that my instruction, with the help of the local cadre, convinced the class of the importance of surviving at sea both crew and ship.

Treasure Island is an island located in San Francisco midway between San Francisco and Oakland. It is under the Bay Bridge. The cadre was not ready for us, so I spent an hour telling my class about how watertight doors.

The ladder doesn't necessarily mean something with rungs; it also means stairs. Half stairwell, the half ladder is called a ladderwell. Use both hands and common sense when going up or down or a person is likely to fall flat on his face.

We finally boarded the USS Buttercup. The class was supposed to keep this landlocked ship from sinking. They did **not.** In the years that the USS Buttercup had been a permanent fixture, no class has ever kept it from flooding. Everyone but me got wet. Even in their dry clothing, they all resemble recently bathed Retrievers; more like poodles with damp hair plastered to their heads. We boarded the bus and headed back to our ship.

That night I was still a little keyed up about my excursion to Treasure Island. I checked and could not find a Zane Grey, or a L'Amour in my locker that I had not read. I'd eaten, and I was feeling drowsy. I knew if I were to climb into my rack and go to sleep this early I'd be awake by three and feel miserable all day. So, I headed to the ship's library. Who knows I might find a western I haven't read.

No such luck.

Chapter Two

When not on duty and out to sea I used to go up to the fantail and just watch as the phosphorus would sparkle in the wake of the ship. It was like looking at the stars on the surface of the ocean. Well, I went up to the fantail, and it just ain't the same tied up to a pier next to the slip where a week ago there was an Aircraft Carrier sitting in what I could only describe as a giant swimming pool at Hunter's Point Naval Ship Yards. Of course, the enormous cement swimming pool is where they put the ship when they want to work on the hull.

Got me some bug juice, Kool-Aid, and shot the bull with the night cook; Pop had to be the only enlisted sailor older than me. He had to get back to work. The few men working the night shift get upset if they don't get their midnight chow.

I had nothing to read. The few people wandering around would not be enough for a card game; maybe two-handed Rummy 500.

Most of the administration offices were down here with me on the second deck. I don't know why I thought of it, but I thought I might visit with priest. Not that we had anything in common. Except he's a Catholic priest, and I'm a lapsed Catholic. *We're in port, and it's not like he has a hot date. I met the Catholic Chaplain at San Francisco International. We did share a ride in a Navy issue sedan driven by the hulk. He wasn't the Hulk, but he was one big Hawaiian. We exchanged lies, maybe I told a few stories that might not be entirely accurate. He did ask me to visit him. I guess old habits die hard. As a kid, if a priest said something it was like it was coming directly from God. I do believe God doesn't like me very much.*

It was night, and most the offices and the people in them were on the beach or in their racks. Well, I thought, it's not like I have anyplace else to be.

I started worrying that this wasn't a smart idea. I may not want to do this. I am already in trouble. Yep, there was a sign stating the this was the door to Fr Donahue's office. He's not in. He's probably hanging out in the Wardroom. Damn! The door was cracked open. I saw a light. I also heard him talking to someone. I pushed the door open. The first thing I noticed was black sox, they were on Father Donahue's feet which were on his desk. On the right and behind the desk was a couch. It was a typical Navy issue couch with two green vinyl covered cushions.

An olive drab fatigue dressed Marine was sitting on the sofa. He had a salt and pepper Crewcut, the side of his head looked shaved. The large Marine's skin gave the appearance of well-worn brown leather. I could no doubt cut butter with the heavily starched sharply creased fatigues. Must be some kinda curse? Two Marines in one day. I was **not** impressed with the first Marine I met earlier the night before, then dragged, carried him until the corpsmen showed up.

No, as this Marine turned towards me I could see gray eyebrows. I was going to say hi to the priest, turn and leave, but I caught a glimpse of a Gunnery Sergeant, an infantry patch over his breast, and parachute wings above that. The Marine stood and turned toward me. I noticed deep laugh lines at the corners of his eyes, a bulbous red nose with broken blood vessels. He reached out a hand I moved closer to him. His hands were strong and calloused. He spoke with a voice used to giving commands, not loud, but I don't think anyone would have a problem understanding him. "I'm Gunnery Sergeant Cortez."

He started for the door. I spoke up, "Gunnery Sergeant, I just stopped by to visit. You don't have to leave. I'm Connor Fitzgerald. Damage Controlman Second Class Connor Fitzgerald."

Stopping and turning away from the door he came within an inch of my face. "You were with Corporal Cole when he had a stroke." More of a statement than a question.

For some reason, I was feeling intimidated. "Yes, Sir. How's he doing?"

"First, Petty Officer, I don't ever want to hear you address me as, Sir. Gunnery Sergeant or Gunny. Can you remember that?"

"Yes, s…Gunny."

"Corporal Cole died at 1700 hours this afternoon. Father Donahue was with him at Oak Knol when he died." Gunny looked over at the priest. "That reminds me, will you be free tomorrow afternoon?"

The priest took his feet off the desk, and looked down at his desk blotter, and replied, "Yes Frank my schedule is clear.

With Gunny's hand on the door handle, "It's just that his family is coming in tomorrow afternoon. I'd like you with me when I meet them. In my thirty years in the Corps I've lost my share of Marines, but usually, the commanding officer meets with the family when possible."

"I haven't been in the Navy that long, but you know the Navy will ship his remains home." Said the Chaplain. "Frank, did you suggest an autopsy?"

Gunny turned back toward the Chaplain, and replied, "I talked to them just before I came down here and told them that. They wanted to carry his remains back, and his mother emphasized that she did not want her baby being cut-up. The parents want him on their ranch. They'll fly back with his body."

"I was with him when he died. The people at Oak Knol did do a tox screen. They did not have the results when I left. "I tried to suggest autopsy, and was told that since this was not combat-related that they would have to get permission from the parents."

"I talked to the parents, and neither one of his parents would hear of it." The Gunnery Sergeant opened the door and stopped. I turned to look down at Father Donahue. He opened his mouth to speak, then quickly shut his mouth as if he had just caught a bug. He once again opened his mouth. "The Navy pathologist, up at Oak Knol said it appeared to him like natural causes. I suggested—that they invite the county coroner to examine the body. It seems they can't do that unless the family requests it."

"Tim, he was barely twenty-one. He was health-Conscious to a fault. Something just isn't right."

There for a couple of minutes, I thought they both forgot I was there. I did the little thing of clearing my throat.

Gunny Cortez turned to me, grabbed a chair I hadn't seen, and placed it in front of Chaplain Donahue's desk. "Now Petty Officer, I would very much like to hear your story,"

I told the Gunnery Sergeant everything that happened that morning, and Al, and I tried to carry him to sickbay. I did mention that when I first saw him, his nose was not just bleeding; it was more like it was gushing. I did not say that I was the one that bloodied his nose.

Halfway out the door, the Gunnery Sergeant asked. "Why did you try to carry him?"

"When we left the laundry, he was walking. He collapsed not long after we climbed the ladderwell heading for sickbay."

I stayed seated as the Gunny left. Once the Gunnery Sergeant was out of hearing distance, I asked, "Father, you got a few minutes?"

"Yes sure." He rolled his office chair back from his desk and turned. He was reaching into a wardrobe; that was between the two filing cabinets. The priest reached behind for a purple stole draped over a hangar.

"Father, no confession. I just want to talk, but it has to be in confidence."

The priest placed his purple stole back on a hangar, slowly closed his wardrobe, turned back towards me as he sat in his chair, and scooted around his desk to sit directly in front of me. "OK Connor, let's have it. Push that door closed please?"

"I didn't mention to the Gunny, but I think I killed him." I declared.

I told Father Donahue the whole story: how he demanded that I give up my seat at the restaurant, how the woman he was with suggested they sit elsewhere, and how he backhanded her. "Father I was doing pretty good until he hit the girl. I know it wasn't smart, but my Irish blood started to boil." I looked over at the priest. "You were with him at Oak Knol? He was a pretty big man."

"I flew with him in the helicopter." Replied the priest.

I couldn't help feeling that by hitting Cole's nose, I was the one responsible for him dying. "But Father, I gave him that bloody nose."

"Connor, I don't think you killed him, and from what you told me there was something else going on with him. When we medevacked out, his blood pressure was through the roof; his heart was pounding so hard that I could have sworn I heard it over the rotors of the helicopter. His heart rate was hard and steady. Then just before we touched down at Oak Knoll, he went into cardiac arrest. I'm sure he flatlined before we got into the ER. The doctors and the medics tried. It seems that if I got in a fight, I'd remember at least that I got in a fight. Connor, you had to do what you thought was right. You were defending yourself, and the young lady."

It's late hit the rack, and if you want, we can talk later. Oh, let me apologize. I just assumed you were Catholic. I wouldn't have presumed you wanted to go to confession."

"I am a baptized Catholic. Catholic schools, I received all the sacraments, including marriage. My faith has waned.

Let me just say that if there is a God, He has no time for me. "Connor I'd like to hear your story. You did not kill Cole. Whatever was going on with him would have killed him no matter what you did."

"Yeah, I mean Yes Sir." I haven't been spending much time in a Catholic Church, and even longer since I've had a conversation with a priest.

"Maybe I should say..."

"Say what Connor?"

"Nothing, but even if I am having a tough time believing in organized religion; I would still like someone I could talk to in confidence."

After morning muster the following morning I caught up with Baily, I told him about how Modesto down in the ship's store said he knew the ship's tailor. I also said how the Marine that beat the tar out of me came into the ship's store. "Baily, you wouldn't believe it. I thought for sure he was gonna finish what he had started the night before, but Cole acted like he didn't recognize me." We were heading for our compartment. I almost fell the stairs to our compartment, but ships do not have stairs, they're ladders. Maybe ladderwells. Baily caught me just before I fell flat on my face. Limping over to the little table we had in the corner of our living space, "the only thing I was able to do to this gorilla was bloody his nose. His nose was still bleeding."

"Fitzgerald! Get to it. Daylight is burning. We gots to get this ship, and our Damage Control teams ready to cruise." Sitting at the little table, Baily offered me a cigarette. I reached out to take it when I reminded myself that I quit two years ago,

"OK, Corporal Cole died this morning. His nose wouldn't stop bleeding, and the doc said he had a stroke." Taking a long drag on his cigarette, looking up at the overhead lights.

"Damn Fitz. You might have gotten out of restriction if you told me that story. Not," Baily said with just a hint of sarcasm.

"Baily, that story is true. cept, I never told anyone but you that I was the one that gave him the bloody nose." I limped over to my locker to get my work boots. "Oh, the Gunnery Sergeant wants to meet with me after lunch tomorrow."

"Fitzgerald, you need to be aboard no later than oh-five-thirty. We're getting underway. I guess the old man wants to see if he can shake this boat apart," declared Baily.

We would be out a few days. My last shakedown cruise was over ten years ago; I wasn't going anyplace. In fact, I returned to the Navy to go to sea; preferably aboard a ship.

"What do you think?" Baily asked like he wasn't aware of what we had been talking about."

"You think we'll go to sea? I heard that the ship wouldn't be able to get away from the pier because of the coffee grounds up to the water line." I thought I would get at least a chuckle.

Not even a smile. Baily finally responded, "Was that supposed to be a joke?"

"You know I came back in the Navy to go to sea. Three months ago, I signed aboard, and the ship was sitting on huge metal horses in the middle of a massive dry swimming pool."

Baily just scrunched his eyebrows.

"You know. The Navy calls that big hole a slip."

"Ya know it's pretty serious if you miss ship movement. Just be sure you're here."

"But Baily…" This sailor is good at talking, but he only listens to himself. He had not heard a word I said. I hope he remembers that he was the one that put me on restriction.

Chapter Three

I was dreaming about a red-haired woman, with just a sprinkle of freckles across the bridge of her nose. She was wearing white, white nurses dress. Above a pocket on the left side under her collar was a plastic nametag. I knew if I could get closer I could read the name.

Someone was pulling on my feet. No…I don't want to wake up. I opened one eye. Not good. I could barely see who it was that was pulling my leg. It was as if I was coming out of a thick fog. I then opened my other eye. The mist was clearing. A short man in khakis. A nose, more a hawk's beak "Chief?" I sat up. Wound up hitting my head on the rack above. So, I eased out of my rack. "Chief Fairchild, what are you doing down here?"

"Why, Fitzgerald, did you think I spent my whole life in the chief's quarters? We need you to the sea and anchor detail."

"But Chief, I didn't think second class petty officers had to do that?"

I turned on the little lamp on the head of my rack. "it's only zero-four-thirty."

"Baily said we didn't have to be aboard till zero-fife-thirty," I moaned. Besides, as a Damage Controlman, our jobs are below decks." Climbing out of my rack and taping the Chief on the shoulder.

"I know, but you are here now." Said a short emaciated looking man in khakis, *Our Chief.*

I barely managed to get two out of three of my morning rituals done before I heard the Bo'sun'Pipe, the call to set the Sea and Anchor detail. I was in a position on the hangar bay to watch the tug pull alongside us. The skipper was on the bridge, and he left the 1MC, the onboard speaker system open. When I first heard that the ship's Captain was a Mustang Officer, ex-white hat. Hearing his description of the tugboat skipper's background, and heritage I no longer had a problem with our Captain's history as being enlisted in another life.

The Boatswain blew his pipe, and we assembled on the hangar deck where the Master Chief sent us off to multiple stations. I was with a short, stocky gunner's mate on the port side of the hangar deck. The two of us managed to catch and secure the lines from the pier. Over the noise and activity of a ship, an enormous ship getting underway. Standing within a foot of each other when he yelled. "I'm Jenkins. How about I buy you a cup of coffee after this?"

I lifted a free hand up as if I was going to wave, and I yelled back, "Fitz, Connor Fitzgerald. Sounds good I might even have a few minutes."

I happened to notice his hand as we were coiling the line. I usually wouldn't pay attention, but this guy was young, and while everyone else, including me, was still rubbing the sleep out of their eyes, there was no stopping this guy. He looked over at me and put a thumb up. He then yelled over the noises of a ship waking after a long sleep, "Where do you work?"

I just gave him thumbs up, and yelled, "Damage Control." There is something about the vibrations caused by engine and hum of the generators like the ship is shaking off a long sleep, that still excites me.

I was coming down the ladderwell to the Mess Deck, when Jenkins, handed me a mug of black coffee. I gulped; that was a mistake. I felt like screaming, but couldn't even speak as all I could feel the burn as the scalding coffee went down my throat. I couldn't tell if it was strong, as the only thing I could feel was the coffee burning all the way down my throat. I could even feel the burning liquid hit my stomach. Not only could I not scream; I could not speak. My face must have shown that I was in pain.

"Fitz! Are you all, right? Guess I should have told you the coffee was hot."

Catching my breath and squeaking, "Ya think."

The cooks were feeding the kitchen help, or better known as mess cooks. Breakfast would be ready for the rest of us in half an hour. Jenkins and I were talking as if like lost cousins, which happens when sailors meet other with newly arrived sailors, the conversation went to 'Where you from, where did you go to boot camp?" He reminded me of my old man. He didn't use the handle to the coffee cup; he embraced it in the palms of his hands. I think that is when I once again noticed that the nail on his pinky finger, it was long, not just long but much longer than that of the rest of his fingernails. It reminded me of a spoon.

I never seem to fail when it comes to putting my foot in my mouth, but I just had to ask, "What's with the pinky finger?"

Jenkins hesitated, looked me right in the eyes, and said. "Oh! I had an infection. It's been a little tender. I think I can cut that nail now. Should have done it before I tried to handle those lines."

It sounded kind of weak to me, but I chose not to challenge him. I did come back with, "if that nail is a problem, maybe you should have one of the corpsmen look at it." The last time I smashed my finger my nail turned black, and some euphoric nurse's aide yanked the nail off.

I'd forgotten what a shakedown cruise was like. First, we steamed to an area as far away from the shipping lanes as possible. I was, and I guess I am once again a WESPAC sailor. After all those years, I'd forgotten how rough the waters were in this part of the Pacific.

Some of the kids aboard thought I was nuts, but like the old-timers, I liked baked beans for breakfast. I had just finished my second plate of beans bacon, and eggs. My mother would have had a fit, I had my elbows on the table, and my hands wrapped around my second cup of coffee. By then I had gotten feeling back in my mouth. I must have been daydreaming.

Jenkins was all but yelling at me, "Hey! Fitz, where are you? You must have been thinking of that girl."

"No. No, I wasn't. How did you know about a girl?" truth was I could smell the jasmine.

Jenkins slapped the table, and declared, "Fitz, You're one of the section chiefs with Damage Control. I'd much rather smell burnt gunpowder, and sulfur, but I was just told that I am to report to you during General Quarters."

"Jenkins, you know where we assemble?" He shook his head. "We're on the third deck." I pulled out my green memo pad and jotted down the frame number. There is going to be a drill this afternoon. Not a real exercise, as we'll be going through Sea Trials. Plus, I haven't worked up an exercise for us yet. It will be more like a meet and greet. Only be a short meeting. We might take a little tour."

Jenkins was quiet. I did notice him always wiping his nose, and he seemed a little jittery. He swallowed the last of his coffee and looked at me. "Well after two trays of beans and eggs, I think I would be doing a service to the rest of my crew, or maybe I should just declare a chemical emergency."

On my way to get rid of my tray, I felt the vibrations; the entire ship was shaking like it had palsy the old man sure like to hear his voice. He was announcing our speed. After 45 knots, he started broadcasting the RPMs. I was headed back to the shop when the ship turned to port or left. Talk about walking up the walls; I was walking halfway up the bulkhead. The skipper sounded proud of himself; every sharp turn put me walking on the bulkhead.

As the RPMs increased everything from the pans in the galley to buckets and mops not tied down came crashing down. The chairs on the mess deck looked like jumping beans. I couldn't hear my voice, but the captain's voice came through the 1-MC loud and clear; he seemed quite proud of himself.

As soon as we secured from sea trials, I had the team assembled at the forward mess decks in front of the locker that contained our protective masks. I had planned to have a fire drill. Just as we were about to pull the fire hoses out the alarm whooped instantly in response, blaring out of speakers all over the ship, rousting sleeping Sailors from their bunks—as it was designed to do. Then the alarm was replaced by the bo'sun's voice. "All hands to Action Stations! All hands to Action Stations!" We no sooner had we arrived at our assigned Battle Station and set Condition Zebra when another alarm went off, the alarm that indicated that chemicals or gas was detected in the area. I yelled, "Gas!" and made the motion of putting my hands on my cheeks several times. I looked out at the team and saw Jenkins fitting a protective mask to his face. I tapped him on the shoulder. "Jenkins! What are you doing on my Damage Control team?" Jenkins' calm response was, "I've been assigned to your team."

I looked down at the clipboard that I had set on the counter, ran my finger down the roster; sure enough, his name was there. My response was, "Get your mask on we'll talk later."

Within minutes we were secured from General Quarters, and the gas threat was a false alarm. The Skipper came up on the 1-MC explaining that there was an unidentified aircraft approaching the ship. His final words were, "Continue the training exercise."

We were checking out the machinery; making sure the Red Devils had fuel and were in working condition. The Red Devil is used to take the smoke out of a fire, and smoke-filled compartment.

I had only overseen this damage control, party two months. We met twice before. At which time, I was trying to act like I knew what I was doing. It had been ten years since I had been on a damage control team. The job was and is the same, keeping the ship afloat, and fighting fires, patching holes, dealing with Chemical, Biological, and Radiological. Unbelievably, things had changed. There was new equipment I had never seen before. I spent more than a few sleepless nights pouring over new material. The one thing I found out was that it was no longer Radiological; it was now Nuclear

There were twenty men on my team including two officers. Jenkins and two others from Gunnery would muster with us, Damage Controlman Thomas would supervise the Damage Control team in gunnery. All twenty were present for my talk. I gave what I thought was an excellent lecture on how to protect themselves and how to fight in a chemical, biological, and radiological environment. I used Petty Officer Thomas for my demonstration. I had them check their Oxygen Breathing Apparatus, and we talked about firefighting. I reminded the men that there is no place to go to get away from a fire at sea. I also asked my captive audience about fighting a fire aboard a ship. There were a few that responded that you put out a fire t by pouring water on it. I replied, "What about a chemical or an electrical fire? And what happens when you pour water on the fire at sea?"

A young Ensign was waving his hand, and getting red in the face. I replied, "Mr. Simmons?"

"Yes, I'm Mr. Simmons."

He reminded me of a third-grader trying to get the teacher's attention. "Go ahead Mister Simmons tell us what would happen."

"We would sink."

"Excellent. I see you were listening."

We secured from General Quarters, and we all went to the aft mess deck in search of coffee or for the younger one's Kool Aide. I grabbed a cup of coffee and headed for the fantail. Watching the giant screws turn up sea foam always seemed to relax me. It wasn't at all like the last time I stood on the fantail of the ship tied to the pier and watching them load garbage on one of the barges.

We once again assembled at our assigned battle stations and had a few drills. The three down in Gunnery reported back by watch phone.

I thought about the navy bean soup for supper, but to the relief of my shipmates I just made a sandwich out of the roast beef, I must have drunk a gallon of bug juice or better known as Kool-Aide.

I showered, climbed into my rack. I didn't plan to sleep. I was in the ship's library earlier when I bumped into Father Donahue. He pulled a book off a library shelf and told me that I might enjoy it. Why not? Never read much, but after being at sea for a few months, I found myself reading the graffiti off the bulkheads and stalls in the head, (toilets). It was 'The Screwtape Letters.' By C.S. Lewis. He thought I might get a laugh out of it. I remember opening the book, the next thing I heard was, "Sweepers, sweepers man your brooms. Clean sweep down fore and aft."

So, I pulled my blanket up and rolled over. It didn't take a second until I was back in the la la land. "Oh. What is that noise?" I said to no one. I did manage to roll out of my rack without doing too much damage to myself. It was that damn boatswain's pipe.

Walker, a dark complexioned wiry third-class Damage Controlman, literally slid down the ladderwell, "Fitz, Fitz! Did you hear."

It felt as if I swallowed a spiny cactus. I could barely feel the crust on my teeth with my tongue. Sitting up felt like someone was sitting on my chest. Shaking my head and rubbing my eyes I countered, "If you hadn't noticed, I just woke up. What's going on?"

"The Master at Arms, kind of like our sheriff's deputy, was making his rounds, near the forecastle, shining his flashlight in the forecastle, and looking at the huge anchor. Starting to turn away there was a flash or something. He wasn't going in. He said the anchor chain was big enough, but the gear, that was holding the chain links, the sprocket, with its giant teeth, always freaked him out. Something was not right. That's when he shined his light on the gear, and that is when he saw the kid lying on top of the anchor chain."

Running my tongue over my lips and teeth, I asked, "OK, Walker what happened next?"

"Well? What do you think he sounded the alarm? Said Boats was the first one there."

My jaw dropped. I had one shoe on and just looked at Walker.

"You know the Master Chief. Well, Master Chief Benedetto, Captain Prescott, our commanding officer?"

"Yes, Walker I know who our Captain is."

"They're all in the windless room. Some 19-year-old gunner's mate.

"What was the kid's name?"

"I don't know Fitz. He wasn't doing much of anything. He was pale, and it looked like he vomited all over his self. He wasn't saying anything."

I was thinking about the kid I met on the Sea and Anchor detail. "Was he dead?"

Looking at me like I didn't understand English "Well?"

"I hope so. I helped carry the body down sickbay was going to put the kid in cold storage, but Doc Miller said we should leave him on that steel examining table. It's just kinda strange."

"OK. What was weird?"

"That they called the priest to sickbay. The man was dead. The doc looked at him, and he agreed that he was dead. Don't Ya think it was kind of late for a priest?"

I drank tea every chance I got. I got some honey and a lemon off the cooks. By noon my throat felt a little scratchy; which was a lot better than it was when I woke up. I was still getting winded. There's pain when I laugh; just going to have to keep from laughing.

How did they know? At dinner, they had fried chicken and chicken noodle soup. There was nothing wrong with my appetite, but I was still having trouble swallowing, so I had two bowls of very salty chicken soup.

I needed to talk to the priest. I wasn't too sure if I would find the Father in the office. I heard rumors of what it was like in the wardroom. I guess it's like where the officers socialize. I figured I'd try his office. I just needed to find out about the dead gunner's mate.

As I got next to the priest's office, I could hear the priest talking. I banged on the door.

"Enter!" responded the priest. I cautiously eased the chaplain's door open I heard, "Come in Connor. I promise I won't bite."

I saw the gunnery sergeant out of the corner of my eye, "Evening Gunny."

Father Donahue spoke, "Guess you heard we had another death?"

"Yes, Sir. Also, heard that you were called down to sickbay." I suppose I still had that stupid look on my face when I queried, "But you're a priest?"

"Well, Connor you are right, I am a priest. I think I was down there is sickbay more for the doctor than the dead sailor. And besides, does anybody know when the soul leaves the body? I looked over his shoulder as he tried to do an autopsy. Doc was afraid that that valuable information would be lost waiting on the Navy pathologist, he'd never know what killed him. There was vomit around his mouth. It didn't look like his lunch. I agree with Doc Miller that I thought it was an overdose."

I finally cut in. "OK, Ok. Did you get the gunner's? mate's name?"

Looking over at Gunny, and then at me, "His name is or was Mitchell."

I guess the relief must have shown on my face, "It's just that I met young gunner's mate this morning, and I thought it might have been him. I was not surprised when you said overdose. I was talking with this gunner's mate today, and I think he might have been high. I have no proof, but I have been around users. Now I'm not saying this guy I met this morning was an addict, but his speech and behavior reminded me of some of the so-called recreational narcotic users. The kid's name is Jenkins. I always thought that if someone were high on drugs, they'd be lethargic. You know walking around like zombies."

Father Donahue cut in, "That is if he was doing some opiate, like heroin, or Oxy."

Gunny stared at me for a few seconds, then remarked, "Fitzgerald are you saying that you think there is a drug problem on this ship. I mean two deaths in a week. That is hardly evidence of a drug problem on this ship."

My eyes were starting to itch. It seemed like I was rubbing them raw when I looked up to the priest than to Gunny. I was feeling the start of one hell of a headache. With a heavy breath, I commented, "I may be all wet, but I think we have a real problem.

Gunny spoke up with a little sarcasm, "Ya know Father, this ship is the size of a small city, and it has more people than that West Texas town I call home. I'd know if there was a drug problem on this ship. In any city, there is going to be a few, but not on this ship. I mean once we get underway they're not going to be able to go down to the street corner and purchase their little party favors."

The priest rubbing the back of his neck commented, "Frank, not if they have a supply chain right here aboard ship. What do you think Connor?"

"Well." First looking at the priest, then at the gunnery sergeant, I hesitantly spoke, "I do believe there is a problem. My first experience with the Corporal was less than friendly; he reminded me of an animal, a feral beast, and then the next day he didn't recognize the man that he tried to beat up. I saw his eyes when he smacked that woman. When we met the other morning in the ship's store, and he did not recognize me. At first, I just thought Cole was a bully. You know a little guy like me runs into tormentors all the time. But I considered his eyes he had no idea that I was the man that he fought the night before. From what I heard from Father Donahue, Mitchell did suffer an overdose. Mitchell's poison was some opiate. Also, the young sailor that I spoke with yesterday was, I'm sure under the influence, although he was in no way lethargic. It looked as if he was on amphetamines."

Father Donahue spoke up, "Frank, the Doc called me down to sickbay because he needed confirmation on what he already knew. Cole was a weightlifter. He was obsessed with his body. Doc Miller also recognized that his arms and legs were large. His conclusion was steroids. Unfortunately, he didn't get the opportunity to confirm that."

Now I was scratching my head. "From what I remember about the Navy, the Commanding Officer knew what was going on in his ship."

Gunnery Sergeant countered, "A man can't just walk on this ship with drugs, at least drugs enough to supply even just a few men." Rubbing the bald spot on the crown of his head, "coming back from liberty the O.D. or the runners will check what you're bringing aboard."

Father Donahue was looking at the blotter on his desk when he spoke, "Unless there is someone up the chain of command that is looking the other way, or maybe a part of distributing the drugs."

It was as if the gunnery sergeant was drilling his eyes into the priest. "You think there is someone, maybe a senior enlisted man, or a commissioned officer, that is allowing or helping someone bring drugs aboard this ship?"

"Sorry Frank, if it was occasional, or rare maybe not, but we have two dead, and maybe another working possibly under the influence. I may be a priest, but as a chaplain, I have seen this way too much."

Gunny was again scratching a part of his hairless scalp, "Father, out of three thousand ship's company three men does not seem to be a trend or an epidemic. Two sailors and a Marine do not indicate a drug problem."

I guess I just happened to ponder out loud, at no one. My throat was still a little tender, so my voice must have been raspy, "Ya know, I'm just a little guy. I don't make friends that easily. I was thinking about myself who has never been considered an extrovert, how come I know two of these dead guys? Listen, Father, Gunny, I hate to break up this party, but I'm going to get a cup of strong black tea and hit the rack."

Walking back to my compartment, I was thinking, here I am a second-class petty officer, and who do I find myself associating with but a Marine gunnery sergeant, and a priest. I mean a priest. The Church, especially the Catholic Church, with their rules and regulations. I don't want anything to do with those hypocrites that call themselves religious. I guess it's like the first day we met at San Francisco International Airport; he seemed as lost as me. Plus, in all the time we've visited he has never tried to judge me or preach at me.

Boy, I thought my throat was getting better. What else? The mess cooks were sweeping the deck and scrubbing the last of the pots and pans. There was one cook left in the galley. Looked like he was setting up for mid-rats. It seems like the Navy is always feeding. Late night rations are usually for those that work the night shift. But if a person is up the cook will not discriminate. I just pulled up a chair next to the big coffee pots and started sucking on an orange; that is while I waited for my tea bag to steep.

Ski, the portly night cook, handed me a slice of lemon, and observed, "Fitz, you, aw-right

"I got a little sore throat. Must have picked up a cold from the snot-nosed kids I mean newbies."

"Fitz, you're sweating. I think you need for the corpsman to give you some aspirin, maybe something for that throat."

"Nah, I'll be OK. I'm going to drink this tea, and hit the rack."

I hadn't had a drink, I mean a real drink in eight years, but my vision was starting to blur, some Indian began to beat a drum.

I saw Ski making coffee. He was asking me something, but it was like he had something in his mouth. He put the back of his hand on my cheek. I think I was trying to be cute, "Hey Ski, I ain't that kinda guy."

I must have grayed out because suddenly he was squatting at my feet. I did hear him say, "Fitz, you are burning up. You need to get to sickbay. Whatever you got I sure don't want to catch it."

It felt as if I had a mouthful of cotton. I was having a problem swallowing my spit. What spit? My mouth was dry, and my throat hurt. I was terribly close to Ski's face. It dawned on me I was close to his face because he was carrying me. I kept blacking out. My eyes were open; at least I think they were open. I've known Ski ever since I got here. I guess I've known him for at least three months. Never knew his two front teeth were porcelain.

I heard the corpsman ask Ski to help him get me in bed. Sheets! I was under sheets. All we ever got was two wool blankets. I think the corpsman asked if I was having trouble breathing. I tried to be cute. I said, "Breathing is a problem, but it's even worse when I laugh." I don't think anyone heard me. I felt the prick of a needle. It hurt, I could see the IV bag behind the corpsman. I tried to focus on the IV bag. The IV bag was starting to blur, then blackness.

I was freezing; my throat was on fire. I tried to call out, but I was having trouble speaking. I finally managed to get the attention of a corpsman. My throat was on fire. I was even having trouble swallowing water. He then brought me a large mug of ice. I was eating ice chips, or just letting the ice rest at the back of my throat.

I must have blacked out. Dreams nightmares. I think they were nightmares. I wasn't sure if I was dreaming. Someone put the rails up on my bed; I guess I must have been fighting somebody. I'd see the corpsman, then the potbellied Chief Isaac looking at me I knew it was the Chief, his belly was hanging over the bed rails. Sticking a thermometer in my mouth; I think I almost swallowed the thermometer. Next thing I heard was the Chief tell me, "You try that again sailor, and I'm going to find another place to stick this thermometer."

It was hot like I was roasting. I could feel blisters forming on my cracked lips. I couldn't breathe through my stuffed nose. Every breath I sucked through my mouth was like sucking the end of a lit blowtorch. *What now?* Oh, no! It felt as if someone just slammed his fist into my gut. The galley must have gotten a case of rotten eggs. I couldn't wait. I was pushing men out of my way on the way to the closest toilet. I didn't know whether to sit or kneel. There was a smell, and it wasn't all me. It was a sharp acidic odor. Fire, my skin was on fire. I was on my knees hugging the commode. I felt hands on me. It wasn't a nurse. If it was, she was the ugliest nurse I have ever seen. It was some pocked marked sailor, and he was rolling me over and changing sheets while I was still in a fetal position.

At last, the pains in my belly seemed to be gone. I ran my tongue over my blistered lips. Is the ship on fire? *Why do I still smell rotten eggs, and burning the lamb chops? Why haven't they sounded the alarm? Is anyone here?* I had to force myself to open my eyes. I was in the open. The sky was full of fire. It was volcanic ash. I could smell sulfur and sparklers, only they weren't sparklers. They were flames coming out of the running lava.

Blackness! I couldn't see. The pain in my belly was gone. My vision was coming back, but figures were distorted. At first, they looked like stick figures. My eyes were burning, but I thought I saw Chief Isaac over by the podium where they sign patients in. Then I couldn't be sure, but it sounded like that kid. What's his name? Jenkins.

The bed I was in had everything that a hospital bed had except for width; if I were two inches wider, I would not fit in the bed. The head of the bed was slightly cranked up; I guess to help me breathe.

I heard their voices, but I couldn't make out what they were saying. My vision was blurred, but what I saw through the fog made my stomach turn, it was the kid, Jenkins, kissing Chief Isaac right on the lips. They were getting more than a little noisy. Then the blackness. The next thing I remember is some burly corpsman rubbing me down with alcohol.

Chapter Four

I was standing over what was supposed to be a hospital bed in my skivvies looking around, like a blind man trying to find my clothes, when I felt a tap on my shoulder. It was Baily. I turned my head, I shouldn't have. Oh! Did I have a stiff neck? I finally uttered, "Baily, you shouldn't have. Did you break in my locker?"

"No Fitz, I did not break into your locker." Pointing to the bed, "This is everything with your name on it that came back from the laundry. Fraid they had to destroy the clothes you had on when they brought you down here."

I caught Jenkins out of the corner of my eye, with the large Samoan right behind him. Looking at the Samoan, bent over as he was I couldn't help but notice that the big Samoan reminded me of the Hunchback of Notre Dame, bent over the whole time he visited with me. He was talking to me, but I didn't understand any of that pigeon English. I think he said something about getting together to go out before we pull out for WESTPAC.

Doc Miller took my pulse, blood pressure, put that cold stethoscope on my back and then on my chest. He slapped me on the back, and said, seems like you had bacterial pneumonia. That's the one that is contagious." The doctor was sitting on the side of my bed. "We treated that, but guess what? I was looking at your throat, and I saw white specks. You had Scarlet Fever. Fascinating. Kids normally get that."

"I know I'm short, hell I'm small. You mean that I even get a kid's disease?"

Doc Miller looked down at me and replied, "You do know that medicine is not an exact science. Anything can happen. You just one more for the textbooks."

"Doc? I feel pretty good."

Now get out of my sickbay. Seriously, I know you are feeling some pain in your chest. I'm giving you some antibiotics. If you need something for pain, come back.

I used the shower in sickbay. Must have stayed in the hot shower a little too long; somebody was pacing back and forth outside my shower stall. I couldn't get enough of the force of the hot water coming out of the showerhead. That same somebody was banging on the bulkhead, yelling, "Save some of that hot water for the very ill people."

I shaved in sickbay. Looking down at my sickbay bed I was surprised to see my dungarees pressed; I never had my dungarees pressed. I hoped they were not searched. Ouch! They were starched.

I found out when I signed back into the division with the chief that we had been tied up back at Hunters Point for the last four days.

Chief Fairchild said, "We'll be slipping across the bay to Alameda later this afternoon. Get your gear stowed." He must have noticed that lost look on my face. "Fitzgerald, something wrong?"

"No Chief nothing wrong." I was thinking of the ruckus I heard last night. "Like did anybody else get dead."

The Chef just shook his head, and responded, "I know Doc Miller said you were fit for duty but are you mentally fit? Nobody's dead. We just completed and routine shakedown. What little they found was tightened or repaired. We're heading home."

The Chief already had his feet propped up on his desk with his head buried in some paperback. He raised his head up. Now he looked lost. He finally spoke, "What is it, Fitzgerald?"

"Oh! Nothing Chief. Just wanted to get my duty assignment. Where's Baily?"

"He took time off to be with his West and kids. As soon as we get over to Alameda and park, you can take the weekend off."

"The weekend?"

"Yes, Friday, Saturday and It's Thursday, so you get an extra few hours. Don't have to be back until Monday morning for muster? Call that red-haired girl you been talking about."

"How did you know about the red-haired girl?"

"Everybody knows. Think even the skipper knows."

It was early. I stood at the head of the ladderwell to my compartment just watching the activity. Men were going this way and that way. There was a snipe, people that work down in the bowels of the ship are called snipes. I recognized him. I think he was a Machinist Mate. I was watching him from the of the ladderwell to my compartment. He was filling buckets with coffee.

I couldn't take it any longer. "Hey, fella."

He turned, I recognized him. His hair always reminded me of wheat that needed cutting. "Johnson!"

"That's me. what's up?"

"That coffee must be pretty good."

"The truth is, Fitz, I don't know. We ain't drinkin it. We're using it to clean the deck grates. The coffee takes all that green scum right off them. Makes um shine like they were fresh out of the store.

I had nothing to do, so as usual, I went wandering around the ship. I would have gone topside. Back to the fantail, but what will I see up there? I was thinking; sometimes this Navy gives me too much time to think. We are once again tied up in the shipyards. I guess I could watch the barges come and go.

I finished the Screw Tapes the last couple of days in sickbay. I'll go down to the library and see what else I can find. For someone that believes in the devil or Satan, the book could be comic. Who am I kidding? I enjoyed it, and it was a break from the westerns I was reading.

It was still early, but I needed to do something. I once again found myself browsing the shelves of our little library. I felt body heat, turned, and thought my heart would stop.

"Father Donahue. What are you doing?"

"Follow me, while I straighten up a little?"

"Are you the librarian?"

"Not really, but this is where I come six days a week. There's a little chapel in the back of the library where I do my thing."

"OK, just what might that be."

Father put his fingers in his hair and pushed a couple of strands out of his eyes. "This is where I come to do my priest stuff."

"What is priest stuff?"

"I'm a cleric first. But I have more than one boss. I have a couple of other supervisors I have the Navy Catholic Bishop; Chaplain Shaw is the Protestant Minister aboard ship. He is also my boss. Then there is Jesus Christ. Like you, I have a Navy Supervisor; the ship's Captain and Chaplain Shaw. I come down here to meditate so I can say my prayers. As a priest, I also must say Mass every day. That little chapel in the back is where I say Mass."

"I'm sorry Father I'll just find me a book and head back to the compartment. I don't have any duties today."

I followed Father Donahue into the chapel where he proceeded in hanging up his vestments in the small wardrobe at the far side of the chapel.

"Now Connor can we talk?"

"Yeah. I mean Yes Sir. I'm divorced. That's OK. As a Catholic, we are not supposed to be divorced."

"No Connor. If you are living in sin, you are not to receive the Eucharist."

"Well, I'm divorced."

"Just like that, you are divorced." The priest scooted up in his chair, folded his hands and replied, "Being separated and are not having sex, then the way I understand it you are not in a state of sin. I am sure if I talk with the Bishop we can get you back into the Church.

I felt as if I were in the principal's office. I was sitting in one of those tin folding chairs. Father Donahue was sitting beside me just looking out into space. You know twiddling one's thumbs can be quite a feat. Anyway, I looked over at the priest. "Well, Father what else do you want to know?"

"OK, how long did your marriage last?"

"Two years but I spent maybe two months with her. It was coming near the end of my first hitch. I told her I was getting out and that she should wait until I got out to get married. She wouldn't hear of it."

"Priest." It was the XO, Commander Wilson, "Are you in here, Priest?" The voice was deep and demanding. "Priest, Father Donahue answer me?" His voice was dripping with sarcasm.

I scooted my butt around in the metal chair, turned my head to see Commander Wilson, our executive officer.

Commander Wilson glanced at me then walked over to the Chaplain asking, "Who is this?"

"Sir, Petty Officer Fitzgerald was here about a personal matter."

The Commander motioned for Father, and then said, "The Captain is having a briefing at thirteen hundred hours in the topside wardroom, you know the one our aviators use. You do know where that is?"

I was impressed at Father Donahue's composure as he replied, "Yes Sir."

The XO just glared at the priest. Without averting his eyes, the XO said, "That is the dining facility that most of our aviators use when they are aboard."

"Yes, Sir. Chaplain Shaw gave me quite a thorough tour of the ship. There are still places aboard that I would like to visit."

The XO's demeanor seemed to change. "Yes, that is correct. Listen, Father, I came in here with a bad attitude. It is not your fault. Let's just say that the Skipper is not pleased with the progress of this ship, both the equipment and the men. I've served with Captain Prescott before, and he has a nose or a feel for people. The XO looked over at me. The Captain told me that he felt there was something wrong. Said he had a feeling in the pit of his stomach. He didn't clarify, but I think he was talking about his crew."

The XO departed not the same way he entered. He almost smiled on the way out.

Father Donahue motioned for me to follow him out as he locked the door to the chapel.

It was like he was waiting for my approval. So, I said, "I don't see why not."

"Apparently, I am expected in the wardroom. If you'd like, we can talk later. It can't be today or this weekend. I have a dinner engagement, but if it's all right maybe sometime next week?"

"That would be okay. You have a dinner meeting?"

I could not visualize the priest with a date. I must have made a face.

Standing up and stretching. Putting a hand on my shoulder, "It's a dinner engagement not a rendezvous with a woman."

"I didn't think that."

Father Donahue raised his eyebrows, "It's all right. I'm having dinner with Chaplain Shaw and his family. We're supposed to be having a home-cooked meal."

I followed the priest out of the library. Father Tim headed toward the escalator, which went from the second deck to the ready rooms, and the aviator's wardroom. I headed back toward the galley. I felt the vibrations of the engines. The lights flickered momentarily, and the ship transferred from shore power and was once again dependent on the ship's generators.

By the time, I had eaten a sandwich and two mugs of sweet iced tea we were tying up at Alameda.

I was restless. I wanted to get off the ship, but couldn't for the life of me figure out where or what I wanted to do. In the old days, I would have headed for Oakland and the Black Saddle. When I was nineteen, I would try weekly to get into the Black Saddle. Every weekend at least two or three times I would try and be carded by some tall ugly guy standing at the door.

The day I turned 21 I tried again to enter the Black Saddle; that ugly guy didn't even look at my ID.

Ever since my divorce, I swore to myself that I was going to stay away from women. That woman I met might just be an exception. What was that name? Oh, Morag. After all, she was a nurse. Now the last name. I remember she was a Scott. I bet if I call San Francisco General they'll be able to find her.

Once I got ashore, I headed for a phone, the kind you had to pay to use. There was a phone booth. Maybe the phone book chained underneath the phone; it was an Alameda telephone directory, plus most of the pages were missing. I got hold of the information operator. I reached San Francisco General and was asked what floor, what department. After being connected to several people, several departments I was finally connected to the Intensive Care Unit. It seemed that Morag Frasier was off-duty. I was about to hang up when a woman came on the line and said that she could reach Morag, and would I give her a number where she could contact me.

So, there I was pacing back and forth in front of the phone booth. I was leaning against the phone booth when

Jenkins showed up. He startled me when he smacked me on the back. My mind must have been a thousand miles away, when he said, "Hey stranger the last time I saw you, you had tubes coming out of your arms and a plastic mask on your face."

"You came down here to visit me?"

Scratching his chin, Jenkins replied, "Not really, I was down in sickbay to visit a special friend. "Heard you had pneumonia. How do you catch something like that?"

"Don know."

"A couple of guys and I are going over to San Francisco. There's a party on Eddie Street. Goes on all night." He turned and yelled at a group of sailors down by the street, "Greg, right. We're supposed to call Greg."

"Sorry, but give me five minutes. If I don't get my call in the next five minutes, the phone is all yours."

"Listen, Fitz, you can't get hold of your friend why don't you come with us. Even if you do, I'm sure we can fit you in the car."

I was ready to take Jenkins up on his offer when the phone rang. I grabbed the phone, glanced back at Jenkins, and waved him away. In a whisper, I said, "Jenkins I'll only be a few minutes." I thought about it, but I have never been known to play well with others. "Jenkins, you guys go ahead and get your ride. I'll get over the bridge on my own."

I'd forgotten the sound of her voice. And here I swore off women, but the allure of a female's voice especially one with a slight Scottish brogue caused my heart to race, of course, I did just get over a case of pneumonia.

She dragged out my name, "Connor…Aye, I remember. I've been thinking about you."

Right. I'm sure Morag was thinking about me. I asked, "I'd like to invite you out. I know last minute and all, but I've been tied up for a few weeks."

"No, no. I understand. You timed it perfect. I have the weekend off. When did you want to do this?"

I hesitated before responding. "I've got the weekend off too. I knew better than to ask a beautiful girl if she was busy, but, "What are you doing tonight?" The silence. She's waiting on a date right now.

", my flat mate and I were just about to break out the Scrabble board. You're welcome to come over. There's always room for one more."

"I'm not that good at Scrabble, but what the heck. Now you are going to have to tell me how to get to your place."

She instructed me to take the Mission bus to 15th and Mission. Walk past the city projects to Valencia. Her apartment looks out on the old Mission Delores.

What am I thinking? I don't need to get involved with some woman.

Well, I don't have to get involved.

There was a voice; it was mine; you know you miss the smell of a woman. It has been a while, but are women still soft? I used to like the scent of a woman's freshly washed hair.

It's crazy I should just buy a paperback check into the Pickwick, soak in a tub of hot water and read my book.

Sleep under freshly washed sheets.

I can't do that. I already told Morag I was coming over.

I can't get in too much trouble. Morag said that her girlfriend was there.

Chapter Five

Mission and 15th Street I got off the bus. I was staring at a pink apartment complex. That must be the projects that she mentioned.

I could feel a thousand eyes looking at me. Brown boys started appearing on the street.

I remember thinking. It was starting to get foggy. I was having a hard time reading the street sign, but I could see the Mission Delores. Morag did not give me an address; she said she would meet me. "Well, I am here Morag," I said that to myself. She said the projects; then she said the old Mission. Mission Deloris? After all, I did live in the Bay Area. I know where Mission Delores is.

The garages drew my attention, as it appeared to be an Adobe construction. The two large roll-up garage doors were up. It was dark and cavernous. It was an auto repair shop, maybe a body shop. The garage looked out of place in what I presumed to be a residential area. When I got closer, I could see it was body shop. There were two old cars up on blocks. There on either side of the garage were two grime-encrusted windows. From what I saw there were tools including pneumatic tools. Anyway, the windows needed a good cleaning.

The fog was starting to thicken. Turning around and looking beyond the garage, there was a slight hill. The fog was thickening, but it was like night and day. The fog was making it difficult to see the next block. What I did notice was the street turned into two lanes with palm trees and green grass on the median between the two lanes. There were white painted apartment buildings on both sides of the road their Bay Windows reaching out over the sidewalk.

My first time in San Francisco I was surprised to see palm trees. I always thought palm trees only grew in hot places. San Francisco was not tropical; it always reminded me a refrigerator in the middle of the bay.

I had written down the directions that Morag had given me on a used envelope. Dress Blues don't really have pockets. I typically stuck my wafer-thin wallet in a little slip on the right side, and at the waistline of my wool navy-blue trousers. I had folded the envelope and shoved in that little slit with my wallet. I knew I was no longer on Mission Street. While my index finger and thumb were in that small slit at the right-hand side of my waist right behind my wallet.

I was gawking and blindly turned to enter the garage. I was trying to read what I had written on that envelope. I remember getting a broken pencil of Jenkins, but for the life of me, I could not discern what I had written.

I stepped into the garage, looked up to see a browned face boy staring at me. With a slight palpitation, I started to ask if I could use their phone. I did see a brown scared hand move, but that brown face boy was behind me and had something pressing against my throat. That would be a knife, a very sharp knife. I tried to look down, but the pressure against my throat was keeping me from swallowing. I knew that there must be blood oozing as it was running down my neck. I could feel the person shift his weight. I could no longer see his face, but I sensed he was looking up at the back of the garage.

There was a tall, lanky brown-skinned boy, maybe a man in his twenties standing at the head of a narrow wooden staircase near the back of the garage. He was eating something; looked like he was shoving a burrito in his mouth. He yelled spitting some beans out of his lips, "Ese! What's you got? You catch you a gringo sailor boy?"

The one behind me with the knife up against my throat yelled back, "Jefe, I found this white sailor boy snooping around the garage."

Jefe? I knew Jefe couldn't be his name. If I remember my street Spanish; he's the boss. Well, taking two steps at a time, Jefe, the boss, slapped the knife out of Ese's hand, grabbed my jumper and neckerchief in one brown hand, pushed, and dragged me outside the garage to a garbage strewn alleyway. His other hand had slipped very close to my throat, "OK, Chico what are you doing down here?"

"I am supposed to meet someone at the corner of Delores and 15th Street."

"Well, this ain't Deloris. Deloris is two blocks over. You ain't gonna find Delores on 15th Street. They don't cross.

I started to speak; he put his hand over my mouth. "Listen!" He stopped, turned me toward the street. He grabbed the back of my head. I think he was trying to catch a fistful of hair. With his large brown calloused hands, he pointed my head toward a street with a grassy medium. "It's late, maybe too late, to meet some woman down here. Now, Chico, you want to sight-see come back tomorrow and visit the **old** church down the street." He pushed me out toward the street.

I could see the tiled roof and bell tower of the Mission from where I was standing. I started walking when I heard voices. There was one voice that sounded familiar. Stepping closer to the building; trying to stay in the shadows. *That voice it had to be. 'It **is** Al. Aleki Kalama.'* I needed to get a look.

The gang or whatever was coming out of the garage, pushing each other laughing. I heard another voice. I could see a white guy in a windbreaker. I didn't hear Al's voice again.

I did see a gray van backing into the garage. In the driver's seat was a white guy with a ball cap and a brown leather jacket. A slick pockmarked kid was casually walking to the back of the van. He yelled. "¿Qué estás haciendo güey?" Two more gang-bangers came from inside the garage.

They were speaking Spanish; although growing up in Tampa, I used to hear Spanish. Of course, Tampa has their Cuban, and Castilian communities. I lived in San Francisco, but the Spanish they were speaking didn't sound like any Spanish I was used to hearing. They were unloading rifles.

I didn't see any cash change hands, but a large man wearing an orange watch cap was putting packages in the back of the van where the weapons had been.

I don't think anyone saw me as I headed away from the garage; still trying to stay in the shadows. I started thinking.

'When Ese put the knife up to my throat, I did notice a cross between his index finger and thumb. I haven't lived in the Bay Area for a while, but that's the mark of the Pachuca.

I was sitting on the steps of the old Mission when I smelt a trace of lilacs. It was Morag. She said, "I was at the bus stop on Mission and 15th. Watched two buses go by." She turned abruptly while putting out her hand, "Well…come on. I don't live far from here."

Morag's apartment was beautiful and organized. The apartment looked big, but as I looked around, I saw lofty ceilings and Bay windows. There was a padded sitting bench and storage area directly under the bay window.

My hands felt damp and sticky. It had to be grease from Jefe's hands. I couldn't see any oil or grease on my hands but never the less. "Morag, I feel the need to wash my hands."

Morag directed me to the bathroom, which could have been another bedroom. The basin was generous. The lines and style reminded me of my grandmother's bathroom. The fixtures were decorative. How does a person keep brass shining? There are boatswain mates on the ship that shine brass every day, all day, and as soon as someone touches the brass, it turns green. The bathtub was ancient, and it was at least four inches off the floor sitting on four lions paws an iron ring suspended from the ceiling surrounded the tub. There was a floral printed shower curtain on the ring surrounding the tub. I didn't look behind the shower curtain, but I assumed there was an equally old-fashioned shower head there.

Morag and to my surprise, a small, but a sinuous woman with light brown skin, short cropped black hair that just barely covered her ears smiled at me. She was wearing white horned rim glasses. Morag sat in a chair at the far side of a kitchen table. The small woman took off her glasses and stood. What I saw almond shaped sparkling brown eyes; the kind of eyes that sparkled leading me to think she was about to pull a prank. Morag, with an open hand, indicated the other woman, that was now standing at the table, and with hardly a trace of the familiar brogue, "Connor this is my housemate, Tina."

It has been my experience that homely, or ugly women select beautiful looking women to hang around. I guess that way they feel they might get the attractive one's leftovers. I would not call either one of these women homely.

Tina put out her hand. "Does a man shake a woman's hand?" She asked, "Connor can I get you something to drink? I think we have a beer in the fridge.

"No thanks, Tina. Water would be fine."

Not only was Tina attractive, but the sound of her voice was sensual. I think I would describe her skin coloring as golden.

Tina took a glass that had been sitting on the drain board. Turning toward the sink, she looked back at me, and said, "I think there's sweet tea in the fridge."

"Well, Tina you've made my day. Sweet tea would be great."

After putting ice from the freezer into the glass and grabbing a pitcher, she poured what looked like stout tea over the ice. Tina took her glasses to rub the bridge of her nose. I had been looking at Morag. As I turned to grab the glass of tea and was once again taken by Tina's eyes.

I did better than I expected at Scrabble. I never considered myself that good with the English language. I tried to take a foreign language in high school and was told that I should try to learn the English language first.

Morag went over to a double sink and reaching up into a cupboard grabbed a large bag of potato chips. She opened the fridge and withdrew a container of dip.

"Connor, I'm so sorry, but we have nothing in the house to offer you to eat. Tina and I ate earlier at the hospital."

I didn't mean to, but I jerked my head up and looked at one girl than the other.

"No, we're both nurses, and if we work Fridays, we eat at the hospital. One of us shops on Saturday," replied Tina.

"I did get something to eat before I left the ship, but the salty chips and sour cream and chives dip were perfect.

OK, so I found out that Morag was born in a little village not far out of Dundee Scotland. Her Grand raised her. She left Scotland as a teenager. Always wanted to see San Francisco. The sight of blood didn't bother her, so she went to nursing school. She has worked in the critical care unit for five years, ever since she started at San Francisco General.

Earlier Tina had mentioned that her dad worked on freighters. Dumb me. "Why don't we get together with your dad? Go out together? I've always been intrigued by the men who crew those freighters."

Looking up at me with a kind of smirk on her face, "Connor, that's not going to work. See dear old dad won't be getting out anytime soon. He's off paying his debt to society." She almost giggled. "See he has a bunk at San Quintin."

I couldn't help it, but sometimes my mouth does override my ass. "OK, I'll bite what's your father in for?"

With no emotion that I could tell she calmly said, "He killed my mom." She rinsed out her glass. And said, "We're still on speaking terms, and if he hadn't killed her I would have."

Morag spoke up, "Connor Fitzgerald just what are ya doin in the Navy?"

"I joined the Navy when I was seventeen. Got out when I was twenty-five. Spent some time trying to get educated. Worked at several jobs." I chomped of some of the remaining ice in my glass, "If ya hadn't noticed I'm a small guy. I thought about being a jockey. That did not work for me. Oh! I'm married." Things got quiet. It looked to me like Morag's jaw dropped.

Taking a deep breath, "Ya know Connor I don't usually go around with married men."

"If it helps, I'm divorced."

Tina was just sitting as quiet as a mouse. Seemed like she was enjoying herself just watching.

Morag after what seemed like several minutes said, "Aye. It does help a little. Seems like I been meeting up with the wrong men ever since getting off that Greyhound bus." Morag grabbed my empty glass and motioned to me.

"Connor Ya want a bit more tea."

"No thanks. I'm like a little kid."

Both women looked at me. "Ya know what happens when you give a little kid something to drink late at night?"

"Aye, I do. I still should watch what I drink late at night.

Now, what happened with that Jockey job?"

"Well, I was taken on by a stable. I guess the third day there I found out I was afraid of horses. You know I don't even think I weighed a hundred pounds. Those animals weigh over two thousand pounds. Plus, they knew."

Tina spoke up, "You went to work in a stable?"

"Sometimes when a jockey is starting out he works for a farm. They call a place that trains racehorses, stables."

"So, you are telling me that the horses did not like you?"

"I could tell they didn't like me. When the horses were let out to pasture, they would stare at me. I knew the horses were laughing at me."

Morag countered, "Horses can't laugh."

"You're wrong Lass. I could see them huddle together and stare at me."

Tina came out of her bedroom carrying a light sweater and was heading towards the door.

"Tina! Where are you going all dressed up? I said. "Is it my company or is it my bad jokes. That story about the job as a jockey was true. You know that the first time I joined the Navy, I barely tipped the scales at a hundred pounds. The recruiter had me eat ten pounds of bananas before I ever let anyone weigh me.

Morag came up behind me. "Connor, Tina's shift starts at eleven. The last bus passes by here at 8:30," explained Morag.

"Morag, I don't like to bring this up, but those bruises on your wrist are new. Has somebody been bothering you?"

"It was Russell, Russell Cole. He found out where I lived and just grabbed my wrists."

"Morag, that bruise on your wrist, can't be more than a few days old."

She looked at me. Her eyes were starting to water, "It was just a few days ago, I don't think Russell will be back?"

My stomach must have made a noise when it came up to my throat. It wouldn't have taken much for Morag to convince me to stay overnight. Especially when finding out her roommate was going to work, but Russell Cole had been dead over a month. Why is she lying? I don't need to get involved with another woman that finds it so easy to lie.

I felt an electrical shock as Morag placed her hand on my shoulder. With those big green eyes, she looked at me, and said, "You didn't eat, and you told me on the phone you had the weekend off."

"Well, Morag I just remembered that I was supposed to meet some buddies tonight. I think we're going to that Japanese restaurant; the one at the top of Nob Hill." I lied. "How about a picnic tomorrow. I'll even pick up some fried chicken. Some potato salad. Do you think you might like that?

"Sorry, I need to get groceries tomorrow, and I've got the swing shift."

She leaned over and kissed me. Her lips just barely brushed mine and turned me down. My heart dropped. Now I've been turned down before, but I really thought Morag and I had something.

"Your friend is celebrating his birthday now of night?"

I don't remember mentioning a birthday, I replied, "No, it's actually tomorrow night."

"Ya know you can stay here tonight. Tina won't be using her bed."

No, I was thinking. *Staying here overnight with a beautiful woman is a bad idea. I'll check into the Pickwick.*

I was moving toward the door when Morag moved close to me. She leaned her face down toward me. She was getting close, so close that I felt her hot breath on my neck. I could smell her breath; it was sweet with a hint of cinnamon. Morag just brushed her lips against mine.

I **was** going to soak in a hot tub, but I think tonight I'll just take a cold shower. In the light of day, I can find out what this woman's game is? I didn't think I would ever be moved like that again. That warmth that stirring in my loins. Noo, not tonight, just stand under a cold shower.

"I don't have to be in until the afternoon. I just think a picnic would be better when I had the whole day. Goodnight Leannán."

This girl is strange. "Who did you call me?"

"Not a who Connor. Sorry, it means Sweetheart or Lover."

"I have to go."

I intended to walk back to Mission Street and catch a bus. No problem. Well, a minor problem. The fog was so thick I could not see my hand even when I put it up to my face. My sense of direction has never been good. I don't know how I did it, but a little breeze came along, just enough to thin out the fog. I had been looking down, trying to look at my feet.

I sensed rather than saw those pink buildings of Valencia Gardens. I mentioned the pink apartments to Morag. She corrected me. Telling me that they weren't pink, they were rose-colored. At any rate, Mission Street should be right ahead. Now if I don't fall on my ass, the bus stop should be right at the corner.

Sure, enough, the bus stop was right where I thought it was. There was a schedule atop the poll, but I wasn't quite tall enough to see it, and the fog did not help. There was a bench near the curb, but a short distance from the bus stop.

With a little effort, and working up a sweat I managed to drag the bench over to the sign. By now I was dripping, and the fog was getting thicker. The wetness of my body and the chill coming in through the mist I couldn't stop my teeth from chattering.

Climbing up on the back of the bench, and almost falling. I was finally able to read the bus schedule. Seems, that, I missed the last bus by half an hour. *The last bus! That means that I am going to have to walk to the Greyhound bus depot.* I had no problem with the distance, it was only a few blocks. I had an issue with the Mission District. I lived in San Francisco, Daily City. The word was the cops didn't patrol this area at night.

So, shivering I put my hands in my pockets and started walking toward Market. With my sense of direction, I hoped I was heading for Market Street.

Ten years ago, they used to run Jitneys. Jitneys were usually long-bodied Chryslers. They were black or gray, and for two dollars they'd take a sailor back to the base, or any other favorite place where sailors hung out. It was Friday night there should be a lot of sailors on the beach. The only problem with a jitney was that the driver would not move unless he had the car packed with sailors. The sailors were packed like sardines. The reason a young sailor would take a jitney was he probably spent all his money on booze.

If a sailor was in the middle and that sailor was beyond drunk the sailor on either or both sides would probably be puked on.

Now to flag down the first Jitney. They didn't have any route. If a sailor was on Market Street, or up at Fisherman's Wharf the jitneys are sure to be there, but 15th and Mission were gang territory. Unless the jitney drivers thought they could pack the car, they would not come anywhere near this place.

I dragged the bench back where I found it and plopped. If I still smoked, this would be the perfect time to light up.

I still soaked in my own sweat. My teeth were beginning to sound like castanets. Well if I start walking I just might be able to get my blood flowing. Oh, no. There was a Volkswagen bug, and I could see that he slowed down to a crawl. Yep. He winked at me. Should I, or shouldn't I? That's all I need is some smelly, hairy guy Pawling all over me. I waved, and he almost wrecked his little bug.

He brought the Volkswagen to a screeching halt right in front of me. I almost laughed watching him climb over the gear shift to roll down the passenger window.

More than ten years ago, when I first arrived in the City by the Bay, these guys used to terrify me. For some reason, I wasn't frightened, or flustered.

He managed to stick his head out the window, and as I expected, "Hey sailor can I give you a ride?"

I surprised myself, and replied, "Look I'm straight, but I'll give you a couple of bucks if you give me a ride to the Greyhound bus depot?" The Greyhound station is right around the corner from the Pickwick. To my amazement, he did just that. The Picnic was across the street from the bus depot. I did shower. I sniffed my dress blues, they didn't stink. I folded them and placed them on a chair.

San Francisco makes a big deal about foggy nights. But believe me, there is something special about misty mornings with the sun trying to cut through the fog. I think a photographer might call it soft focus. I couldn't see a thing in front of me, but the glare of the sun made my head hurt.

By the time, I got as far as Powel, the sun's rays were cutting through the dissipating fog, and people were turning the cable car on the giant turntable for its trip back up the hill. Why not. I caught the car just as it was starting its climb.

I was at the top of Telegraph Hill gazing over as the fog that shrouded Coit tower lifted like the curtain of the first act of the play. Ah, maybe a hot cup of tea. I still need to get my adrenaline cranked up. I noticed that people that were heavily addicted to alcohol would switch to the most robust coffee. Coffee! Maybe this morning might be a day to start with coffee? I never considered myself an alcoholic. I always said that I could put the whiskey down. My Da said I was lying to myself. The truth is that even when my wife left me, I never felt the need to get drunk, but I did try. My mind stayed in a numbing haze for a month.

There it is. A Deli! I can smell the coffee from here. Somewhere behind the smell of coffee, there was the aroma of fresh hot pastries. I pushed the door open to the sound of jingling bells.

The smell of coffee assaulted me as I entered the deli. Yes! This morning is a good morning for coffee. The smell of coffee beans typically assaults my senses just as the bus crosses into San Francisco coming off the Bay Bridge. I just might be convinced to change my mind. I didn't see any sweet pastries or doughnuts, but I did see baskets of rolls, Kaiser rolls, and hard rolls. Ah, the famous sourdough bread. A ruddy-faced fat man was wearing a white paper hat, and a white apron at the counter and he was slicing meat; they do have more than bread. There was another man, not so big with curly black hair coming out also wearing a white paper hat. He appeared to be making the rounds of the small tables pouring coffee. A blond-haired woman was dressed in a white hair net at a cash register.

I picked up two sourdough rolls, two single-serve cream cheese, and waited in line for coffee. The tables were small, two chairs per table. It seemed to me that there were two people at each and every table. There were also hushed conversations at each table. Most everyone appears to know their table mates. Ah…There was a table near a picture window with one elderly man sitting there staring out the window. I carried my rolls and coffee over to the table. The older man wearing a yamaka and a brown Cardigan sweater looked up at me and smiled. Until he looked up, he had been reading a newspaper with a cup of coffee beside him. He motioned to the paper and made a gesture to me, as he was offering the section to me. Before my butt hit the chair, I had slathered a sourdough roll with the cream cheese and was chewing on a sizable chunk. The man's head was back in the newspaper before I nodded recognition.

Morag had to work. Of course, her shift didn't start until three. She is a lot like me. If I got the duty even if it is only for a few hours, I don't want to involve myself in anything else. She did say that she had to do the weekly grocery shopping.

I spent the day wandering the hills of San Francisco. I figured I would treat myself to one more night in a hotel. The sun was setting, and I was heading for the hotel. I remember thinking, *the sun is just now setting. The night is young. I really do need to find some entertainment. I mean if all I'm going to do is go to some hotel, take a bath and read a paperback, except for the tub I might as well do that back on the ship; where I might be able to get some popcorn and watch the flick on the hangar bay.*

If there is any doubt that I walked all the hills of San Francisco, my sore aching feet would argue with you. I was starting to feel a little chill. This city always seemed to me to be a refrigerator. I hadn't realized that my short walk had also caused me to work up a sweat.

I found myself across the street from the Terminal Restaurant at the USO. I didn't want to go back to the ship, and I really didn't have much money left. Sometimes, most times the USO has tickets to different clubs or concerts. I picked up a ticket that would get me into one of the Jazz Clubs. You'd think with my obsession with Westerns that I'd be more into Country and Western music. Naa. I used to like Marty Robbins or straight Western. No, I prefer to listen to Jazz. I did get the rare opportunity to see and hear to Brubeck, and Rushing. Brubeck would come up with chords on the piano that was not what would be expected, but always entertaining. Rushing's vocals were original. Jimmy Rushing had to be in his seventies. He still sounded good.

Sunday morning, I made it over to Mission Delores for Mass. There might have been something in the back of my mind that I just might casually bump into Morag; no luck. Of course, she was a Scot; not known to be Catholic. I only caught the final blessing. I guess Scots don't go to Catholic Mass.

I took the bus that leaves out of the Greyhound Depot. It wasn't even 0930 by the time I was back on the ship.

Someone told me once that I had no idea what the real world was like, and I was not streetwise. Oh yeah, Mavis, my ex-wife. That was over ten years ago, before my last WESTPAC cruise. As for being streetwise, or naïve. I am, but I knew what was going on. I just had no desire to be involved. I knew the people that partied. I later found out that some of those same individuals were shooting cocaine in their veins; sorry, but I did, and maybe still do like the taste of single-malt scotch when I could afford it. I smoked cigarettes but had no desire to smoke pot. I am hung up on time. I do not like drinking, smoking, eating or snorting anything that is going to distort time for me. Oh, I've been what is called wasted. For me that is drinking too many intoxicating beverages, and passing out, or getting sick; sometimes both.

I did take Bennies, or Benzedrine once on our way to Australia, and we were being shadowed by aircraft from a country that didn't like us. We went to General Quarters and set Condition ZEBRA. That's when all fittings marked with a black Z are closed; the ship is completely watertight. The rest of the trip was at the Condition 3, the larger ships also use the term Condition 3. At Condition 3 half the weapons are left at the ready, as well as half the crew, the other half go back to their regular duties. We could still move about the ship provided we shut and secured the doors behind us.

The aircraft that were following us appeared to be long-range bombers that would fly away from the ship, and within minutes' other bombers would replace them. Then the MIGs replaced the bombers until the had guys got bored and flew home.

I was officially in a miserable mood sitting on the couch, in my compartment aboard ship staring into space. The only noise I heard was the flap of the fly's wings. My ears seemed to be clogged; my face felt as if it was on fire. I heard what sounded like the rushing of the sea in my ears, but it was only the sounds of blood rushing to my head and my breathing. My face was getting hot. I was pissed. The gangsters' or what they called themselves, Cholo, acted like family. They were into something…Selling drugs, buying weapons. The van I saw? There were no Navy markings on the van, but it was that dull Navy gray.

My head felt as if it was spinning, my face felt on fire. My thinking was confused. Thoughts were bouncing. The Pachuca mark between that kid's index finger and thumb. The large man that sounded like Al, the Samoan called Jefe, Alejandro. Who was this Alejandro? My Irish was up now. Pachuca's, street gangsters. I looked at these kids. They are not kids. They are vicious street thugs. I didn't care. I needed answers. And those, those voices? Was that my new friend Al. I mean even the glare on his shaved head. I didn't hear the smaller man talk.

Chapter Six

I was in my skivvies, thinking about laying on my back, with my blues folded at the foot of my rack. Thinking, *I would like a cigarette, even an adult beverage.*

I met her once, went to her place played a board game, was just fixen to have a real date with her. Time seemed to be muddled. *Has it been a week since I saw Morag? It felt like yesterday that I was sitting on the steps in front of Mission Delores.*

My head was starting to throb. I was laying on my back and was having trouble breathing, about to grab one of my books, but my chest started hurting. I rolled on my side. Breathing came a little easier. I could hear a gurgle in my chest.

I don't remember marking my place in the book I was reading, but I woke to silence. I didn't look, but I knew I was the only one down here. I had to pee but was having trouble getting up. I did manage to get to the head. I staggered up to the mess deck. I should have been hungry, but the sight of the bacon floating in grease nauseated me. I started to get coffee but thought that a cup of stout tea might be better.

Sunday aboard ship in port can be like a ghost town. I could go and drink coffee with the priest. But then again, this is Sunday. I could go to Mass. I realized just then I have no idea what time Mass starts. For that matter, I don't think Father Donahue would be holding Mass in the library on Sunday morning.

I heard a commotion up on the hangar deck. I put my cup in the scullery, or the place where they wash the trays and mugs, and headed up to the hangar deck.

I saw the priest in his vestments. He **is** a priest. No longer in khakis, or the dress blues of a Naval Officer, but as a priest.

It's funny, not ha-ha funny, but weirder, but ever since my divorce I tried to tell myself that religion wasn't necessary. Then out of nowhere, I see the priest dressed up to do his priestly thing, and all those Catholic School memories come back.

I had no idea that there were that many Catholics, especially in port. The sun was shining through the large hangar bay doors. There was barely a trace of the well-known Bay area chill in the air. The altar was set up on the aft starboard aircraft elevator. The rays of the sun were at Father Donahue's back; giving him an unearthly or more like a supernatural appearance. There was barely a breeze. I remember other military priests fighting to keep the altar linen down, with one hand holding the pages of the Sacramentary or the book the priest uses while saying Mass, from causing him from losing his place.

It had been awhile since I attended Mass. I did feel at home. It was like I was with family. It amazes me that I get these feelings. I was five-years-old when my grandparents took me out of the Mercy Home for Boys and Girls. I knew I would miss my friends, but I would not miss that cold icy penetrating wind that came from Lake Michigan in the winter. Of course, the bitter cold of the Chicago winters was equaled by the hot, humid summers. It really isn't where a person lives, it is the people he lives around. Walking into that rose shingled house in St. Petersburg Florida was the first time I had that feeling since leaving the orphanage.

I don't know what I expected. Drinking coffee with Gunny and the priest was out of the question. Father Donahue had just finished saying Mass, and I'm sure that he would much prefer to spend the rest of his day with others. Someone told me that Gunnery Sergeant was on leave. Once again, I find myself wandering the ship. The ship's library was out of the question, as they had all kinds of groups meeting in the library.

I had just walked past Father Donahue's office when I heard my name called. I turned, and Father Timothy Donahue had his head sticking out of the half-closed door to his office. "Connor!" he yelled. "Were ya looking for me?"

Turning to face him, "No, ye, yes sir."

He opened the door to his office and motioned for me to come. Turning and placing his vestments on hangers. With his back to me while straightening his locker, "Connor I saw you at the back. There was room up front, or are you like the many that must sit in the back of the church. They are mostly the ones that feel a need to escape my sermons."

Feeling a little awkward, I replied, "It's just that I feel funny not being able to receive communion."

"Other men don't receive communion; some are just coming into the church."

"I know, but there are two parts of the Mass; the Word, and the Eucharist. If whatever the reason I couldn't or didn't receive…Well, then I just didn't feel like I went to Mass."

Putting his stockinged feet on his desk, and adjusting his glasses, he stared at me for the longest time. When he finally spoke, "Connor, I thought you told me that you didn't believe in God?"

He caught me off guard. Responding I said, "No, Father. What I said was that I had lost my faith. I guess in a way I feel the Church turned her back on me. I thought it was Mavis, but it was me that didn't have what it takes to make a marriage. I didn't know she was unhappy. No matter, one person shouldn't decide to get a divorce; it should take two

"Connor, something else is going on, and it is not just your struggle with your faith." The priest put his feet on the deck and walked over to his coffee pot. Looking down at the pot and then at me and asked, "What is the real problem?"

I was staring at the highly waxed tiled deck. "I think I told you the story about the night Russell Cole and I disagreed. He bruised my face and my ribs. I bloodied his nose. The next day…"

"Yes, Connor I remember."

Father Timothy Donahue locked the door to his office and unlocked a desk drawer. The priest pulled out a well tanned Meerschaum Bulldog Tobacco pipe. Opening another drawer, he pulled out what looked like a small leather pouch. He put his index finger and thumb in the bag and removed an aromatic smelling tobacco. He put a pinch of the tobacco into the pipe, tamped it. Out of the same desk drawer, he pulled out a box of wooden kitchen matches like the ones in my grandmother's cupboard. Drawing in on the pipe and letting out an aromatic puff of smoke he looked over at me. The priest raised an eyebrow and with the used wooden match between the same index finger and thumb asked, "Connor, sorry I should have asked first. Do you mind if I smoke?"

"I don't mind. When I used tobacco, I would have smoked cigarettes, cigars, and I even did a little chew. I didn't know you smoked."

"Ah yes. I'm down to once a day. If you are sure it is not going to bother you, please tell me your story."

"Her name is Mavis. I had just started on my second enlistment. I liked sea duty, but someone told me that if I didn't pick a shore station, I would be assigned one. So, I volunteered for instructor duty. I made first-class petty officer in record time. I took command of the only ship in the Navy that never goes to sea and always sinks.

I met Mavis my second year at Treasure Island. We dated. At first, I would take her out once every other weekend. Then it was every weekend. We finally saw each other daily. Any free time I was with her.

We had talked about marriage. I tried to tell Mavis what life would be like married to a sailor. She assured me that she had no problem with me being a sailor. That was until my tour as an instructor was up, and I headed back to sea.

Mavis drove me in my classic Studebaker to the ship the day we departed on our WESTPAC cruise. That is the last time I saw her. Mavis wrote for the first couple of months; daily. Then the letters stopped coming.

I requested leave to go home. For all, I knew my wife could have dropped dead. Wouldn't someone tell me if she was dead? I wrote letters not just to her, but to the few friends we had in common. The answer was the same; no response from her and our friends said they hadn't seen her. Her friend Janet stated that she thought she was pregnant and had gone back to Iowa.

We were married, but I never met her parents and did not have a clue on how to get in touch with them. I not only made an allotment out to her, but I also paid rent to the rental agency.

The ship got back to the states in September. I went back to our apartment and found a note on the kitchen table addressed to me telling me that I had deserted her. A few days later there was a knock on the door, and a man in a gray suit handed me divorce papers. She didn't want to see me. I don't remember the person's name. The man in the cheap suit told me I had to sign the papers."

We both turned and looked up to the sound of pounding on the door to the Chaplain's office. Father Donahue yelled for whoever was at his door to come back later as he was counseling someone.

What I heard, "This is Commander Wilson. Father Donahue, I need to talk to you. It's about one of your people."

"Sorry Commander. The door is locked. Just give me a second." Replied the priest.

Commander Wilson, the Executive Officer moved, no, more like shoved the priest out of the way. He looked over at me and said, "Who's this?" the XO stared at me for what seemed like minutes. He finally said, "You're Fitzgerald.

What are you doing here now? Don't you have someplace else to be? Church services were this morning."

I looked up at the priest, and before he could say anything, I said, "Sir, I have a personal issue to talk with Father Donahue about."

Commander Wilson mumbled something under his breath and turned toward the door, His hand was on the doorknob, when he asked, "Father do you know Gunner's mate Jenkins?"

"Yes, Sir he is one of mine."

"Have you seen him recently?"

"Yes, Sir I believe I did. I saw him this morning at Mass."

"Have you seen him at any other time. I mean within the last day or so?"

"Yes sir, he came to confession last night."

Commander Wilson released the doorknob and scratched his head. With a little hesitation, he queried, "What did you talk with Jenkins about?"

The priest sat up straight, and replied, "Sir you know whatever I hear in the confessional is private and sacred."

The XO stepped out the door, turned and said, "Sorry. I do know that I just thought that he might have said something, not in the confessional. Like did he ever mention Chief Isaacs; You know our Chief Corpsman?"

The two of them just stared at each other. I was trying to make myself as small as a mouse.

Once the XO was out of sight, the priest motioned to me to continue. "Mavis and I had a little place out in Daly City. I went to our home in Daly City; it was empty. Her clothes were gone the only thing left to her was a note on the kitchen table. The letter stated that she was not cut out to be a Navy wife, and I was to go on without her.

I had taken leave. So, I was not expected back aboard ship for a month. I was drinking and smoking back then. I looked for my Studebaker; it was no place to be found I later found the closest liquor store. I had planned just to have a drink. I was never much of a drinker. I drank that bottle of Scotch; it was not a cheap bottle. I got sick, but once I got over being sick, I bought another bottle. Under the influence of little food and constant drink, I went into a blue funk.

I don't know when I started drinking the cheap stuff, but I woke one day with a raging headache and several empty bottles on the floor. I don't know when I started drinking the Thunderbird, but there were empty bottles of Thunderbird on the floor with cheap whiskey bottles. The whiskey bottles had labels on them, but I had no idea what the labels said. officers

Everything was a haze. I seriously thought about desertion from the Navy. Then one day with a serious headache I washed up, put my uniform on and headed back to the ship. I had made up my mind to get out of the Navy. I don't know maybe I thought if I got one of those civilian jobs Mavis and I could make a go of it."

A large ceramic ashtray appeared from one of his desk drawers, and he tapped the ashes out of his pipe. Father Donahue must have put a wet paper towel in the ashtray, as I could hear the sizzle of the hot ash as it hit the ashtray.

As I pulled myself from the Naugahyde covered couch, Father Donahue stood and queried, "Connor I do enjoy your company, but for someone who has stated that his faith has waned, why do you want my camaraderie? Don't get me wrong. One of my jobs is to help you reconnect with your faith, and I will always make myself available.

It's not just that I need you to help me back to my faith, but other than the Skipper and Gunny, you are the only one aboard close to my age. Oh, there's Danish, a cook. Rumor has it that he was a mess cook for Noah."

Chapter Seven

Father Donahue followed me out of his office, turned and locked the door. We didn't speak until we neared Officer's Country. I headed to the compartment that I shared with forty other men, while the priest headed to his room that he shared by himself.

I was really feeling puny. I had stripped down to my skivvies, folded, and placed my dungarees, and shoes in the little locker. I was slouched on the Navy issue plastic leather, (Naugahyde) couch. If I still smoked, I would have been smoking. I was tired, more than tired. I mean I met a woman was about to go on a picnic. Before that, the local street gang grabbed me.

The last thing I remember was thinking that there is nothing, that we are truly just combination of atoms. But then again how would that account for bad luck. I don't believe, but if I don't think how I can believe in bad luck?

The compartment was dark except for the little red light on the emergency lantern in the corner of our break area. The last thing I remembered was a feeling of drifting. It felt nice. If I hadn't known better, I would think we were at sea. My eyelids were feeling heavy.

Lights! They **are** bright. "OK! OK. Get your asses up. Hit that deck!" That voice. It was my friendly supervisor, Baily. I was in the fetal position on the cold Naugahyde couch.

I was hugging myself; my jaw hurt from trying to stop my teeth from chattering like castanets. Opening my eyes, yep, Baily was much too bright and cheerful. There Baily was with a grin cheerfully standing over me.

"Ya know Fitzgerald, this job provides a bunk, or rack with blankets. You don't have to sleep on a Navy issue couch." He walked back into the compartment, pulling on the blankets and teasing the men up.

I was pulling my folded dungarees out of my locker when I replied, "I know, I know. It's just that I had a rough night. I was totaled. I was lucky to have enough energy to get undress. I came over here to catch my breath. The last thing I remember is staring at that little red light on our battle lantern."

I didn't know what was unique about that morning, but I was genuinely considering not taking a shower. No one should be that cheerful at O-Dark-thirty on a Monday morning. I mean what the hurry was. It was starting to feel as if we, by we, I mean the entire damage control division were the only souls awake at zero dark thirty.

I did manage to scrape my face with a razor. Take care of some other personal needs. I stuck my nose under each armpit and decided that all I needed was a little deodorant.

Baily was pacing back and forth like some mother hen. There were whining and grumbling. My shipmates were stomping like disappointed two-year-old's. Fortunately, no one jumps up and down screaming or crying.

I climbed the ladderwell from our joint bedroom and managed to push myself through to the mess deck to the coffeepot. Right above our compartment was what we fondly call the Acey-Deucy Mess; that's where the first and second-class petty officers can avoid the lower pay-grades while eating a meal.

I was about to sit at one of the tables when I looked up and saw both Chief Fairchild and our Division Officer Mr. Hales, who is a Navy Lieutenant. Navy Lieutenant James Hales had been assigned as our Division Officer shortly after I signed into the division. As part of Mr. Hales introduction, he mentioned that a scholarship to the University Florida, a football scholarship had given him an opportunity to play pro football and that he lasted a season with the San Diego Chargers before he blew his knee out. That's why every time I see our division officer I think of football jerseys. I always visualize him about to run in the last quarter of a football game. I wouldn't have been surprised if he yelled, "Let me go on the coach."

Chief Fairchild still reminded me of a hungry fox. The chief was as short as me. He pulled over an old wooden apple crate. The Chief might have been short, but he had one impressive voice. Chief Fairchild had us come to attention. The Chief went out into the passageway, and when he returned to the division he had a wooden apple crate, he put the box in the middle of the room and stood on it. The chief wasn't very tall but made up for the height deprivation with a powerful voice. He proceeded to address us, "I know, and I agree we are the only ones awake aboard this ship, but I wanted to talk to you before the ship's crew got the word about the inspection. Mr. Hales and I got the word last night that we are going to have a visit from the IG Inspection team. The team will be here next Monday morning.

"Some of you old-timers Know what an IG Inspection is. You people new to the Navy are about to find out. For the old sailors, a reminder, and for your brand-new people… The Deputy Chief of Naval Personnel and Commander, Navy Personnel Command on behalf of the Chief of Naval Personnel, is responsible for an inquiry into and reporting on, the effectiveness and efficiency of field activities in the command. The BUPERS IG serves as the principal advisor to the CNP and DCNP for inspection matters and is responsible for coordinating and conducting inspections of field activities. In this capacity, the IG serves as Chief Inspector and exercises overall direction and coordination of the Command Inspection Program for CNP commands and events. Originally scheduled to hold with the Operation Readiness in Hawaii.

"We are going to have our inspection in conjunction with our visit to San Diego. Failing will not get us out of this deployment. However, we will not fail. It is imperative that we achieve an excellent, and earn the big E."

All that. The acronyms! That's why nobody understood me as a civilian. My entire military life was made up of abbreviations.

"Don't look so glum. I know, you all know, or if you didn't know someone has mentioned that we are overdue for an Inspector General's inspection. Well, the time has come." Someone had his hand up. "OK, Chambers. For you or anyone else who is not familiar with an ORI. That is when we play war. This is not an ORI. This is the part where people are sent to inspect our paperwork. Check our bookkeeping."

Mr. Hales moved to the front, and spoke, "This is the part when they inspect our record keeping. The IG team will watch as we go through our daily routine. The inspectors will inventory our equipment to make sure we have what we are authorized. That means if we are short we will get a bad mark. If we are short, we must assure the inspectors that we have those items on order. If we are over, we will have hell to pay. So, make sure we do not have more than is authorized. We get rid of the excess." The chief took a deep breath and pointed to Mr. Hales.

Mr. Hales looked like he was pleased that he got to say, "That is all. I have arranged that you men will be allowed to eat with the mess cooks. Eat before the Bo'sun'Pipe blows."

My team surprised me. In the brief time, I had been their team leader I never gave them an opportunity to show me their talents. I was sure that they were the best; Of course, I credited myself for that. I started to assign men to different tasks. There was a group of eight guys in front of me; Fireman Cantu had his hand up. I motioned for him to speak, "Boss, why don't you find out what each of us is good at?"

Well, I did. What I found is there were a few that were good at typing. I discovered that I was not the only one with a degree. I had been with these men for a little over three months, but I never treated them like a team. Not only did we organize the paperwork, but we inventoried and documented: chemical suits, protective chemical masks, oxygen rebreathing units. The oxygen canisters stored per directives. During our inventory, we had found the additional Red Devil, and a bag of tools; looked like tools used on the flight deck.

I would have liked to appear as if I was in total control. It wasn't until Third Class Petty Officer Stewart spoke, "Hey Fitz, we can't have the extra Red Devil or the tools anywhere near our workspaces."

Rubbing my neck, and scratching my head, as if I were searching for bugs, I replied, "OK Stew, you have something on your mind?"

"First as far as extra equipment, like if it were a protective mask or even a wrench, we could put it in our locker, or even hide it under our mattress, but a gas driven machine? I was thinking we just leave it where it is; in the mechanical storage hold. We called it our mechanical area. People didn't usually come into the hold unless they are checking on stored items.

There are numerous types of doors: on deck, some appear to be a large safe like doors with many latching dogs around its perimeter. There were frame numbers on both sides of the bulkheads. I attempted to spin the locking wheels; Stewart moved me aside. As he turned the wheel, I watched as the locking pins slid out of the bulkhead and the heavy metal door crunched open. With a hiss of compressed air, the door inch open. The pungent odor was harsh and immediate. I looked over at Stewart and just shook my head.

After pulling the door all the way open, we put the Red Devil next to other gas-operated equipment. This area has always had a musty odor, but at that moment my gag reflex was working overtime.

I recorded the frame number, and we placed our unauthorized machinery behind the boxes and crates and cases of chemical suits, and next to other gas operated equipment that to which we were not assigned. We were ready, at least my team was ready.

Mr. Hales, our Division Officer is rarely seen, except for morning formation, and is seldom heard. That's why I was surprised as was most of the Division when he showed up in our tiny office. For a big man, it was almost amusing to see him edge his way through the crowd of Damage Controlman. Mr. Hale had us gather around, with Chief Fairchild on one side and First-Class Petty Officer Baily on the other. Like I mentioned before we had no problem hearing the Chief; that is when he chose to speak. He announced that we did an excellent job and the Liberty section had the weekend off.

As we were turning to leave Mr. Hale spoke, "Before you leave this ship, double-check and make sure all paperwork and equipment is ready for inspection. The inspectors will be here early Monday morning."

I volunteered to take Chambers' duty as PPO, (Police Petty Officer). The primary obligation of the PPO was to make sure that all sailors behave when returning to the ship after a night of deliberately getting intoxicated put to bed, and they did not cause too much of a disturbance. Chambers was married and besides it was only for one night. I figured

I'd get up early Saturday morning and take a trip across the bay to San Francisco. I found out that there was a place close to the Greyhound bus station that I could still get my blues dry-cleaned and rent civvies. It might be nice to wander the hills of San Francisco like a civilian.

I guess I was feeling a little melancholy and wanted to take one more look at my City by the Bay. I might even go over to that Delores next to the old Mission. I did not intend going to Mass. The weather forecast as sunny. The weather guy also said that there would not be fog. Most places forecast fog; San Francisco will predict when there is not going to be fog.

It was early. The men wouldn't be staggering back for several hours. A random thought hit me. I'll wander by the chaplain's office, and see if he one of his friends has him any of that special coffee. It was early. They hadn't started serving chow yet, and the ship was already starting to feel like a ghost ship.

Most of the Divisions released their people early. I guess that meant the everybody was ready for the upcoming big inspection. I must be old school. I remember a Chief on another ship, a ship I served aboard many years ago; I think his name was Samson. Chief Samson was a Chief Boatswain. He would say, "Ya know kids, a good inspector, especially one that is part of the Inspector General's team can always find something." It just seemed to me that two days before an inspection was not the time to sit back. In my time in the Navy, I have been through a few IG inspections. Arrogance is the kiss of death.

So, I once again find myself wondering the ship. Trying to think of something we forgot. I was in the process of checking the tags on the fire extinguishers. I didn't come close to all the fire extinguishers, but I did check the ones in the most prominent places. I was about to check our oxygen rebreathing apparatus. I was in the process of testing our chemical suits when I said to myself; everybody else was gone. 'I've got to stop this.'

I was walking through the forward mess area and decided to see if my friend, the Chaplain was still aboard. As I came near his office, I noticed that the door was cracked open. I pushed it open and saw a black man in dungarees squatting in front of the only locked filing cabinet in Father Tim's office. So, I did the usual to get his attention, "ahem," cleared my throat. He turned his head. There is no way I could squat like that. At least not for any length of time. His heels were flat on the deck, and his butt was resting on his heels.

He rose with ease, not even a grunt. He was lean yet lanky. I could see that he was well muscled. At first, I thought he was very young, but something in his bearing said military, he was not new to this rodeo. As he walked over towards me, I could see age lines around the corners of his eyes. Thomas

I spoke first, "Hi, I'm Fitzgerald. I just came down here to see if the Chaplain was busy."

He reached out a hand, "I'm Yancy, Darryl Yancy, Chaplain's assistant. Not long ago I was just another yeoman, working as one of the Captain's many clerks. Everybody is running around crazy getting ready including Chaplain Donahue. If it is an emergency, I'm sure I can get hold of him."

"Naw. I just wanted to visit. I'm Connor Fitzgerald Damage Controlman Second Class. Maybe we can get together for a cuppa someday when we get back to acting like real sailors."

As I turned to go, I heard what the sound of someone from the deep south was. "What didja stop by for?"

"Sorry, Yancy I just came by to shoot the bull with my favored priest. No emergency. I noticed a little twang in your voice. It took me a few minutes. Tell me if I'm wrong. You from Georgia?"

"Yep. Atlanta, a small town about thirty miles outside Atlanta. Woodstock. Where you from?"

"I'm not sure."

"Come on Connor. Everybody knows where they're from."

"OK. I'm not sure where I started, but I was six-years-old when my grandparents found me in Chicago. They took me to Florida, and that's where I was until I joined the Navy, the first time."

"Yes but…"

"Yancy, that's enough for now. It looks like you're in the middle of something."

"You're right we'll catch up later."

I dug into my collection of paperbacks. I do like westerns; I love the ones about Cowboys or more like the stories about the lone cowboy riding on his trusty steed. I was working on my collection, a second time. I found one I hadn't read.

This one was set more in modern times. It is a Navajo Policeman in New Mexico.

The book was good, and it is true I sometimes crave silence, but the Acey Deucy mess was like a tomb. The only thing I could hear in the compartment below, where I lived was grunting, groaning, and farting of forty sleeping men, Forty Damage Controlmen, and all our earthly possessions. My eyes were getting heavy. I had to get up and go topside for some fresh air.

It was getting close to the bewitching hour; that is when my chicks would come home to roost. I was standing at the head of the Afterbrow, with the OD, Officer of the Day. In this case, it was Chief of the Day. Enlisted people on large ships such as carriers use the gangway on Afterbrow just as an officer stands at the quarterdeck as the officers' board ship a Chief Petty Officer, in this case, Chief Wilkens stand at the gangway to the Afterbrow. I was standing with Chief Wilkins as the crew was making their way up the gangway. For the most part, they were well-behaved. One of my guys got a little loud but other than that all went well I counted my chicks, and everyone was tucked in. Of course, the married men including the Class B married would be staying ashore. Class B was the men that had girlfriends where they would be spending the night.

All my people were aboard, at least those I expected to come back aboard. Walker was about to pee in the garbage can when I grabbed him and led him up to the head.

I headed up to the mess deck grabbed two mugs of coffee and went back up to the hangar deck. Chief Wilkins was sitting at the desk in the little room right off the gangway.

He gave me half of the newspaper he was reading.

The OD's runner returned from his rounds. We were all sitting in the little OD's shack when we all got up to the sound of screaming. What I heard were two voices yelling, "Calm down sailor. You're lucky we didn't leave you in jail downtown."

The Chief went down to greet them, he turned back to his runner and told him to call the Petty Officer on duty for the Gunner mates.

What I saw were two large, muscular sailors wearing armbands that identified them as permanent shore patrol, and between them was Tom Jenkins, my friend from the line handling party. Tom was cursing and screaming and kicking. The two Shore Patrolmen was holding him at least a foot off the ground. Right, then Tom Jenkins reminded me of a two-year-old throwing a tantrum.

From what I overheard Jenkins, was arrested by San Francisco's finest for intoxication and attempting to sell a controlled substance. Chief Wilkins called two Marines up from corrections, and Tom Jenkins was taken away to spend the night, more than likely the rest of the weekend in the ship's brig.

The way I remember it that was the excitement for the evening. I was sitting in the OD's shack trying to read the rest of the newspaper and trying to keep my head from bouncing off the old gray metal desk.

Chief Wilkens tapped me on the shoulder, and said, "Connor why don't you hit the rack, Chief Brown is here to relieve me. I told him you were the PPO for Damage Control. If any of your people get rowdy, he'll send the runner to get you."

"Chief, I do not believe any more of my men will be coming aboard. I am sure that the people that are not aboard now are snuggled up with a warm body, preferably of the opposite sex. Your runner knows how to get hold of me. My compartment is right below the Acey Deucy mess."

I had a stiff neck from sleeping on our plastic couch. At least I was wearing my work jacket. When looking up, I could see that all the lights were on in the compartment. The last thing I remembered was that most everyone was asleep. Walker was the only one left. I thought I saw everyone come aboard, but I didn't remember seeing Walker. I've often thought that Walker's snoring could wake the dead.

Zero-six-hundred we had weighed anchor and were on our way to San Diego. There were no drills on our way down the coast of California. None of the squadrons were aboard. We did have the ship's helicopter, but the pilot was part of the ship's company.

I missed breakfast, but there were coffee and doughnuts on a table in the Acey Deucy mess. There was also a low-lying cloud of cigarette smoke. I quit smoking shortly after my divorce, but I was getting a nicotine buzz. I couldn't wait to get down below and smell nicotine.

We had tied up at North Island in San Diego. I was sitting at a table with a couple of my teammates when a large man in khakis that had been washed so many times that at first, I thought he was one of the cooks until I noticed the anchors on his collar. One of my teammates elbowed me and casually motioned with his head at the chief's belt line. There was no visible belt line. If he was wearing a belt, it was well hidden by his protruding belly.

He was coming our way. Sure enough, with a cup in one pudgy hand and at least Three powdered doughnuts in the other, he sat next to us. He set his coffee cup down, put the doughnuts down, licked his fingers and put out his hand. We shook hands, and then he announced, "I'm Chief Snyder. I'll be following you around. The rest of the team…" Raising his hand and pointing to the other strangers, made up of first and second-class petty officers, "are the other bean counters. We're going to check your inventory just to make sure you have the equipment you need to do your job. I can assure you we will not be running any drills."

Chief Snyder handed his clipboard to Petty Officer Thomas, a young black sailor that has been my shadow since I signed into the Division. As we headed down the passageway of the second deck heading for the machines that sent and delivered foam to the flight deck, I looked back at a puffing red-faced chief. Thomas tapped me on the shoulder, and in a stage whisper, "Fitz," with his thumb pointing back over his shoulder at Chief Snyder who was falling further and further behind, "I think if we don't slow down the chief is going to have a heart attack."

I stopped, pretending that I needed to say something to Petty Officer Thomas. As Chief Snyder got closer, we proceeded down the passageway at a slower pace.

The Chief **had** been about two paces behind me, but when I looked back over my shoulder, the chief had vanished. Thomas was ahead of me heading over toward the foam machine. I called out. Thomas…where is the chief?"

Thomas was on his toes, looking over my head. He pointed with his thumb, "Back there."

I turned and saw the chief bent over and sucking air. I asked Thomas to find some cold water.

"Fitz. We're not that far from the forward mess deck. The galley is open for lunch. Maybe we can get the old-timer some iced-tea."

Facing Thomas, and raising his shoulders, I replied, "Why not?" Turning to Chief Snyder, I commented, Chief Snyder, why don't we take a little break. The old-timer was puffing like a locomotive. It was close to the lunch hour, Winded Chief Snyder responded, Hey, guys that's great. I'm not hungry, but a cup of coffee would be great." Bending over and coughing, the Chief straightened and motioned for me, and Thomas to lead the way.

The Navy in their wisdom had replaced the old long tables where ten or more sailors would squeeze in on a bench where if you weren't careful you might be eating off your shipmate's tray and replaced them with tables that seated four. We found a table close to the large coffee urn.

After the chief had finished two steaming cups of black coffee, he apologized, and we proceeded on our tour of the Damage Control storage areas aboard ship. We slowed our pace down.

Turning to Chief Snyder, I commented, "Chief, we have protective masks and rebreathing units in several locations. We'll take our time, finish the second deck than we'll use the escalator and head up to them oh-three level."

Thomas tapped me on the shoulder and asked me, "What about the chemical suits?"

'We'll finish the oh-three level and show the chief our pumps and Red Devils." Turning to the chief, I remarked, "On the oh-three, we share some equipment with the aviation Damage Control teams."

Thomas proceeded to rearrange the forms on his clipboard. "Got ja Fitz."

Chief Snyder turned and looked at me. "Is there equipment stored anyplace else?

"Yes, Chief. On the deck below our Division is another storage area where we have more chemical suits two more Red Devils and a pump."

We visited the chemical storage areas on the oh-two level, an area that we had joint custody with n the aviation Damage Controlmen. Thomas went down his list, the chief asks a few questions, and then inquired, "Is atropine stored here?"

I explained, "We had joint custody of this storage area," pointing to several locked cabinets, "atropine is kept in the lower cabinets. In the upper cabinets, chemicals specifically used in the aircraft. I understand that there is another inspector with the aviation people. If you'd like I can coordinate with the air-dales?"

Chief Snyder responded, "No, that's alright, Jackson, First Class Jackson is inspecting aviation."

Chief Snyder had his hands around the steaming mug of coffee. The Chief's hands were shaking, and he was holding the cup up close to his face. The Master at Arms assigned to the mess deck came over to the table we were sitting. Bending down to quietly spoke in the Chief's ear, "Chief, I understand they have an excellent meal down in the Chief's mess."

With rank has its privilege; First and Second-Class Petty Officers get to sit in their own private dining area, CPOs or Chief Petty Officers have their own cooks, and they pay for the service and the extras they get in the CPO mess.

I looked over at Chief and asked, "Chief did you want to stop for lunch?"

The Chief looked up at the Master at Arms, then at me, "No I'm fine. Just needed a cup of Joe."

The Master at Arms, looking down at the Chief replied, "No problem Chief. I understand they are fixing roast beef with all the trimmings tonight if you are going to be aboard?"

As the Master at Arms started to turn away, the Chief said, "Sounds great." Looking over at Thomas and me, Chief Snyder responded, "I don't expect to stay aboard long. I'm sure we will finish the eyes-on by this afternoon. I may have to stay onboard just to tie up the paperwork."

Once the Master at Arms walked away, Chief Snyder looked up, and then to his right and then to his left. The Chief motioned for us to get closer as if we were going to share a great conspiracy. "Listen, I am so very sorry. I tried to tell the Navy that I didn't think I was ready to come back on active duty.

"I've been retired for over two decades. The Navy says they need us. Oh, I'm not the only one, mostly corpsmen. At any rate. After twenty years in the Navy and a few years with the Denver Fire Department seems my lungs are screwed up. They found something in the lungs." The Chief took a sip of his coffee and started to get up. Plopping back down, he looked over at me and said, "I promise not to be too much trouble for you. Normally it is not this bad. You know breathing is so overrated."

Thomas spoke up, "What's the deal? I always thought that the whole idea for you lifers was to put in your twenty and then retire to some tropical paradise sipping a My-Tai."

"Who are you calling a Lifer?"

Squinting his eyes and putting his finger under his nose, Thomas continued, "Well Fitz returned after a few years. I'm pretty sure he is going to stay this time."

Chief Snyder stood, caught himself on the table. "OK. I retired, and my return was requested. What's your story?" Standing up Chief Snyder stretched, and then commented, "I'm rested. You guys ready to look at more storage areas?"

Looking over at Thomas, who always seemed to need a haircut and a comb. Looking at the old Chief, I responded. "Ok, Thomas. Pay attention. I am not going to tell this story again." I left the chief and Thomas standing at the table as I took the coffee to the scullery; I often wondered if they washed the cups. I swear some days I can taste the previous night's supper.

The Chief looked up at me, and asked: "How long did you stay out?"

"After ten years, I found myself looking down at a giant cement hole with an Aircraft Carrier sitting on a metal horse."

Thomas stuttered, "What-wha did you do in those ten years?"

"Lived off the GI Bill while I attended college. I'd have stayed in school, but Uncle Sam informed me that since I got a degree that I would have to go to work; they were finished paying me.

Chief Snyder remarked, "You couldn't find a job even as a college graduate?"

"I attended a small teacher's college up in the panhandle of Florida. Would you believe there were not that many teaching jobs? I wasn't locked down to a location, so I got a job teaching at a little state-run school in Mariana Florida. That lasted a couple years."

Thomas remarked, "I've heard a lot of people get burned out teaching."

"It wasn't that. I just got tired of being bullied by fourth graders."

I motioned to Chief Snyder, and asked, "You finished Chief?" He shook his head. I grabbed the empty cups and took them to the scullery." We have one storage area left. More chemical suits, more protective masks, and several oxygen re-breathing units. That's it. Oh Yeah, there are several First Aid Kits with the usual items, besides the gauze and mercurochrome there is morphine. We also have several cases of Atropine. The storage room is in a watertight compartment on the third deck, directly below our Division."

The Chief seemed to have gotten a second wind as we descended to the storage area. We proceeded to the third deck and the last of our inventory. With smooth precision, the locking pins slid out, and the massive metal door cracked open with a sinister hiss of compressed air. The first thing I felt as the door swung open was the bite of the stifling air against my skin. *Something's wrong! This space is not refrigerated, but it should at least have circulation. The draft was warm, not only was it warm, but It was dank and humid, the salty-sweet smell of urine and excrement.* I didn't say anything, but the scent reminded me of a toilet in a Hong Kong waterfront bar.

The cavernous space was crammed with boxes. The boxes or containers were stacked, close together and at least three or four high forming a maze of narrow passageways with walls of corrugated steel. Several divisions used this old storage hold. We not only kept The Red Devil, and the pumps down here but, chemical, suits, protective masks.

The lighting system was inadequate. I've been told that every ship no matter how new it has ghosts, or things that never work right. Less than half of the fixtures worked, and those had been fitted with energy-saving sodium-vapor lamps. What little light they produced was largely eclipsed by the towering rows of shipping containers.

The lights flickered out. I was waiting for the battle lanterns to come on; they didn't. There was a suffocating, putrid odor of rotten eggs. The hold was not used to store meat. Yet the rancid smell of rotting flesh seemed to be everywhere.

I yelled, "Thomas are you anywhere near the filing cabinets."

"Yeah, boss. I can feel one of the filing cabinets."

"The filing cabinet is not locked. In the top drawer, there are flashlights." I thought that I was not as prepared as I thought. All my team should have been carrying torches.

Shining the light from one of the flashlights directly into my eyes, I commented, "OK, so you found the flashlights." Chief Snyder had already pulled a handkerchief out and was holding it over his nose. With a muffled voice Chief Snyder blurted, "When is the last time anyone has been down here?"

Trying to ignore my gag reflex, I responded, "Three days ago, it was Friday." I became aware that there was no circulation in the room. I never thought about it, but the ship's blowers provided fresh air throughout the ship through vents and tubes that were in every compartment. The air in this storage area was still. "We, that is Petty Officer Thomas and me, dusted, poured bleach down the drains, we even mopped the deck."

I started to gag. That smell was strongest from someplace behind the rack of shelves. "I guess it could be a dead rat. Although if it is a dead rat, it must be huge." That would upset the old man. The Navy doesn't take rodents kindly. Our deployment would be delayed until we found destroyed every rat, mouse, and cockroach on the ship. Plus, we would have to scrub the decks and every corner.

Chief Snyder yelled, "Fitzgerald!" Signaling toward me and then pointing, "Those shelves. There is something on the deck behind the shelf."

They were not really shelves, they were cabinets. Atropine and morphine were in a secure steel container, much like a person would see on a hospital ward. The Chief was now frantically waving at me. "What is it?"

Just then the lights flickered back on. I yelled, "Thomas get over here. I think we need to stay together. I don't really want to be caught in the dark again."

"Thomas, are you near the filing cabinets?" "Not now. I already gave you a flashlight." Chief Snyder had a handkerchief over his nose and mouth and pointing behind the shelf nearest the bulkhead. I shined my light on the deck next to the chief. What I saw looked very much like some sailor taking a nap. At first, I thought someone had come down here either to get drunk or get high. He was sitting against the bulkhead with his head resting on his chest. It was Petty Officer Jenkins, a very pale Jenkins. The lights were now on in the storage room, but Jenkins was still in the shadows. Looking down, I had to blink and rub my eyes. Above Jenkins' black sock in his left ankle was a hypodermic needle.

I wasn't the only one, but the stench of vomit hit my gag reflex. I looked up and saw Tyrell holding his nose.

The lights were now on, and it was no trick of lights and shadows, Jenkins sitting against the bulkhead with his chin on his chest, and a hypo in his ankle. There was vomit down his dungaree shirt, and around his lips. I could see blood mixed with the vomit and around his nose. I walked over towards what used to be Jenkins. Going down on one knee I saw a light tan powder on his cheek and near his nose.

I could feel my stomach come up to my throat. I was about to brush white powder off the dead man's shirt. There was also white powder on Jenkins' cheek. It felt as if my heart stopped as I felt a firm grip on my wrists.

"Stop!" I looked up to see Father Donahue; he had his hands wrapped around both my wrist.

My mouth was dry, and I felt as if I were going to vomit, then I asked, "What are you doing here?" I fought to release my wrist from the priest's grip. Father Donahue's grip felt like a vice.

Master at Arms, First Class Petty Officer Petty ran by my door yelling that there was an accident."

The lights flickered and were on once again. "Father, I was just going to check to see if I could find a pulse."

Father Donahue released his grip and gently moved me back. He was putting on rubber gloves, when he said, "I'll check for a pulse."

I looked up and saw a crowd. I could see Father Donahue saying something in Doc Miller's ear. Some wiry sailor in dungarees was snapping pictures. No flash and I could barely see the camera; I assumed he had a camera as he was dancing around the body with something in his hand.

I looked back at Tyrell and cynically asked, "Tyrell, did you invite the entire crew down here?"

"I just called the corpsman and the Master at Arms." Countered Tyrell.

The only person I remembered seeing was the priest. I don't remember seeing anyone else enter the storage hold.

The priest was still bent over Jenkins. He stood up and walked over towards me. "I'm sorry Connor, but I had to stop you. Russel Cole had that same white powder under his bloody nose."

"Honest Father I just going to see if he had a pulse. Besides I suspected him of being a coke head."

"If I'm not mistaken, that powder is not cocaine."

"I ain't a doctor, but I can tell he is dead." Commented Petty Officer Tyrell Thomas.

I'd never seen Thomas move that quick before. For a black man, he looked pale. He grunted towards me. In a whisper, "Fitz, I'll call Chief Fairchild."

"Thanks, I would have forgotten about him."

Chief Snyder had squatted next to Jenkins' body, the chief put his hands on his knees, rose. Without turning Chief Snyder observed, "Looks like vomit next to his body."

Father spoke up, "Don't anyone touch the body or the vomitus."

Tyrell spoke up, "The what?"

Responding calmly Father said, "The vomit."

By the time the Master at Arms arrived the storage hold had looked like Christmas; the blowers were still not working in the storage area. Master Chief Benedetto, looked as if he just got out of the shower.

Rubbing the bald spot on his head, the Master Chief looked down at me, "There's to be an inquiry, but...A formality, I presume. The Skipper ain't gonna like it. We are definitely gonna be late getting on the station."

"Chief, why would they have an inquiry? I mean he offed himself, right?"

I looked over to see Thomas on the outside of the hatch with a cup in his hand. I could see steam coming out of the large white ceramic mug. Weird, Thomas doesn't drink coffee. I was amazed to see Chief Snyder squatting against the bulkhead. I thought for sure he was too fat and old to squat. I'm only 35, and my knees give me a fit if I must hunker for any length of time.

Chapter Eight

I don't think any of our Damage Control team slept that night. A few were up in the Acey-Deucy Mess playing Dominoes. I had trouble trying to read. I wandered the ship again. The Chaplain's office was locked. I even wandered around where the Marines hung out; no, Gunny.

The Admin inspection we just completed was only a start to the testing that will come. Seems the paperwork had to be done right and accounted for first, then we get to go to sea and have another ORI Team grade us on how we respond in combat.

I remember thinking, *if we are lucky, all our paperwork is in order, all our equipment, and our personal gear is serviceable. We may just pass inspection.* I still didn't feel confident about winning that 'E.', or getting excellence.

I remember thinking, what now. If everything were running as expected, we would be loading stores and prepare to set sail for Hawaii, where we would once again be tested. This time we get to play war. I also remember thinking that if we stayed tied up there in Alameda much longer, the coffee grounds would be piling up above the waterline.

It always seemed a bit repetitious, but once the inspection teams give us our admin marks, we will play war off San Diego, head back to San Francisco, then off to Hawaii.

Women! I thought I was over women. I just couldn't keep that green-eyed redhead out of my mind. Still cheap, I'll give her a call when we get back to Alameda. It's probably the way too early to ask for a date. WESTPAC cruises usually last nine months. With what is going on over there right now, there is no way to know how long we will be in the land, or waters of fried rice. *I mean could I expect her to wait for nine months or longer? I wasn't even gone that long when Mavis left me.*

Back at sea. Before leaving North Island, the rest of the air squadrons came aboard; that is everyone but the planes and the pilots. We were scheduled to meet them at sea for them to crash and dash, touch and go. Of course, everything is made into an acronym. So, this would be called Carrier Qualls. The remaining two squadrons were out of Whidbey Island Washington Point Mugu California.

Along with aircraft mechanics airplane electricians, and air traffic controllers. Our ship's company would receive cooks from each of the air squadrons.

It had been a long time since hearing the scream of jet engines, the thump of aircraft smacking the flight deck. There seemed to be strangers in every department aboard ship from the machine shops to the electrical shop. If my memory does not fail me, they wouldn't be strangers for long.

Once again found myself wandering the lower decks of the ship. This time it was the quiet that I was trying to get away from. Impossible I missed the noise. Not only the aircraft, and the pneumatic tools. But the sounds men. Talking, yelling, composed conversations, and lively stories.

What better time to visit the priest and Gunny. I was at his office, but the door was locked. I knocked, but no answer. Just as I was about to walk away, I spotted Petty Officer Yancy with a stack of folders in his arms. "Hey, Yancy!"

"You looking for Father?"

"Yeah, thought I might visit."

Yancy had keys in his hand under all the folders. He motioned to me with his head to grab the keys. "Would you unlock the door for me?"

"No problem. Where is Father?"

"He's giving a class in the library. It's just starting. You can just walk on in…"

Why not. It is something to do. Besides the noise level down here is not quite as bad as it is on the mess deck or my compartment.

There were more than a few people, some sitting on a metal chair and a few standing. I tried to act like a mouse; staying as far away from the crowd as I could.

Father Donahue was sitting at a small table in front of the crowd. He did mention that he taught high school, and I could picture him in front of unruly high school students.

It was just a buzz at first then I started to pick up the gist of the lecture.

Father Continued, "These foes of the early church make great historians…

"These historical enemies of the Church also make wonderful allies when it comes to combating historic anti-Catholic and anti-Christian myths…"

The priest went on for about half an hour. He then opens the floor for questions. Looking over at me he raised an eyebrow and pointed to a corner of the room where Gunny was sitting.

What I heard of the early Church I found interesting. In the back of my mind, I am still trying to justify my feelings about the Catholic Church. No about all churches.

Father was saying something…I must have spaced out. I don't know what I was thinking. It has happened before. When married with a newspaper, or a book in my hand, or maybe just staring at the television, Mavis would ask,

"What are you thinking about?"

I'd say, "Nothing."

Her face would get red, and she would remark, "That is impossible. You're hiding something."

Father Donahue's voice penetrated my consciousness. I sensed he was looking at me. "OK, men let us take our trash with us, and could of few of you fold and stack the chairs?"

I grabbed and folded three of the folding chairs, stacked and secured them to the bulkhead. Gunny had always impressed me as the most focused man I had ever known; apparently not now. I probably should have left him alone, but like a bull, I just went charging in, and of course, I just had to break the spell, "So, Gunny how did the inspection go?"

Another thing I thought I would never see; he flinched. Turning to me I got to see his big brown eyes. Shaking his head like that old wet poodle, he said, "Oh, Connor."

"Earth to Gunny." I was making an effort to be cute. "I asked how the inspection went?"

Gunnery Sergeant doggedly replied, "The audit report contains 5 material weaknesses 3 significant deficiencies, and 2 instances of noncompliance with applicable laws and regulations. I received a marginal but was told if I corrected these problems, my detachment would be combat ready. I know this is my fault, but Corporal Cole was the Armorer, and his direct supervisor was the Lieutenant. I must be getting too old for this. I did not think I had to supervise a commissioned officer."

Gunny motioned for me to accompany him to the coffee pot. "I understand you found a body while with the IG Inspector?"

"Yes, we did. Petty Officer Jenkins must have been there a while; he was pretty ripe." Gunny offered me a cup of coffee. I nodded, "Sorry Gunny. My stomach is not quite up to Navy coffee right now. I was sure that would blow the inspection for us. I mean he, that is Jenkins had to have been sitting in his own waste for more than a few minutes. I was sure that Chief Snyder that was our IG Inspector would make something out of us not checking our assigned spaces. I think finding a body may have helped us. Gunny I know you are less than pleased with the results of your inspection. The Lieutenant was in charge. It's not your fault. This is your last cruise. You're going to hang up your Marine Greens, and your Parade Dress Blues."

With a stern look, Gunnery Sergeant Fernando Cortez's eyes seemed to be shooting daggers at me. He turned away for a second, and when he turned back, he had half a grin on his face. Gunny's response was, "Listen, I was and remain proud to wear this uniform. If there is anything I will miss; it will be putting on that uniform."

He put his meat hooks of a hand on my shoulder. "No, The Detachment did not pass. I will make sure that all the fault found will be corrected, and now I will take charge. That college boy will just have to back off and let this Marine take charge. You know I think the inspector was going easy on us. There was so much wrong when he went through that I believe he missed something."

"Father Donahue was standing right behind me. The priest saw, "What are you getting at, Frank?"

"Well Cole was a qualified Armorer, but the books that I showed the inspector were too neat. There weren't any cross-outs. I mean even the cleaning equipment was clean and in order, not just on paper, but in the storage containers. The Armory was one place that the inspector could not find fault. It just didn't look right to me."

"Gunny?"

"What is it, Connor."

"I can't prove it, but I think Lieutenant Reese is selling weapons."

Gunny was inches in front of me. I'd only known him for a few months, but I have never seen him move that fast."

"Petty Officer, do you know what you are saying? Never mind you are accusing a Marine Officer of stealing and selling weapons."

"Yes, Gunny. That is why I haven't told anyone." I acknowledged.

I carried the large coffee pot to the deep sink in the utility closet next to the library. I washed the coffee grinds down the deep drain and was rinsing the coffee pot when Gunny tapped me on the shoulder.

"Ya know Connor, after almost thirty years in the Corps, having done everything from cleaning toilets to handling ledgers. I know how to balance the books, but there is something wrong. Crazy huh. Something's wrong because it is too right." The Gunny proceeded to rub his head.

"Gunny, that makes no sense at all."

Father Donahue had locked the library and turned to the Gunny and me, "You guys going to turn in?"

Gunny spoke up. "Not right away. I need to check the Armory. We passed the inspection, and the audit went well, but I just got a gut feeling something is wrong."

Father turned to me, "What about you, Connor?"

"One question." I could see the priest raise an eyebrow, "Why did you stop me from touching Jenkins. I mean I knew he was dead, but didn't think it would harm anything if I double checked. I wasn't going to move the body." I kind of scooted in a metal chair, "I can see a priest being called if someone dies, but it was pretty obvious that Tom Jenkins was dead."

"One answer. I saw the brownish powder on Jenkins' shirt. Corporal Cole had the same powder on his shirt. The powder is drug, and from what the pathologist and I discovered over at Oak Knoll was that the powder on Cole's shirt, as the powder on Jenkins shirt, was very potent opiate."

I just had to know, "Father, you told Gunny and me that Cole's parents did not want Cole cut on."

Father replied, "The Pathologist at Oak Knoll is required to check for toxins. He, the Pathologist shared his results; that's how we identified the drugs in Cole's system.

"I'd seen Jenkins rubbing his nose. His nose seemed to be always running. I thought it might have been cocaine."

Gunny was just standing there. Father started to walk away then stopped. "Whatever that substance is, and I think I know. It can enter your system through your skin. Countered the priest.

Gunny remarked, "Father, you're a priest. How do you know so much about chemicals and drugs?"

Rubbing his scalp, Timothy Donahue pulled out three of the folded chairs and motioned for Gunnery Sergeant Cortez and me to sit. "OK. I think I mentioned that I was a high school Chaplain and science teacher. Well, long before that I worked as a scientist. To be exact, I spent a few years working for the CDC as a Cytologist, a biologist that spends most days analyzing cells and their environment to detect abnormalities. Doc Miller is a good man and a good general practitioner. But I am probably the closest thing to a pathologist aboard this ship. I have seen that light brown powder before. Cocaine is white and crystal-like in substance. Cole and Petty Officer Jenkins had a trace of a drug called Fentanyl, only about ten times stronger than heroin. From what Doc Miller and I could tell, there was both heroin and Fentanyl in his system. Fentanyl has been around for a long time. It is used to relieve severe pain. It seems to have gained popularity on the streets. And it can be absorbed through the skin."

The next couple of days were spent re-educating some of the crews that came aboard with the air squadrons. New faces, and some old familiar faces. We ran a few drills just to see what training was needed.

I passed Father Donahue in one of the passageways, he reminded me of the rabbit in "Alice in Wonderland, I'm late I'm late for a very important date." Running two and Fro, more like walking very fast. The only one I noticed moving faster was Ensign Simpson. Father was carrying folders, while Mr. Simpson if not carrying folders was carrying bundles of mail; besides being the Transportation Officer, he was also the Mail Officer. I liked Mr. Simpson, but on more than one occasion would get annoyed. I just felt I had to knock that smile off his face. He was much too cheerful.

The activity aboard calmed to a mild roar. The passageways were literally deserted. And I was in my rack with my blanket pulled over my head.

I felt the ship shudder as if it got a chill. I reluctantly opened my eyes and propped myself. Most of the men were scrambling about in different stages of dress. Sticking my head out of my rack, yelling, "What's going on?"

Somebody yelled back, "Skipper came on the 1-MC a few minutes ago, and said that since this would be our last full weekend at home, he wanted us to take the weekend off. Oh yeah, Baily was down here, and we are supposed to get dressed up and stand on the flight deck as we tie-up."

My beard is sparse, and with my ruddy complexion and blonde hair, I should be able to get away without shaving.

However, my immediate supervisor, the chief or the division officer always seem to know when I try to skip shaving. So, there I was with pieces of toilet paper stuck on my bleeding face; the result of trying to shave three men back from a mirror with an old razor. The salt spray stinging my face as I stood along the edge of the flight deck.

There it was again, that shudder, then clunk, the sound of metal rubbing rock; reminding me of the sound of fingernails scraping across a chalkboard. I was close enough to the edge of the flight deck to see sand and mud coming to the surface of the bay. Close enough to see the people on the pier, squinting as the reflection of the sun off the water and through the mist was making it difficult for the crowd to see the ship.

The klaxon and the bell went off as we all did an abrupt about-face and ran to our Battle Stations, only to find out that we, that is the ship, dug itself into 27 feet of sand on the starboard side, and 18 feet of sand on the port side of the ship.

There were two harbor tug boats on either side of the giant carrier; they did nothing but turn up more sand. Two seagoing tugs were brought up against the ship. I heard scraping, but not much else. There was Coast Guard Cutter in port, and with the help of destroyers, the carrier was finally pushed up against the pier.

Liberty was granted to the married men. This time I did not volunteer to stay aboard; I was volunteered. The only place I wanted to go was across the bridge in San Francisco.

I just couldn't keep that red-head out of my mind.

Chapter Nine

I got out of my dress blues and changed into undress blues. I did manage to go ashore, but only as far as the Acey Deucy Club. Since I didn't drink I had a something carbonated, might have been a Sprite.

It was Friday, and I was not scheduled to be on watch until 0800 hours Saturday. I could have taken the bus to San Francisco, but that would not have allowed me anytime to spend with Morag.

A few of the men that went ashore, in dress blues with the name of the ship, displayed on the left sleeve at the shoulder were being teased by bartenders, waitresses, and even cab drivers. The stories going around were, "Will that be on-the-rocks?"

Damage Control teams are made up of men from different divisions. Our only excitement was responding to a fire in the Wardroom. Seems like one of the junior officers tried to heat up a sweet roll in the toaster.

I had not planned to go anywhere. I intended to sleep in. Sunday in port meant brunch. In other words, I could go to breakfast and lunch at the same time. Sleep in, if I got to the galley before noon.

It was 2200 hours or 10 PM, the galley was open for mid-rats; a meal served for the night workers. I made myself a sandwich and was about to sit down at a table when Chief Fairchild stopped me and asked, "How many men have we here?"

"You mean aboard ship?"

The Chief seemed to be getting a little frustrated, when with a sigh, he said, "Yes, here aboard ship."

"I'm not sure. We have a few that are on duty; maybe six. I think I saw Schultz and Murray. They just got back aboard. Why?"

Looking kind of sheepish, "I want all men in dress blues and shined shoes on the flight deck by 0800 hours. Seems as if we are having a change of command."

There goes my sleepy Sunday. I thought I'd go ashore; maybe as far as the Navy Exchange and pick up a Sunday paper. It had been a long time since I pulled the Sunday paper apart to read the comics, I kind of missed that little magazine that was in the middle of the newspaper.

No…I was put in charge of trying to contact our sailors ashore. It would have been nice if everyone had phones, but the need for phones did not seem to be a priority. For some sailors, mainly Petty Officers and Commissioned Officers the San Francisco Bay Area was their Duty Station. Yeah, I even got hold of them.

At 0730 hours on a chilly Sunday the Damage Control Division, except for our Division Officer, Mr. Hales was present on the flight deck. Looking down the rows of sailors and, the sailors of the Damage Control Division I could see more than a few blood-shot eyes.

We had come to attention, and out of the corner of my eye, I saw Captain Prescott walking up to the raised stage with a podium. His usual grin was missing. I couldn't tell, but it seemed to me that his eyes were downcast. There was another Captain at the left of Captain Prescott. Captain Prescott stepped behind the podium turned and saluted the other Captain. Turning and facing the crew, Captain Prescott announced, "Officers and men Let me introduce your new commanding officer, Captain Daniel Briggs." They saluted one another and shook hands. Captain Prescott continued, "May I say it has been a pleasure to serve as your commanding officer." Our Captain and former Skipper made a sharp turn and left the stage.

At first glance, Captain Briggs was more likely to be taken for an attorney than a naval officer. His long face and narrow cheekbones gave him a clean and efficient look that his neatly trimmed black hair seemed to reassert. His lips were thin, giving him an intelligent expression that reinforced the image of humorless efficiency. The laugh lines around his mouth were the only giveaways of imaginative spirit that hid behind his subdued brown eyes. A shade under six feet tall, he had a compact physique that was neither skinny nor overly muscular. I could visualize him in front of a jury. Our new Captain appeared to be about thirty, or possibly thirty-five. He just seemed young for the commanding officer of an Aircraft Carrier.

I did manage to go ashore and get a Sunday Newspaper; comics, magazine and all. It was a little humorous; Father Donahue was saying Mass near the fantail, and Reverend Shaw was holding Protestant services near the forward elevator.

Walking past the quarterdeck, I became aware of several sailors carrying Sea Chest, better known as footlockers, and luggage down the quarter-deck gangplank. The sailors were placing the bags in the back of a gray van. Captain Prescott was climbing into a black sedan.

I was on the Naugahyde covered couch in the compartment when a tall skinny pockmarked faced kid in dungarees banged on the open hatch to the compartment. Trying to catch his breath he asked, "Are you the duty Damage Controller? Are you Fitzgerald?"

Putting my feet on the deck, folding and placing the Sunday paper on the table. I was lost in reverie until I heard someone clearing his throat. "Are you First Class Fitzgerald?'

"Yes, I am. Damage Control First Class Connor Fitzgerald. What can I do for you?"

"Captain wants to see you on the bridge."

"Me?"

"Yes, Sir."

I couldn't help it, "You see any gold or silver on my collar?"

"No, sir. I mean no,"

"Relax, I'm only having a little fun with you. What in the world would the Captain want with me?"

"You best ask him. He seems to be a little frustrated."

"Where is the Captain now?"

"He's waiting for you on the bridge. I'll wait here while you put on your shoes."

Wiggling my foot into one of my shoes, I replied. "I think I can find the bridge."

This skinny pimple-faced kid looked down at me and said, "Captain Briggs wants me to bring you to him personally."

By the time we reached the bridge, I had grabbed my knees and bent over to catch my breath. After an uncontrolled spasm of coughing, I could speak. "Just give me a second."

Putting out his hand the pimple-faced kid grabbed my outstretched hand and said, "Sorry I'm Quartermaster striker Johnson."

Entering that small area known as the wheelhouse, I looked over to see Captain sitting in a large padded chair. His head was resting in his open hand. He appeared to be in deep thought. I did notice that the Captain was much older than I had perceived him to be when I first saw him earlier at the Change of Command Ceremony.

As his head came up, it felt to me that his large brown eyes were looking right through me. The Captain put out his hand and grabbed my hand stating, "You are just the man I was looking for, Connor Fitzgerald. First, I need to ask if you can arrange to have protective masks and chemical suits stored here on the bridge; that would be in addition to gear each member of the bridge crew has been assigned? Secondly, follow me into the chart room."

I just had a feeling that all was not as it seemed. I felt my face redden as I thought, *'How does the Captain know my name? Didn't he ask for the duty Damage Controller?"*

There were tables with maps and charts on them. There was a long table that looked like the kind of table found in the boardroom of a large corporation. At the large table, there was a blonde, almost white-haired lean man wearing a Navy-Blue windbreaker. The blonde man had a striped dress shirt under the windbreaker

Reaching out his hand toward the man in the windbreaker, Captain Briggs said, "This is Special Agent Gabriel. He is with NCIS. I believe you met him when you found one of our crewmen had overdosed."

What could I say, "Yes Sir? I remember."

Captain Briggs indicated with a gesture that I was to sit in a chair across from the Special Agent. He then said, "I received information that you think you saw Marine Lieutenant selling weapons to a local street gang. I'll let Special Agent Gabriel ask you a few questions. Fitzgerald, you are not in trouble."

"First, let me explain something. The recent Inspector General's inspection found some discrepancies in the records for the small arms in the Marine Armory. We have not been able to locate Lieutenant Reese. He is officially on temporary assignment at Leggett Field. He is supposed to report aboard tomorrow. I would like to gather as much information as possible before he gets back." Exclaimed Special Agent Gabriel.

"OK Special Agent. Why am I here? I can tell you what I saw and what I heard. I'm pretty sure Gunnery Sergeant told you about what I saw."

"It's true. I would like to hear the story from you. I would also like to know how you managed to get near enough to a San Francisco street gang?" Asked the Special Agent.

I guess I must have sounded a little defensive with my answer, "I met a woman, and was looking for her address when I literally tripped into a garage run by these people. They thought they had sent me on my way when I noticed a gray van pulled into the garage. So, I hid." I got a raised eyebrow from Captain Briggs.

"I was at the side of the garage, close enough to hear what they were saying. I wasn't sure it was the Lieutenant, but I was sure I recognized Ship Serviceman Kalama." I answered.

"How did you know it was Ship Serviceman Kalama?" Said the Special Agent.

"His size." I could see the expression on the faces of both the Special Agent and the Captain. "Kalama picked me up at the airport the night I signed aboard, and he repaired my dress blues. He is the first Samoan I have ever met. The shaved head and his size also drew my attention."

Special Agent Gabriel warned me, "Please do not tell anyone of this meeting."

Captain Briggs added, "We may need your help. I spent most of the last night into the early hours of this morning trying to learn all I could about this ship and its crew. Captain Prescott is a good man and a good commanding officer. What happened to him could have happened to anyone, but he did leave me a thick folder full of things that were bothering him about this ship and its crew."

Special Agent Gabriel spoke up, "We need your help. Captain Prescott called in NCIS several months ago. I've been aboard since Petty Officer Jenkin's death. The local authorities and the FBI think that the drugs that were found with Jenkins were purchased ashore. We did not expect to find any problem with weapons. Gunnery Sergeant Cortez feels otherwise. We told The Gunnery Sergeant that we would consider it. Finally, I would rather you not say to the Gunnery Sergeant that we are actively investigated the arms allegations."

Captains Briggs waved me out of the room, with the last remark, "We still need those extra protective masks."

Taking a deep breath, and letting it out as quietly as possible, I replied, "Yes sir, and I'll bring up several sizes of chemical suits." I was about to exit the room when I turned and asked, "What about firefighting? The Captain looked up and raised his eyebrows. "OBAs or oxygen breathing apparatus, flame-retardant coveralls, and gloves?"

"Thank you, Petty Officer, but we have OBAs and gloves. But if the bridge should get hit we probably will not have time to put on that gear. It would not hurt to add a few pairs of the flame-resistant gloves."

I didn't know how to tell my new commanding officer. But once the horn, the bo'sun's pipe, and the bell rang the bridge crew like the rest of the ship's crew should be in battle uniform, which includes a protective mask by his side, and their chemical coveralls within a few feet to me put on immediately.

The noise level aboard ship was almost hushed as we pulled into the shipping lane. I along with the rest of the enlisted members of the Damage Control Division was combing the ship, workspaces, living areas, and common areas inspecting firefighting equipment, and the sprinkler systems.

The waters off San Francisco were as usual; just a little rough. It was explained to me once that with the current coming down from the Arctic and the warmer waters met, well it could get a bit rough.

On the second level, I noticed an office door open. I was just about to shut the door when I saw Special Agent Gabriel, I couldn't be sure as he was leaning over with his head in the trash can. He apparently decided that he didn't really want his breakfast. From the doorway, I glanced around the office checking for fire extinguishers and sight testing the sprinkler system.

Chapter Ten

WE spent seventy-two hours tied up at Ford Island. A bus to Hotel Street, where I wandered around, and for some crazy reason I debated with myself about getting a tattoo; no that really was a dumb idea. A cab to Waikiki; where I rented a swimsuit and laid in the hot sand and warm waters of Oahu.

I ran into a few shipmates, who tried to convince me to go to one of the favorite clubs on Waikiki. I turned them down, but they did persuade me to go to a restaurant on Waikiki that was reputed to have some of the best steaks on the islands, or for that matter anywhere, or so I was told. Walker another Damage Controlman said, "Fitz they guarantee that the steak will be cooked exactly the way you like it."

I found out later that the reason they could ensure that the steak would be cooked the way I liked it is that the restaurant had a large pit in the middle of the dining room and everyone grilled their own steak. The meat was tender and flavorful, and I did cook it to perfection.

Our ORI went well. All the departments got excellent scores. The Marine Detachment managed to correct their discrepancies before leaving the Bay Area. The inconsistencies that were corrected were mainly administrative. Weapons were missing. After filling out a ton of paperwork, the weapons were marked as lost at sea. We were officially certified for combat. On our way out of Pearl, the conversation seemed hushed the traffic up and down the passageways orderly. The Boatswain Mates were swabbing decks and shining brass. Amazing the ship is prepared for war. The whole ship shook like a wet dog every time the Cats, the catapult would pop when launching an aircraft. Seemed like we no sooner left the channel out of Pearl and the airplane drivers started with their Crash and Dash, touch and go.

It started, the bo'sun's would blow his pike, the Captain would yell General Quarters. We would secure from General Quarters. Then again. If it wasn't the Captain on the 1MC, it was the Exec. We'd get a little break. Maybe enough time to piss, or grab something to drink. Then it would be the Officer of the Deck. Each time General Quarters was called we were reminded that it was a drill.

We were never actually called down from General Quarters Zebra was set while we were at General Quarters, which meant that all hatches were secured, nobody traveled through the ship. Not only were the hatches secure so was the ventilation system. All the time we would feel the cats pop, and the aircraft launch. Then I could have sworn that I heard the breaks of a jet as it hooks the arresting gear.

We were then put on Condition 3, doors were not entirely open, but a person could travel through the ship by opening the little door in the hatches marked with an x. Half the duty sections were manned. Hot meals were served, and there might have been a short time that some of the crew sleep in their racks.

We were given a reprieve, we were still at Condition 3, but we could walk around the ship, always keeping our protective mask and helmet close by.

We were going to be late, but we did stop in Subic to pick-up supplies. The ship went into two section liberty. It was Cinderella Liberty, we all had to be home by midnight.

There are several clubs on base. I made it a point to visit each one. No longer being a drinker, I got restless. The entertainment was good. It always amazed me that the Filipino singers could imitate most of the popular American singers.

Once back at sea we resumed the General Quarters drills. About two days out the exercises stop. That is until 0430 the following day. The klaxon went off the bell rang and the bo'sun's blew his pipe. "General Quarters, General Quarters, Battle Stations. All hands man their Battle Station." The surprise, "This is not a drill. This is your Captain. I say again this is not a drill."

We had seven minutes to set condition ZEBRA, we did it in five. I do believe that if a mosquito snuck aboard it would not be able to get through the ship with all the hatches watertight.

The Skipper came up on the 1MC, "We are three hours out of Yankee Station. We are in the Gulf of Tonkin."

Petty Officer Wright was a sallow looking lanky man whose hair always reminded me of cut hay. Out of nowhere, Wright makes an announcement, "I believe that we are now members of the Tonkin Gulf and Yacht Club."

The Skipper stayed on the 1MC telling us what was going on. "There are three carrier battle groups on the station." Then there was silence. Then there was nothing from the Skipper, not even static from the speakers.

It was strangely quiet. We had been launching and retrieving aircraft while those of us not involved in flying operation stayed locked down at General Quarters, Condition ZEBRA all hatches secured. Anyone trying to move about the ship would be shot. **No**, but we were acutely aware of the penalties for breaking ZEBRA.

Two hours out and we got a short reprieve. The Captain had come back down to Condition 3.

I just had to at least get up to the hangar deck. I had prickly heat, for us adults, it is called a heat rash, I do not believe there was no place on my body that did not have the red itchy bumps.

I just had to go topside. So as soon as the hatches were open, I made it to the weather deck, which on a carrier is the hangar deck. I was standing on the port side of the hangar deck, looking at the gently rolling sea. The Skipper came across the 1-MC informing us that we were traveling at fifteen knots. I was drenched in sweat. The armpits of my dungaree shirt were white with salt.

I headed toward the fantail. I was starting to cool off. With my wet shirt and the slight breeze, I was beginning to feel a chill. There was a full moon. I knew the other ships were out there, but all I could see was the silhouettes of the darkening ships in the distance. It had been quiet, other than the sounds of the engines and generators. What seemed to be out of nowhere I heard the sea explode as if a whale was breaching the surface. I turned in the direction of the sound what I saw was not a whale but something much more significant, a submarine. I knew they were out there, but once at sea we never see them.

The breeze had once again stopped. I think I was probably at the point where I didn't have any more sweat to sweat. I lived in West Texas for a short time. Then the only difference between this heat and that of West Texas was the humidity. There was no humidity in West Texas. There didn't seem to be a cool spot anywhere on the weather decks. I was facing west, into the setting sun, but the sky was still painfully bright. The Pacific Ocean became so calm it looked like glass. Even with the hot wind created by the moving ship, I felt no relief. The chill I felt earlier was now nothing but heat. The back and armpits of my coveralls were dark with sweat. There was sweat running down from under the helmet I was wearing. A shower was out of the question, as we went on water hours shortly after leaving the Philippians. I felt like a soggy—sea creature.

I knew it was a violation of regulations, but I opened the collar of my shirt and pulled it out of my pants. I took my helmet off. Within minutes the sweat had dried to salt, and I got myself back in combat mode. Just as I was turning to go back down to my workstation, I saw another submarine, breach the surface. Like in the movies the ocean bubbled, and the water was cascading off the subs. I had always known that they were there, but it was rare that anyone ever saw them.

Even in my old life, I would never smoke a cigarette on the fantail while we were in any battle condition. We had been placed on Condition X-ray. We could move about the ship, but our assigned battle stations had to be manned. There was a seaman from one of the deck divisions leaning against the bulkhead on the fantail, he was wearing a headset, I could have been mistaken, but it looked as if he had drool sliding down his chin. I couldn't be sure, as it was dark, but it seemed as if his eyelids were half closed.

I loved looking at the wake of the ship. I liked watching the sparkle of the fluorescence being turned up. It made me think of the stars only the stars under the ocean. Looking out at sea, I saw the water start to bubble. I saw a patrol boat, and the froth of the wake that was coming from that patrol vessel it was less than a thousand klicks and heading directly for me I could only assume it was a torpedo. I tried to get the attention of the sailor standing watch. I don't think he was even aware that I was there. I didn't stick around, I yelled, then shook the seaman standing watch, who seemed to be in a daze, "Look we are going to get hit." He blinked his eyes as if he were staring into the sun. I ripped his headset off and yelled into the mouthpiece, "Bogey! Directly aft and to the port side of the fantail."

The bo'sun's voice was almost immediate. "Battle Stations! Battle Stations!" all hands man your battle stations. Followed by his whistle the horn and the bell.

I literally ran, slid down the ladderwells yelling for my team. Several of my fellow damage controllers followed me. We ran and slid down more ladderwells, we were using the ladders like a Damage Control Striker's pole.

The passageways and ladders became orderly one-way streets. The only thing I heard besides my pounding heart was the sounds of boots. At least half the crew was already at their battle station. I was passing men as they scampered up and down the ladders, donned life jackets, and groped for their military helmets. I know the Boatswain called Battle Stations, blew his pipe, and I know the bell went off, and the siren sounded, but it seemed as if I was underwater and didn't hear any of it.

It was the port side. With a shriek of rending metal, hull plates buckled and collapsed. I felt it but could only assume that the ship's stern lifted and hung in the air for a second, apparently suspended on a mushrooming bubble of steam and fire. The keel began to bend. Then the spell was broken, and the stern crashed back into the waves, throwing plumes of what had to be seawater fifty feet into the air. The whipsaw effect torqued the keel in the other direction, and the steel backbone of the ship groaned like a wounded animal, a resonating sound that rose through the deck plates at an incredible volume.

I heard scraping steel against steel. I found myself in the middle of pipes, pumps, relay panels, and electrical junction boxes. My team had caught up with me. We were standing during massive boilers. The Snipes, those that worked on the machinery below decks, were in battle dress, most of them trying to work while encumbered by the helmet and gloves. I should have been focused, but I couldn't stop thinking that after all these years that men went to sea. We had 1,200-pounds-per-squareinch steam in the boilers ready to launch aircraft, propel the ship and provide hot water for showers and washing dishes. Oh yeah since my prior time in the Navy, it was decided to build nuclear aircraft carriers.

The space aft of the boilers, where After Steering was located, right in front of the steering engine was a gyro repeater and a ship's wheel, just like the one on the bridge, except the helmsman faces aft, or to the rear. There was a machinist in grease-stained coveralls just staring at the wheel. Another machinist had his hand against the housing that supported the shaft. I was sure the engineer was feeling the same throbbing vibration of the enormous propeller, that my team and I were feeling. I could feel the vibration through the soles of my boots, and the thick steel housing of the bearing's oil sump.

I think it was the chief engineer that was on a panel next to the after steering where there was a battery-operated radio/telephone which was the closest thing we had to a hand-held radio, "Captain, we need to shut down the port screw."

The sound of scraping metal on metal brought back the sound of my tenth grade English teacher dragging her long fingernails across the chalkboard. The sound turned to a shriek as it rapidly got louder. I was sure I felt the mangled propeller screeching as it attempted to turn. The chief gave up on the radio- phone and tried the old-fashioned way, the tube; he went back to the radio-phone. He must have told the Skipper about the battered propeller shaft and that he recommended that he not even attempt to bring the ship up to speed.

I was more than amazed that the hull of the ship was not breached. The engine was beginning to sound like my old Studebaker when I shattered a piston. It looked as if Mister Hales was about to say something to me when his words were drowned out by the first explosion.

I could feel the ship lurched to port. I don't know which was worse, the explosion or the ear-splitting shriek that came from the shaft and the damaged propeller. With a screech of rending metal, hull plates buckled even more and collapsed. The Isaiah Dove rolled a little farther onto her port side and then sluggishly, she reeled back to starboard. She settled onto her wounded side and began to take on water. The leak in the damaged hull was not noticed at first. The torpedo did not explode, the engine did. There was only a small breach in the hull, Mister Hales and Chambers managed to patch the hole.

Standing on the steel, deck plate precisely one inch above the damaged shaft I could hear the hiss of rushing water and feel the sea as it passed under the hull. There was barely a trickle of seawater coming through the hull. Aft of where I was standing, I could only imagine the massive damaged bronze screw churning the water into a froth as it drove the ship forward. That sound and that feeling were in the past as I was now standing on what felt more like a wounded creature, and sounded like a cry or maybe a death scream.

Walker was busy fighting the fuel fed fire with a dry chemical fire extinguisher. And under our feet was one of the four 30-ton propellers spinning and pushing the giant ship. The shaft to the fourth propeller continued its death cry. Walker and Johnson looked up at me as the vibration was increasing, and getting louder. The deck tilted to the right as the massive ship heeled into a tight starboard turn.

I found myself along with Johnson and Walker up against the bulkhead. I still found it hard to believe that 90,000 tons of steel could move and turn at 45 knots; not tonight. I always had the feeling that the ship was going much faster than the published speed. In fact, this carrier was by far the fastest ship in the strike group. I only hoped that the aircraft were tied down. I know that while I was on the fantail, we were not at flight ops; no aircraft were airborne. I was thinking, *'I sure hope that there isn't some pilot trying to land his plane on our slanting deck.'*

I was so preoccupied with the thought of one aircraft trying to land on a sloping deck, I didn't anticipate the explosion. On the starboard side. But the explosion did not come from outside the ship. I couldn't see past the smoke and steam. The sound of the steel was like that of an injured beast.

I saw the machinist that had his hand against the housing of the line shaft. He was staring at his feet, where oil was pooling. Even with the steam, I could smell diesel. I anticipated the fire, but I was not ready for the explosion. The fires raged through the powerless steel hull that—ten seconds ago I thought the only problem might have been a bent shaft. The machinist with the rag looking down at the oil pooling around his boots was now a living torch. He was walking towards me, apparently not aware that he was on fire. As he stepped out of the flames, it looked to me as if his face was melting like wax. His lips were peeling back exposing his teeth, his eye sockets turned to dark empty holes. I found the foam extinguisher and attempted to put out the fire. I got the fire out, but the machinist looked like a piece of charcoal. He was still alive, not screaming just moaning.

Johnson, Walker, Mister Hales and I were still busy trying to secure the patched hole in the hull along with the remaining engineering crew. I turned to my right and saw Mister Hales with a big hammer putting plywood and old scrap metal and aluminum against the rushing water that was coming in the bulkhead. I don't know when or how Father Donahue got there, but he was cradling the scorched machinist's head in his lap. I've become used to and could tolerate many smells, but I don't think I'll ever get used to burning flesh. Looking over at the priest I saw that he was closing what eyelid was left; the machinist was quiet.

While Mister Hales and I were busy trying to fortify the torn hull, I glanced over my shoulder and noticed that my entire team was present, and they had somehow managed to get the submersible pump, working to take water out of the compartment. I also heard the of the Red-Devil sucking the smoke out of the engine room. Between me, Mister Hales, and two of the engine room crew members, we managed to strengthen the patched the hole in the hull of the ship.

Walking away from the shored-up bulkhead I asked, "Mister Hales, what happened to our guns? The last I heard we still had guns."

"Yes, we still have the five inches. The missiles are supposed to operational too."

Mister Hales was shaking his hands as if he were trying to get something nasty off them, He turned to me and muttered, "What happened to our linebackers?" "Sir!"

"You know the guys that are supposed to protect the quarterback?"

"Oh! You mean the two destroyers and that heavy cruiser that are supposed to protect us from something like this."

Mister Hales replied, "The last time I was topside it looked like rush hour with all the ships out there. **And** no one spotted a stranger out there?"

The Damage Control Officer, Mister Hales, then turned to me. "We need to flood the compartment across from us to straighten this ship, so she can launch our aircraft."

I overheard the Mister Rosch who was speaking on the radio/phone. I presumed Mister Rosch, the engineer, was talking to the Captain, as he was saying, "No sir, one of the twins is down... I'm sure I can get twenty knots out of the other engine Yes, Captain, I can get that shaft to turn, but if I run it too long…Yes, Sir, I understand that we may have to bring it online. Sir, it is not just the engine that is the problem, the shaft to the number 4 screw is shot."

The fires were put out, the hull was shored-up, primary fire boundaries were set up, and we managed to flood the compartment directly across from the damage and flooded engine room. The corpsmen took the dead and injured out of the engine room. Trying to wipe the sweat out of my eyes I once again looked over at the after steering wheel. I'm sure the commanding officer was made aware of the fact that there was **no** after steering.

I'd all but forgotten that I usually spend most of my time while at General Quarters on the forward mess deck. I felt sure that the people I trained from all the other divisions were doing a great job. They have been prepared to take charge, for just a situation like this one we found ourselves.

Wright, Chambers, and Mister Hales with together to patch the engine room. Chambers, Wright and Mister Hales managed to get our equipment out of the engine room, cleaned serviced and once again stored in number 4 hold.

I managed to wipe most of the soot off my face by splashing water on my face. The team and I left the gloves out so that we could inspect them. We probably should have donned our chemical suits, but fortunately, no chemicals were detected anywhere on the ship.

I heard the Boatswain announce over the 1MC or the public-address system for all the fire teams, and damage control teams to meet at our usual spot on the hangar deck. The teams gave verbal confirmation that the damage, except the one propulsion system and that all spaces, were seaworthy. We were dismissed by Mister Hales. The Chief and I walked back to the fantail, where I could see smoke on the horizon. It appeared that one of our Destroyer Escorts was lost, not really lost as we saw the smoke of the sinking Destroyer. I got a crazy feeling in the pit of my stomach and literally broke out in a sweat wondering if that ship's crew made it to safety.

I didn't think it was possible for the huge bird farm, that I called home to make a tight a U-turn in the middle of the South China Sea. That sounds casual, but it was far from casual. It was an effort to make that turn. Even worse I was once again standing on the fantail, I could hear the hiss of the catapults as they were sling-shooting our jets into the blue.

When launching aircraft on an aircraft carrier, it is preferable that the ship is facing into the wind. On that day the winds were calm, and the ship was having trouble even making 10 knots. I suppose the skipper was sending our birds out to hunt down the elusive PT Boat that sent a torpedo our way and destroyed one of our destroyers.

Chow was being served, but I had no appetite. I was thirsty, boy was I dry. I was heading for the large container that was used for Ice tea. Father Donahue was standing near the big coffee urns with both his hands wrapped around a big mud of Cookie's black coffee. The Priest's usual ruddy complexion was gone. He was looking sallow. His hair was disheveled. When I spotted the priest, he was trying to blow strands of his black hair out of his eyes.

I don't usually drink coffee, I prefer strong hot tea, but for some reason, I decided not to have the ice tea, and join the priest with a cup of coffee. Hell, I wouldn't turn down a stiff drink. I don't smoke anymore, but if somebody offered me a cigarette, I don't think I'd turn it down. The priest was standing near the service line. I motioned for him to come over to the table where I was sitting. I could see that his khakis were grease stained, his blue-black hair was unkempt. As he came closer, I also noticed specks of blood on his khaki shirt.

"You know Father, I'd forgotten that when I signed up again, I knew I would be in harm's way. Maybe not forgotten, but I think I was deliberately ignoring not only what we were paid to do, but that is also fighting against the enemies of our country. I'd become complacent, and of course, there is always the sea."

Father Donahue wiped his soot-covered forehead with a handkerchief. "How is that?"

Running around playing sailor, drilling, and training is really not the same as fighting to keep the ship afloat. Which as I said there is always the sea. I've heard she is a fickle mistress."

"I know you are right Connor. I knew this was not going to be a leisure cruise."

The priest must have been listening to me as he adjusted the protective mask strapped around his neck and picked up his helmet. He just stood there for a moment.

Most everyone was busy trying to get the ship, ship shape. There were pots, and pans strewn all over the galley. The decks and passageways were covered in grease and at least an inch of water.

The priest looked around, then asked, "What do I do with his cup?"

I pointed to the scullery. "Don't worry about that I'll take your cup.

"One more question, Connor. Is it safe to put up me? helmet and gas mask?"

"Yes sir, but keep them close. No matter what Congress says we are at war."

I've spent over ten years doing what I do. That is keeping the ship seaworthy. When the ship goes to Battle Stations, all items are tied down. We were secured from General Quarters and placed on Condition 3 where the fittings above the waterline are left open to improve ventilation and habitability. And as far as tying things down, we allowed ourselves to lose our focus. We that is the crew should have been able to set condition Zebra within seconds. That all comes back to me. My job is to make sure all officers and crew are not only prepared but able to keep the ship safe and seaworthy but to ensure that the crew can lock-down the ship, not in a few minutes but in seconds. The excuse that my team was not the only team that fell short was no excuse."

The priest pushed the stray hair off his forehead and started to turn and head toward his office, then stopped and turned, looking back at me he asked, "Is it my imagination but have we slowed down?"

"No, the ship has only one of the engines running, plus we are operating without one screw. Oh, by the way, I am pretty sure we are going to be rationing water. All the desalinated water is being used to launch those jets."

The priest raised his eyebrows then remarked, "Ya know Connor I can hear them, the scream of the engines and the sounds of the catapults as our aircraft are slung off the ship, but I have yet to hear the arresting gears recovering any planes. I usually feel it as one of those birds grab the arresting gear."

It was an effort to make 8 knots an hour. Even though it felt like we had a following sea, it still seemed to take forever to reach Okinawa. The Skipper got on the 1MC and told us we would once again be in Dry-Dock. I was kind of curious, I didn't know there was a dry-dock in

Okinawa. I was not that confident if the ship could make it to the Yokosuka shipyards. The Japanese were still upset about Hiroshima, and Nagasaki and would not allow us to enter any of their harbors carrying nuclear weapons.

We anchored off Naha Okinawa waiting on the barges to unload our nukes. Okinawa is part of Japan, but I guess they don't care if there is a big mushroom cloud over Okinawa.

It took three days for the barges to unload our Nuclear weapons. Standing on the fantail while taking a break from unloading our nukes. I watched as the liberty boats from the other ships that were also anchored out in the bay were moving back and forth from the ships to shore. The Captain went ashore, but the rest of us remained aboard loading the barges with our nuclear weapons.

Chapter Eleven

The Catholic Chaplain looked as if he not only shaved but somehow managed to find time for a haircut. Gunny and Father Donahue appeared to be in a huddle. Gunny was sitting beside the priest's desk bending over the desk talking about something that seemed quite important.

I knocked on back of the open door and cleared my throat. When Father Donahue looked up, and Gunnery Sergeant Cortez looked up, I queried, "If you people would rather I come back later…?"

Gunny voiced. "Come in Connor. We were going over this chart that Father procured from the Quartermaster. The Skipper hasn't made the announcement yet, but he is proposing that we steam on our own power and head for the dry docks at Yokosuka."

"I'm surprised we didn't have more severe injuries, but we seemed to make it through our first combat experience," Father Donahue remarked.

"OK, Father. What does that have to do with how we get to Yokosuka?"

"Well, First Class Quarter Master Brown was in the Chart Room when the ship suddenly lurched to port when the engine exploded. He tripped over one of the tables and broke his leg. The priest was just staring at me. I guess he was checking on his fresh haircut as he rubbed the back of his neck. "Anyway, Petty Officer Brown says it is not safe to try and make Japan. He says that if the seas get rough or a storm pops up. Anyway, to finish that thought, Brown stated that the Sea of Japan is notorious for surprise storms."

Gunny asked, "So if it is not safe to go to Yokosuka under our own power, what can we do? I mean we have to get this ship into the yards."

Rubbing his eyes, Father Donahue looked up at me and queried, "I know I look old, I am old, but I haven't been in the Navy that long. We are not the only wounded ducks the Navy ever had. So, what or how did other ships handle it? I bet there were a few in the worst shape. What did they do?

I wasn't worried about how we were to get to a repair facility. I just figured the Captain would get us there safely. After staring into space for a few seconds, I finally replied, "My job is to keep this ship from sinking and to make sure the crew is safe. Now if it were my job to get a wounded ship into a repair facility, I think I would first check the weather, then call up not one but a couple of the fleet tugboats." I saw both the Priest and the Marine staring at me. Father had even raised his eyebrows. "That is why the Navy has seagoing tugs. Let them push, shove and tow. They are powerful ships."

Gunny replied, "I'm just a Marine. I'm sure the Captain will do the right thing."

"What do you think, Father? I guess if I could make decisions about how to get from point A to point B, plus launch aircraft, I'd be the Captain." I declared.

Gunny Cortez mentioned, "I'm not so sure."

Father Donahue spoke-up, "What's that supposed to mean?"

Rubbing the balding spot on his head, Gunny responded, "I shouldn't say anything, but one of my Marines. And believe me, he was reprimanded. He knows better than to talk about out what he hears around any of the command staff."

Picking a pen off the blotter on his desk, Father Donahue impatiently snapped, "OK, Frank, what is this, Soap Opera? You know you didn't have to bring it up. What did the Marine say?"

"Let's just say that all is not going well in paradise. Anyway, there seems to be a little hostility between the Skipper and Commander Ryan, the Air Boss, maybe just a difference of opinion."

Father Donahue put his pen down, I shook my head and rubbed my eyes. We were both staring at the Gunnery Sergeant.

"Well from what I understand the Air Boss wants all the aircraft to fly to the Naval Air Base at Yokosuka. There was also talk about the ship getting stranded at sea. The Commander said something like if he was the Commanding Officer. The XO was there, and it seems that he pissed-off our new Captain Briggs when he said he agreed with the Air Boss."

It doesn't take much to confuse me, but I just had to clarify what I was hearing. "I was just on the hangar deck, and the only thing there is pallets of nuclear ammo and weapons. Seems to me that the aircraft have already moved." Gunny looked at the Chaplain, then at me. He said, "No Connor, our planes and most of the aircrews are tied down at Kadena. At zero-dark-thirty this morning a launch carried the crew chiefs ashore."

If I squinted against the rising sun, I could see one of the fleet tugs brush up against the ship, and the seamen on the tug throw a line to one of our deckhands. I was near the forecastle and watched as the deckhand caught the line and tied it off. I've handled my share of lines, but what I really like is watching one of our boatswain mates handle the lines.

I can only imagine the conversation on the bridge with the XO, the Air Boss arguing with the Captain. Ship's Captain? That's almost blasphemed. What probably happened was Senior Chief Bosun, told the Captain that they would be using the services of our fleet tugs.

I was staring out at the barges that were unloading our weapons. I couldn't help but notice the powerful boats. If I've been in the Navy, I couldn't keep my eyes off the Fleet Tugs. They were much longer than harbor tugs. The first time I saw an Ocean-Going Tug I thought it was a fishing boat. It was just then that I was rudely brought back to the present when some shave-tailed Ensign yelled at me to load the remaining pallets with the few weapons we had left on the hangar deck.

Like a good sailor, I tied down the last of the nukes, motioned to our forklift driver to take the last pallet to the elevator closest to the barge. I watched as the pallets were loaded onto the barge. I really thought that those fleet tugs were going to be our lifesavers and push/pull this carrier to Yokosuka.

While stationed at Treasure Island I met a, as he called himself a Sea Going Tug Boat sailor. He couldn't believe that there were so many men assigned to an aircraft carrier. He told me that it was a little crowded with the eighty-five sailors that were aboard his Tug. He said that most of the seagoing tugs had a complement of forty men.

I watched as each of the two fleet tugs moved the barges with the nukes toward the weapons storage area on the other side of the island. So, I was thinking, *'There go our lifeguards. Maybe not lifeguards.'* I just couldn't stop thinking about our little trip across the Sea of Japan. We made it through the South China Sea, but we were in good shape then. With that damaged shaft and the bent propeller, what if even a little squall comes up. I'm not a seaman, as a matter of fact, I'd be counted with the snipes, people that work below decks. I **was** a Boy Scout, I do know how to tie knots. I also know that if the seas get rough, we will need power. If we lose the engine we have, we will be at the discretion of the sea.

It didn't seem to make me feel better, but that man on the bridge is the Captain. He has the experience. I don't know for sure, but I don't think he would be wearing an eagle on his collar if the powers didn't think he could drive a ship. Even if the ship is three football fields long and weighs over 90,000 tons.

With the last of the barges, the Sea Going Tugs disappeared into the sunset. My dungarees were damp with sweat. There was a gentle breeze coming in from the east. The wind was mild. It was humid, but I did not smell of sense any rain. As the sunset over the horizon, the sky changed from a light pale blue to darker blue. Looking up I could see the stars. The lights on the shore were coming on one at a time giving the impression of little fires. I could hear the pier-side bars; some sailors were getting liberty; not on this ship.

By the time I got to the galley, they were starting to clear the chow line. Pop called out to me asking if I wanted a tray of food. I said no. Like I said earlier there is a rumor going around that Pop was a cook on the Ark. His hearing must have been failing as he called me over and gave me a ham and cheese sandwich. I really didn't feel hungry, but I think I inhaled that sandwich. I downed two mugs of iced tea and headed for the showers.

Zero-dark-thirty, or 0430 in the dark of morning we, that is the crew, and I were awakened by the sound of the Bosun's pipe. All hands prepare to get underway. I was on the hanger deck as the first rays of sunlight appeared above the horizon. I could hear the anchor being weighed. Considering the rising sun, I could see the shadows of two harbor tugs. They snuggled alongside the carrier as deck hands from both the tugs and the carrier did the things that deckhands do. The tugs turned us around in the channel. I could feel the vibration of the engines, the flicker of the lights as the electricians changed generators.

We were officially at sea. The ocean stretched out wide and glossy in front of us. The sun was not officially up, but the moon that shined between breaks in the clouds lit up a silvery path. The sea was so calm it looked as if I stepped over the rail I could walk on the ocean. From what I heard there were no storms expected. The vibrations died down to a buzz. The Special Sea detail was secured.

No matter the rating or job title there is the at least one person trained and assigned from every department aboard ship with their secondary function, damage control. Besides keeping the ship afloat, fighting fires and staying current in Chemical, Biological, and Nuclear warfare, we may also be called upon to work with the ship's carpenter. This ship has carpenters, but I guess it could be said that carpentry might be our secondary job. Chips, our ship's carpenter does not want me near his tools. I don't think he wants any DC people anywhere near him.

After we had been at sea, my team and I were busy repairing some of the battle damage. True we were headed for dry dock, but we still had to make sure that the ship was seaworthy until we got there.

I was once again taking a break on the fantail with a mug of iced tea, in my hands. I could see a destroyer on the port and another on the starboard. I had a queasy feeling in my stomach. I wasn't sick, but I think if I saw at least one ocean-going tug in the distance. It looked to me like the tug was going the wrong way. We were wounded, and we needed as much help as we could get. The seas were still calm. As the sun just then coming over the horizon, it seemed to be brighter than usual. The sky was blue and sunny, not a cloud. As we were leaving the channel, I caught sight of a school of Dolphins swimming alongside the ship.

It looked as if they were playing leap-frog.

I was just heading down to the storage hold when Baily came up to me and told me, "Take your team and some caulking up to the bridge. Seems like the old man is getting wet."

I must have looked surprised when I mentioned, "If you're talking about the windshield, that is safety glass and is over an inch thick."

Baily smacked me on the shoulder, "Well grab what you need. I heard that Tyrell worked in a body shop repairing windshields. Make sure he's with you."

"Shouldn't someone other than us do that? Maybe someone trained in installing glass."

Commander Wilson was sitting in the Captain's chair. I couldn't be sure because his back was to me, but I'm pretty sure that it was Ensign Simpson standing behind the helmsmen. I walked over to the port windscreen, and I noticed what looked like a hair in the glass as if there were two sheets of glass instead of one-inch bulletproof glass. Along with what appeared to be a hair was condensation, water was building up inside the glass. I'm not sure of the engineering that went into that glass, but it was supposed to be shatterproof.

When my team and I walked onto the bridge, the sky was clear bright and blue, reminding me of a robin's egg. As I walked over to the port windscreen, I could see the once blue of the sky was getting darker. Within seconds, it appeared as black as night within seconds, I could no longer see the moon or the stars. The wind was starting to pick up. The sunrise I was expecting did not come. It came on suddenly, but I got the feeling that I was in an elevator in free fall. It didn't hurt, but it felt to me like the ship was being lifted above the surface of the ocean. Mister Simpson grabbed the mic," Set condition zebra. Stand -by for heavy seas."

I went to my knees, it felt as if someone put a foot right behind both knees. I Noticed Mister Simpson lying on top of the helmsman. Seawater and foam were covering both Mister Simpson and the helmsman. Water was slouching bake and forth of the deck of the bridge.

I'd never seen Mister Simpson move so fast. He punched the button set into the 1MC, General Quarters, set Condition ZEBRA!" He looked back at me, and made another announcement, "I need medical personnel on the bridge." Without taking a breath, he picked up the secure line to the Captain's quarters, "Captain to the bridge." He released the mike button, turned. That's when I noticed the XO was lying face down on the deck. By the time Ensign Simpson reached the Commander and put out his hand. The Commander rose and put his butt back in his chair.

The ship felt as if it was on the surface of the sea, and the sounds of engines and the generators were normal or what I was used to hearing. I was about to step outside when I felt pressure in my ears. It felt as if I was ascending in an airplane. I raised my head and pinched my nose, and blew, trying to clear my ears. It felt like the ship being lifted out of the ocean by a gigantic hand. I grabbed a stanchion, (a vertical post used for supporting decks). I yelled, "Everybody! Get down and grab onto something." I'm not sure, but I think that same giant hand turned us on our side. I know it had to be no more than a few minutes, but the ship righted itself. There for a second, I wasn't sure anyone was going to get out of this alive. 90,000 tons, three football fields long, thirteen stories high, and it was as if we were a toy in some little kid's bathtub. As the ship laid on its side I could feel my heart pounding, I remembered the prayers of my childhood. Before I got to my feet, the ship righted itself. It was hot, but at that moment the sweat that was pouring from my forehead was cold. My heart rate seemed to once again be normal.

I checked my watch, and it indicated that it was 0930. Captain Briggs opened the door to the bridge, and It was so dark outside, so dark that I couldn't tell the sky from the ocean. If my feet were not on the deck, I wouldn't be able to say whether standing upright or upside down. It was quiet, eerie quiet. My ears were starting to ache, I was having trouble clearing my ears. I knew the engines were running only because I felt the vibrations under my feet.

The only kind of light on the bridge was the red light over the skipper's chair and the green illumination of the compass in front the helmsman. The Captain was saying something, I knew because I could see his mouth moving, but I couldn't hear a word.

The XO, Commander Wilson, was now on his feet and very animated as he was talking to the Captain. They couldn't have been more than a couple of feet from me, but I still heard nothing. Mister Simpson was back behind the helmsman pointing at the port windscreen. I think he was yelling at me, "We're in the Hollow!"

My reply, "The what?"

"It's the tube of the wave. When it breaks, it will hit the ship with more force than before. Mister Simpson looked back at the helm. I couldn't hear what he was saying to the kid at the wheel. His gestures made me think that Ensign was telling the helmsman to steer into the wave. He turned back toward me. I figured he was looking at me, but I followed his gaze; he was looking at the Skipper and the XO. He pushed the button on the 1MC and made an announcement, "All hands secure all loose items and brace yourselves." I worked with the Ensign and was surprised to hear his command voice.

I tried to get the Captain and the XO's attention. Too late. I heard a crack, a deafening crack. By the time the screech came, I was face down lifting my face off the deck with a quick look around I saw that my whole team was face down on the deck with their fingers locked around the back of their necks. The ear-shattering screech seemed like it was never going to stop. It reminded me of my high school English teacher, to say she was a big woman would be an understatement, but I swore it was her dragging her long fingernails across the chalkboard. There was no shot fired, but the glass on the port side of the bridge exploded.

I've often seen waves cover destroyers, but never an aircraft carrier. I've watched as the ocean came across the flight deck. However, I have never seen waves come anywhere near our stacks. I often thought that if the sea were to breach the ship's stack, it would snuff out the fires under the boilers. The people in the know told me that couldn't happen.

I had known before I dove for the deck that Ensign Simpson was trying to keep the helmsman on his feet while he was fighting to maintain the ship heading into the oncoming sea. Looking over at the Ensign I could see that his khakis were covered in blood and he was literally holding the helmsman up. He gingerly placed the helmsman on the deck, he pushed the button on the 1MC, and announced, "Medical personnel to the bridge now! CCS take rudder control." With some effort, Ensign Simpson was trying to keep the ship turning into the oncoming seas. I could see, more feel that the rudder was not responding to the wheel. The bridge was no longer in control of where we wanted to go.

The helmsman was conscious but appeared to be dazed. Mister Simpson talked into the sound powered tube directly to tubing. "You've got the con engineering. Standby, for maneuvering orders. Get to it, people! That is all." He released the mike button.

I could hear the response from engineering, "Sir the wheel is not responding." While the motors were working, it was easy to steer from engineering. All engineering had to do was get course corrections from the bridge. When the electrical power failed, however, it was a different story. It generally took four men to provide power by turning hand cranks which rotated the pumps; two men would take turns on the crank while two rested. I understand that it took about 20 seconds to move the rudder from one side to the other if done manually.

I looked over to where the Captain and XO were. The Captain's head appeared to be resting his head on the backrest of his oversized chair. The XO was sprawled on the deck with his head cocked at an unnatural position. There was a pool of blood under his skull.

My ears were still ringing from the burst of the windscreen. It felt as if the ship was shivering. I no longer felt the vibrations caused by the engines. My ears popped, I could no longer hear the whine of the generators. It was still dark even at 1000 in the morning. The battle lanterns blinked and then came on. The purpose of the battle lanterns was to come on when the generators could not produce electricity. If the boilers could not create steam, the engines would not work, and without the engines, the generator would not come online. Emergency battle lanterns would only last a few hours. 10 o'clock in the morning there is no natural light. I was not sure whether I was looking at a darkened sky or we were still under the ocean. About thirteen hours, that is how long the emergency lanterns were supposed to last. Then would come a darkness. Even if we had daylight on the bridge the rest of the ship would experience a darkness blacker than anything that could be imagined. There was the hint of light, coming from outside the sky was now a cobalt blue. Thank God for the illumination from the battle lanterns.

The priest was standing over the helmsman. It appeared he was trying to stop the flow of blood from the helmsman's cheek. There was a corpsman wrapping gauze around the XO's head. Chief Isaacs was waving an ammonia stick under the Skippers' nose. I did not see any of these people enter the bridge.

Chapter Twelve

The Stokes Stretcher got a workout on the bridge. I'd forgotten about the Chart Room. I watched as the Navigator was carried out and a bloodied Second-Class Quartermaster followed the two Corpsmen taking the Navigator, Commander Carter off the bridge. I saw Ensign Simpson try to help the Corpsmen load the helmsman on the stretcher. There was a sizeable blood-stained gauze bandage over Seaman Jones creek. Once I saw what was left of his face, I recognized him. He was one of the men I grilled steak for at the Waikiki restaurant.

The sea was now calm, the sky had gone from a cobalt blue to what looked to me like a dark purple. I felt no movement other than a slight fore-and-aft roll of the ship. My knees were weak, but I managed to step outside the bridge. The sea once again appeared calm. The dark purple of the sky changed to a slate blue. In all my years I had never seen the sky look like that. There was an eerie silence. Even when the ship was in drydock, it was not entirely silent. There was always some kind of sound. One last look at the sky. The slate blue had changed again to something ominous, no longer dark blue, but more like night. It was

1030 in the morning. I was barely able to distinguish a glassy sea. As dark as it was I expected to see stars or maybe a waning moon. There was nothing with no breeze and no blowers the bridge felt like a sauna. I could only imagine what the crew trapped on the lower decks felt.

"Captain on the bridge!" barked a tall, wiry Boatswain Mate First Class. He was standing at the entrance to the bridge with three men behind him. Captain Briggs entered and went directly to his chair his left arm was in a sling with his left hand on his right shoulder. I could see under Skipper's shirt. There was more tape around his rib cage. To the right of the First Class, Petty Officer was another Boatswain Mate. I detected a crow and one chevron near the shoulder of his dungaree sleeve; in other words, he was a Boatswain Mate Third Class. The third-class petty officer stepped in front of Ensign Simpson and placed his hands on the unresponsive wheel. I turned and saw a black Lieutenant Junior Grade Tap Ensign Simpson on the shoulder.

Ensign Simpson glanced at me on his way off the bridge. The First-Class Petty Officer took a post directly to the right and rear of the Captain's chair. I wasn't sure what I was supposed to do.

Captain Briggs motioned for me to come over to him. In a calm voice, he spoke, "You are First Class Petty Officer Connor Fitzgerald." That was not a question. It was a statement. "Fitzgerald, you did a great job today. I want you to notify all the damage control teams to make a written report of all damage primarily structural. I need your teams to at least make us seaworthy. I've notified Chips, *the ship's carpenter*, and he is bringing a crew up to finish repairs on the bridge." I was amazed at how composed he was. It was almost as if something like this happened every day.

I felt it first, that vibration. It was as if the engines were starting. Then the whine that I always associated with the generators. The next thing I heard was a grinding sound. It was like trying to get my old Studebaker into gear without using the clutch. There was static on the speakers. I looked back to see the Skipper had his hand-held radio up to his mouth.

As I stepped off the bridge, I looked back to see Captain Briggs wave for me to come back. I heard him directing the Boatswain to use the hand-held radio to contact all decisions and have them report their casualties. He also directed the Boatswain to pass the word that there will be a meeting in number one ready room for all department heads.

The Skipper announced over the 1MC to bring the ship to Condition 2. It wasn't quite stepping down, but by opening some of the circle X and Y fittings, the blowers would start to get some circulation through the ship.

The vibrations were becoming stronger. The whine of the generator was growing more active. I looked back and saw the battle lantern go off. Stepping off the ship's bridge, I was sure I felt air being forced by the blowers. The air was hot and musty. The generators were on, but I did not detect movement. It seemed like the ship was still dead in the water. I hesitated. Looking back into the ship's bridge I saw the Captain staring at me. He held up his hand as if he wanted me to stop. I saw him push the button to the 1-MC, "All department heads report to Ready Room 1.

For those who are strangers to the upper decks, that is the aviation Ready Room directly below the flight deck."

Down in the Division room, I grabbed one of the Damage Control Strikers and had him locate all the Damage Control teams and have them to report to me here in the Division.

I'm not that fond of coffee, but I filled a mug with the vilest black, foul-smelling liquid, I assumed it was coffee, as it came out of the 30-gallon coffee pot. I'm not sure if it was the thick black, bitter coffee or pure caffeine that popped my eyes open and jacked my heart rate.

It sounded like a herd of elephants at the door. The door opened, and I was faced with several DC team leaders that I recognized and more than I few team leaders from other specialties that I did not recognize. They reminded me of accountants as each one of them was carrying a clipboard. The team that was covering the engine, boilers and machine rooms reported that other than a few dings and some leaking oil, an engine that was overheating and evaporators that were not evaporating there was no serious problem.

My reaction was, "Leaking oil, overheating engines, and evaporators that weren't working…Tell me what can be more severe?"

Petty Officer Wright spoke up, "it appears that the Clutch-Brake is not working."

I'm sure that there was a big question mark between me eyebrows as I countered, "A what?"

I didn't know this before, but the Clutch-Brake is the device that engages or disengages the engine from the propeller shaft. I guess it's like a clutch that engages a gear.

The engine is running, but it's like in neutral."

I just had to know, "Where does that leave us?"

From what I understand, the auxiliary pumps and the machinery that runs the blowers are running. We just can't get the ship out of natural."

I shook my head and then asked, "Who was up near CIC, or the radios? Are we able to broadcast?"

Chambers answered, there was never a problem with radar or the radios. It was the radar dish and the antennas. Seems like we lost one of the dishes and the antenna somewhere back in the Sea of Japan."

Like I didn't have anything to do. What I was doing was wandering around the hangar deck. Staring out at a sea that made me feel as if I could step off this sauna and on a calm, cool sea that was as smooth as a baby's behind. The truth is that I was concerned. I heard the anchor being weighed, and the anchor chain being played out. Then nothing. After a few minutes of the anchor being dropped, it was being pulled back up. There was not enough anchor chain to reach the bottom. If we had power, we could hold our location. With no power and not being able to secure ourselves, we will be pushed with the winds and the currents; even a ship as large as a carrier is subject to being tossed about by the sea.

The sky was a bright blue. The sea was starting to get choppy, and we were drifting. The generators were generating, the machines were buzzing, with just enough vibration to lull me into imagining that we were steaming, but the engine was now engaged with the propeller. The fact was that we were drifting, and we were picking up speed. I couldn't help thinking of our Division Officer. Lieutenant Junior Grade Hales relates everything to football. If he were here on the fantail and realized that this giant ship was drifting. We had absolutely no control of where we were going. He would probably come up with another football analogy. "Where were the tackles, the guards, or the running backs.

I was starting to get scared. The current could take us anywhere. We could wind up in enemy waters. Nobody thinks about us sitting out here. Oh, the airplane drivers, or the grunts. We are out here providing our own aircraft. Hopefully or that heavy cruiser is still out there for cover fire.

Now I got to thinking. Where is the Navy? Why are we out here in the middle of the Sea of Japan with no escorts or no protection? Boy! Could I use a stiff drink? I was about to go back to my duty station.

I started down the hangar deck. We were in Condition 2, and the elevator doors should have been closed. It wasn't like our airplanes were aboard, Except for our helicopter. I think I might have heard it first the slapping of the waves against the hull. Then I felt the ship bounce. Bounce weird description for a carrier, but it happened again. It was a bounce.

I walked over to one of the open elevator doors. There was foam at the crest of the waves. It couldn't have been more than a few minutes that the water raged, the foam at the peak was thicker, and the ship felt like a Merry-Go-round that was out of control.

I did see the light in the distance. Straining my eyes, I saw that it was one of our destroyers. Closer in toward us was the Heavy Cruiser. I was wrong the Navy was watching out for us. Nobody told me but what we went through had to be an earthquake. I mean the ocean rising, the waves going over our stacks. Those guys over there on the destroyers should be drawing Sub pay. It is amazing that they are still doing their jobs.

I was back down in the hold. The equipment was cleaned and serviceable. We dragged the Red Devil and carried the pump to number 4 storage hold. I should have been paying attention. I liked keeping my mechanical equipment in a hold, A place where oil can be changed, and small machinery can be worked on. I should have asked the day we found Jenkins 'body, how all this freight got here.

My last time in the Navy I do not remember sharing spaces with any other division. I knew the Marines were sharing some of this space. I never ask what was in it, but then again, the only Marine I ever saw down here was the Marine Lieutenant.

Supply had a couple of containers down here, as well as Aviation Supply. Looked around and it occurred to me that I was in a warehouse. There were so many containers and what looked like weapon storage cabinets. There was enough space where we stored our machines, but cabinets and large shipping containers were so close together that it was almost impossible to move between them. Oh, Yeah, there were empty packing crates stacked in the corner. The day I received my third chevron I was called in to see Chief Fairchild. The Chief had me sign a bunch of papers. I was signing for Protective, masks, Oxygen Re-Breathing Apparatus, the OBAs that are used when entering a smoke-filled compartment. I wasn't sure, but did I sign for everything down here? The chemical suits, the Red Devils and the pumps used to suck water out of flooded compartments were either signed out to the sailors and their divisions or utilized my Damage Control. Is this just a floating warehouse? Am I responsible for all this cargo?

Using the hangar deck to get to the forward mess deck where we were busily observing each other or, playing cards, I looked out on a calm sea. There were small gentle waves. I just then realized that we were moving. I walked over to the elevator and looked down. Yep, there was that fleet tug that I'd heard so much about. I ran over to another side of the hangar deck and looked forward, Another one of those deep-water tugs.

The Heavy Cruiser was still way off, but the destroyers were close enough that I could smell them frying chicken. I wasn't hungry before, but now I was wondering if they were going to have mashed potatoes with their chicken. Condition 3 means that we won't have to eat combat rations. I wasn't hungry until I smelt chicken frying. On the way to the forward mess deck, I ran into Petty Officer First Class Quartermaster Johnson, who informed me that we had drifted almost one hundred miles off course while our engines were not working.

I had wandered, up near the forecastle, the wind had picked, and the sea was becoming choppy. I was watching a deck-hand, on the tug on our ship's starboard side do his thing. I raised my head and saw one of our deckhands playing out the line to the deckhand on the tug. I was startled at the sound of someone behind me clearing his throat.

It was Master Chief Blood. A look at his weathered face I wouldn't be surprised if he wasn't Noah's leading seaman.

He shouted over the wind and the waves smacking against the ship, "These Ocean-going Tugs are something else. It is hard to believe that the tug your looking at can push this Bird Farm all the way to Yokosuka. We've got another tug on the port side near the stern. One of those tugs can do the job. Back in the day, I was a Seaman assigned to a Sea Going Tug."

I turned and looked up at the Chief, commenting on Ocean Tugs, "I met a guy when I was assigned to Treasure

The island that said it was the greatest assignment he ever had." "Aye that it is. They were nothing like the one's today. For instance, that one beside us displaces about 1200 long tons. It's 206 ft. long and has a speed of over 18 knots, carries a crew of 85. The tug aft is much like its sister. Back in my day, our crew complement was 40. I think we were lucky if we could make 10 knots. We still had the power. Even at 10 knots, we could push a couple barges from San Francisco to Subic. We tugged our share of warships.

I don't think I have ever seen the Chief without the stub of a cigar in his mouth, the stub was usually not lit. I watched in fascination as he struck and lit a wooden match then lit the cigar stub that was between his lips.

At the foot of the ladderwell, I noticed an unkempt group of men in total disarray, sitting at a table in the middle of the mess deck attempting to play Spades. By the time I was during my second hand of Spades, the Captain had secured us from Condition 2.

Wright and Chambers looked over at me. I was still looking at my hand, but I could feel their eyes staring at me. I looked up at my cards, "What? Did I cut one? I know, I got a piece of spinach stuck between my teeth."

Chambers took a breath, and said, "No, Fitz. Aren't we at war anymore?"

"I'm not sure, but I think we are far enough away from the fireworks. Besides I think all are airplanes are gone. Plus, there are a couple tug boats out there that are pushing and pulling us towards Japan."

Somebody suggested that we play a game of chance. I replied, "I don't think so. Besides we are secured from General Quarters, we have been for some time, but I bet Cookie wouldn't say anything if you guys wanted to clean this pigsty up."

Tyrell remarked, "Hey you a First-Class Petty Officer, no wife too. You mean you ain't got no money to play?"

"I'm just not good at gambling. Soon as someone lays money on the table, I might as well just give you all my lunch money."

Back down in the hold, I joined Chambers, Wright, and Tyrell as we cleaned checked and re-checked and re-checked our equipment. We secured the machines, locked all the cabinets. I must be losing it I once again looked out at what I thought was an area that only a few people had access to. This area was used to store things that couldn't be stored elsewhere. How many times did I come down here to pick-up equipment? Where and when did these shipping containers get here? I've seen spaces like this used by the crew to store mahogany, they purchased in the Philippians, suits bought in Hong Kong, or even the booze some of the crew buy to take home. I guess I shouldn't be that concerned. I remember that in a time long ago I bought myself a couple suits and some other clothing, and stored it in a hold just like this one.

I had to talk to the Chief and make sure that the only things I signed for were Damage Control equipment. As I headed for Chief Fairchild's office, I could still feel the motion of the ship. I still felt vibrations from the engines, but I knew that we were not moving with our own steam.

I banged on the door to the Chief's office. I didn't hear anything. I pounded again and heard a gruff, "Wadjawant?"

"Chief, it's Fitz. I need to ask you a question?"

"The door's unlocked."

"OK. What did I sign for? Am I responsible for all that stuff in the hold?"

"No! Just the stuff that belongs to Damage Control. You are securing the equipment and the masks, and chemical suits.? Oh yeah, we can't let the OBAs get into the wrong hands."

"Yeah Chief."

"What!"

"Yes, Chief. All our equipment is secure. I've got chains and heavy-duty padlocks on the machinery."

The Chief grabbed his hat. I was sure he was going to get up. He put his hat on, pulled the bill of his chief's cap down over his eyes, and put his stocking feet up on his desk. While I was visiting the Chief, the Captain put us in Condition 3. Which meant that maybe I would stop cracking my shins or sprain my ankle. As it is I do believe my shin has a permanent dent.

When we are in a wartime situation if not at Zebra, or Battle Stations we cannot set a Condition lower than Condition 3. That must mean that we are closer to Japan than Yankee Station. No airplanes, so we are not sending any planes into a war zone. The only way we could be secured from Readiness Condition 3 would be to secure us from Battle Stations. I had no longer figured that out, and I heard the Skipper come over the 1MC with the announcement that we were indeed off General Quarters.

I was once again wandering the ship. I am tired, my eyelids feel like lead, but I know that if I allow myself to sleep now. With the vibrations of a powerless engine, I'll once again be wandering an eerily quiet ship, with the only company I will have is the sentry, who doesn't want to be the sentry. The last time I got in a one-sided conversation with the fantail watch he just stood there with drool running down his chin never said a word. He was almost shot. I've got a couple of books in my locker. I know if I try to read a book right now I will not get past the first page before I go into la la land.

I finally found myself sitting at a table next to the galley. The old-timer was sitting across from me. Pop was probably older than, Gunny and Father Donahue. Cookie pushed a large mug toward me. I put both my hands on the white ceramic Navy issue mug. I eyed the old cook, "Pop, the very last thing I need is coffee."

"Conner, ya better take a whiff of that. It ain't coffee."

Pop, I appreciate this, but you know I haven't let a drop of alcohol pass my lips in years."

"Boy Connor, you are hard-headed. Just take a sip. It's hot. If Ya don't like it, ya won't hurt me feeling. I got a feeling this is just what you need."

Well, I did. And after I let it cool a little I gulped the rest of it. It was tea. The taste was indescribable. I think if I tried to describe it. It was some sort of tea. The tea or whatever might have had a hint of mint. Lemongrass, not a lemon. Whatever it was, it seemed to calm my stomach, I'd had a whopper of a headache coming on, it was gone. I had been exhausted, but my mind wouldn't stop. *Silly things. Girls, women, fun to be with, but such drama. Then there is my new friend. Ever since the day he tailored my blues and swore to be my new bruder, the only time I see him is when he is acting like that Marine's bodyguard. I can't help feeling that something is seriously wrong. That maybe I should have made more of an effort to be his friend. I mean it's not like I have so many friends. That's one of the reasons I came back in. I just couldn't get into what the civilians were doing. Hell, I'm only 34. You'd think that I was kid away from home for the first time.*

Whatever Pop gave me seemed to get rid of the cobwebs in my head. I think I remember climbing into my rack. I saw the pillow. That's all folks! The next thing I remember is staring at a man that looked like a fox, or a fox that looked like a man. Damn, the lights were on again. "Oh! Shit!" Did

I say that out loud? "Chief?"

"Yeah Fitzgerald, I love you too."

My rack was in the middle so I couldn't sit up. I just kept my head down and slid out the foot on my cradle. Maybe not a cradle; more like a shelf. I just had to say it, "You know Chief in all my time in the Navy, I've never seen a Chief Petty Officer spend so much time in the enlisted compartments."

"I am not that crazy about being here, but you have been summoned."

"Is it the ship? Have we got another hole in the hull?"

The Chief appeared to be wiping the sleep out of his eyes when he replied, "No Fitzgerald. It seems there is a very large Samoan that is yelling his head off asking for you."

I had one leg in my dungarees when I ask, "Where is he?"

"Right now, there are two brawny Marines, and a First-Class Master at Arms holding him against a bulkhead in the ship's laundry."

I was having trouble tying my shoes, when I looked up, I saw Chief Fairchild heading up the ladderwell. "Hey, Chief." I yelled, "Where are you going?"

The Chief stopped with one foot on the top rung of the ladderwell, looked back at me, and responded, "I ain't going anywhere near that man. I'd kinda like to experience my retirement."

***What** is going on? I was just thinking of that oversized Samoan. I thought maybe he got in with the wrong crowd. Never, never fraternize with an officer. That Marine Lieutenant Reese seemed like an arrogant so and so. One of those that thought he was privileged, or more like he was entitled.*

Chapter Thirteen

I did manage to get dressed. The fact that I don't have much of a beard helped. I just threw cold water on my face and ran my fingers through my hair. Up the ladder and past the galley. For a none coffee drinker, the coffee this morning was smelling good.

I was standing at the top of the ladderwell to the laundry. It seemed extremely quiet. I didn't even hear the presses. The washers never shut down, except maybe during General Quarters. Just silence. An eerie silence. I eased myself down into the laundry. The presses weren't making any sound because they were shut down. Bags of dirty laundry were strung out on the deck.

Then I saw him. Two husky Marines were on top of Al, one laying on either arm. I called out, "Al!" Al stood up brushing the Marines off like they were bothersome insects. The First-Class Master at Arms was smacking a nightstick against the palm of his hand. Special Agent Gabriel was pointing an automatic pistol at the big Samoan. The pistol in Gabriel's hand was not a 45, it was maybe a 9mm.

I called out to Al, "Al, calm down. Just let these Marines go. Let me come over there?"

"Hey, Bro. I'm in deep-shit. I don't want to be locked up." The big Samoan was almost crying.

Eyeing the Marines, "Could you guys back off?" I looked over at the Samoan, "Al, just stay still. Let me come to you." At first, I thought Al was staring at me, then I followed his gaze. He was looking over my shoulder at the Special Agent. I glanced back at Gabriel, "Special Agent, you think you could put the weapon down?"

The Special Agent countered, "I don't think that is a good idea."

"Just holster the gun. I'll take care of."

Raising his voice, Gabriel commented, "There is no way you are going to restrain," looking at the Samoan, "that man."

I cleared my throat and glared at the Special Agent. And with more force than I intended, "Just back off. I've got this."

Gabriel looked over at the Marines, then at the Master at Arms, "Alright stand back." Glaring at me, "I swear, I'll drop you if that man so much as reaches to scratch his nose.

Then after you, I'll plant one right between his eyes."

I felt my voice was still forceful, and I didn't even pretend that I was making a request, "Where are you taking Petty Officer Kalama?"

The First-Class Master at Arms answered, "We are going to hold him in the brig until the Captain holds Captain's Mast."

"How about one of you Marines lead the way. Special Agent Gabriel, you and the Marine Corporal, walk about three paces behind us."

I had no idea what I was doing. I think I might have read it or seen a movie that if you act like you know what you're doing people accept it. It seemed to be working. I'm the leader of a Damage Control Party I should be aware where the brig is. I do know where the brig is I just chose not to spend that much time down there.

There was a conversation going on between the Special Agent and me. He wanted to shackle and cuff the Samoan. One of the Marines held up handcuffs but indicated they did not have a way to bind his ankles.

Looking back at the Marine behind me and eying Gabriel, I insisted, "Let's just get Al here, secure. I do not think any of us need to have a big discussion on how we are going to do it." Looking up at Kalama, "Petty Officer Kalama seems to have calmed down. I think it would be a good time to help him get into his new living area."

The First-Class Petty Officer tapped me on the shoulder and said, "If we are going to keep Kalama incarcerated we need to bring him by the compartment to get a change of clothes."

"Why don't we just get," I patted Kalama on the back, "get settled. We can ask one of his mates to get his toiletries and skivvies. Or I can get them and bring them back for him."

I stepped back and allowed the Marines to gently direct the big Samoan into what looked like a private cell. The Master at Arms put his arm out and led me away from the cell and insisted, "Petty Officer Fitzgerald, I need you to wait for me before you go to Kalama's compartment."

We needed a witness to break the padlock on Al's locker. First Class Petty Office Modesto from the clothing store and I watched as Petty Officer Kalama's personal items were inventoried. I had to get permission from the Corporal of the Guard to take Al a change of clothes.

By the time I got Al's personal items to him, Al had informed me, "Hey, Connor. I saw the Captain. He said he didn't want to talk to me, but I could stay here till we got to Yokosuka. Guess what? I'm gonna a get cake and champagne till we get there."

I always liked Kalama, and my heart broke. I knew he was slow, not stupid, probably the best tailor I ever knew. But he did not understand a lot of things. People used him. Once he liked a person, he was loyal. I just couldn't let him think that he was going to get cake and champagne. I just had to tell him. "Al, the Captain, was telling you that you ain't gonna get your supper, probably not your breakfast either. They are gonna feed you hard crusty bread, and they will give you water."

Special Agent Gabriel was sitting at a small table with one of the Marine guards, thumbing through a Stars and Stripes newspaper I went over to him and asked, "Special Agent Gabriel. Can the Captain do that?"

The Special agent's look was that of annoyance when he said, "The Navy can still put a man on bread and water."

I know my teachers used to accuse me of sharpshooting them. In other words, they felt that I was challenging their authority. I got the definite impression the Special Agent was feeling the same way.

I had to reply, "No sir. I know that, but the Petty Officer has not officially been found guilty of any crime or violation of the Uniform Code of Military Justice. And he no longer appears to be resisting arrest." I think I must have started pacing, I do that when I get angry. I just couldn't leave it alone. "I wasn't here when he was arrested. Has he officially been charged? Does he even know what he is accused of?"

I pissed off the Special Agent. Why stop now?

Special Agent Gabriel stood up from the table and ran his fingers down the crease of his khaki trousers. He turned to me and said If you want to do your buddy a favor tell him to hire a civilian lawyer. The Captain declined to charge Petty Officer Kalama because he is recommending a General Courts Martial."

The Special Agent headed for the ladderwell, stopped and turned to face me, "Petty officer Kalama is a flight risk, and the Captain has the power to incarcerate him until an Article 32." The Special Agent started up the ladder.

I just could not let it go, so I responded, "We are in the middle of the Sea of Japan. Where is he going to go? And since he hasn't been charged yet, why is he on bread and water?"

"Well, Petty Officer you need to make a formal complaint. Take it to the IG. If you know what's in your best interest, keep those complaints to yourself. The Samoan was found in the process of selling drugs aboard a Navy Warship. Which is not your concern unless you are his attorney. You know if you want to involve yourself in this matter remember It would be easy for me or any investigator to find fault with someone filing a complaint like that." The Special Agent backed down the ladderwell, came within an inch of my face, so close that I could smell his breakfast. He stepped even closer and whispered, "You know Fitzgerald maybe you are involved. It is evident that your buddy there is not the brightest bulb on the tree. Here you are. A ten-year break in service. Maybe you figured a way to make that money that you couldn't make on the outside. Maybe you just couldn't cut it as a civilian?"

I did not answer, but I am sure the Special Agent and I will **not** be exchanging Christmas cards.

My ears were ringing by the time I left the brig. I knew. No, I didn't know, but I had a feeling that that big Samoan was into something. I couldn't prove it. My gut tells me that Marine Lieutenant is up to his eyeballs with whatever trouble Al is in. I can't prove that either.

The Marine Corporal of the Guard and the duty Marine Turnkey were both just staring at me. I looked back at them shrugged and commented, "I know I let my ass override my mouth."

As if they were trained in synchronized nodding, both the Corporal of the Guard and the Marine Turnkey barely nodded in unison. I heard somewhere that Marines spend weeks learning how not to smile.

My head felt like it was spinning. I was tired, but I was also angry. I know the Special Agent was just doing his job. I also know that the Navy made sure that their Criminal Investigators were not part of any command. I do have a knack for pulling chains. Gabriele was way out of line in what he said and what he threatened.

It was 1400 hours, and I was on a deserted forward mess deck. Not completely empty. I was behind a table with a disassembled protective mask and several test tubes with microscopic amounts of different chemicals. I was pacing back and forth behind the counter explaining how to detect these chemicals and how the gas and other toxic chemicals can penetrate the hull of the ship.

I was about to explain the procedures for decontamination when Chief Benedetto, our Chief Master at Arms, walked up to the back of my little group and curled his index finger at me. He calmly requested, "Petty Officer Fitzgerald you and I need to have a word."

What could I do, "Yes Chief." I called Chambers up to finish my little lecture, and to remind them that we will have a decontamination drill before pulling into yards at Yokosuka.

Chief Benedetto had turned away from me and was headed down the passageway. I assumed we were going to his office which was above the forecastle. For an old Master Chief, he had me out of breath. We stopped just short of the windlass room.

He motioned for me to come closer to him, and appearing to drill holes into me with his eyes and asked,

"Fitzgerald, did you threaten our Special Agent aboard?"

"Not exactly," I replied.

The chief folded his large hands over his ample stomach, "What does **not exactly** mean? Did you tell him that you were going to complain to the Inspector General?"

"Yes, I did, Chief. Does that mean you're going to write? me up?"

"I should write you up. But it was not the Special Agent that decided to put Petty Officer Kalama on bread and water. You really need to apologize to Special Agent Gabriele. I've been in this damn canoe club too long. I can see no reason we need civilians mucking about on our ships. I was just venting. I'll get back to you. You're dismissed."

The Navy sure has changed in ten years. I expected changes, but I never thought we would have civilians aboard ship to monitor us. To make sure we behaved. I guess I need to find the Special Agent and apologize.

Special Agent Gabriele was given an office not far from where the Captain's Yeomen do the admin work for the Captain. I hadn't been in the Special Agent's office for some time. One of the Captain's Yeomen inspects the fire extinguishers and other firefighting equipment.

I hesitated in front of the Special Agent's office door. I took a deep breath, thinking I really don't want anything to do with this guy, but *I rather not worry about him sending in negative report about me.* So, I knocked. I didn't hear a thing. I pounded harder and heard, "Enter." His command carried a tone of irritation. The Special Agent was sitting behind his desk holding an apple up to his mouth, and in his other hand, it appeared he was holding a candy bar. He was still obviously annoyed when he said,

"Why are you here?"

"I just wanted to say that I was out of line."

"Whatever. Don't think that I'm **not** going to be watching you. You know something, and I'm going to find out what it is. I don't know if I ever told you this, but if you haven't guessed, I do not like you. If you so much as fart, I'll charge you with behavior unbecoming. Good day, Petty Officer."

Well, that went well. I don't drink. I don't smoke. Hell, I don't even have a warm female body to snuggle up to. I never expected the Navy to be comfortable. A person must be exceptional to be part of any branch of the military. The truth is I didn't have anything in common with any civilian; not even a civil servant like Gabriele. If he thinks so little of the Navy, why is he working for the Navy Department?

I am not sure what I expected. The first time I met the Special Agent I remember thinking that putting an investigator aboard ship might be a good idea. Then I got very territorial. Like what's this civilian doing in my home? He is not one of us.

By the time I got back to the forward mess deck Chambers had each member of the team take out and re-install filters in the protective mask. I watched as he had the men fit the mask on their faces.

"Chambers, that was awesome, the only thing I'd like I'd like to add is that we will not have a drill on decontamination. It is not that we don't need to practice it is because our ship is wounded. I don't think we need to tax our resources. Please, go over your handouts for the procedures of decontamination." I started to turn away, then turned back, "We do need to practice. If we are lucky, we can put off any drills requiring the use of desalinated water until repairs are completed on our ship."

We broke for chow. At least there was potable water in the galley. The Doc and corpsmen also have clean water.

I know that most branches of the military have a master menu that they follow. Which means if they, that is whichever branch is serving pot roast in Alaska they will be serving the same thing in Hawaii. I talked to one of the cooks when I first came aboard. He corrected me when I called him a Commissaryman. He told me that he was to be called a Culinary Specialist. The title has changed, but as far as I'm concerned, the people that prepare my food are still cooks. The Chief Commissaryman turns a menu into the Captain every month for his approval.

Chili was being served. It is not that the Chili was not good, but generally, Chili is served on this ship during battle conditions. They had hot sauce on the tables, so all was good. I also like crackers with my Chili.

The team member from other divisions went back to their regular duty stations while Damage Control spent the rest of the day inspecting the ship for any leaks, or fire hazards.

Even though we were moving, and I could feel the vibrations from the engines it felt weird. It was getting late, and I was feeling restless. I headed topside, or at least to the hangar Yanked and to the fantail. I thought I might keep the watch company.

I always expect to watch the foamy path the ship made. The tugs beside us were making a frothy trail, but this massive bird farm was barely making a ripple. The seas were choppy. The ship lurched and dropped and slammed into the white-caps. My stomach also lurched. It was not natural that the ship was not under its own power. I wonder what it would be like to ride on a barge. Being pushed and pulled at the fate of the elements. Even under our own power, we are still subject to the elements. For me, it is like letting someone else drive your car while you're in the car.

Well, I think I've had enough fun. I started thinking of that big Samoan. I don't know why, but maybe because he was one of the few aboard that offered to be my friend. The big naïve Samoan was looking for a Sea Daddy. He found one, and he is probably going to pay with his life. That thought just came to me. His life? I don't know what the penalty for selling drugs is, but for Al, Kalama incarceration would probably be worse than death.

I went to the top of the ladderwell that led down into the brig. The Sergeant of the Guard greeted me at the top.

He had a simple request, "Fitzgerald, where are you going?" "I just thought I might visit with Petty Officer Kalama."

"Sorry, my orders were to keep him in isolation. No unauthorized visitors."

What else do I do when I need to talk to somebody? I had a big mug of Father Donahue's special coffee in my fist, sitting in a metal folding chair between the Priest and Gunny.

I thought I was just thinking to myself, *"The security of rigidly structured, military life. Is it true that I am not capable of making my own decisions? Of course, I never have been able to coordinate colors. So, with the Navy telling me what to wear I don't worry about making sure I'm wearing matching colors. What tie goes with this, or can I wear loafers, and if I do wear loafers should I wear black or brown?"*

Gunny was the first to speak up, "What are you mumbling?"

Father Donahue was gaping, both his eyebrows were raised.

"Was I speaking out loud?" I questioned.

Gunny leaned forward and opened his mouth as if he were about to speak, but the Priest spoke first, "Don't worry about it. I don't think either one of us understood a word."

"Father, Gunny, just let me calm down some. It appears I lost it with our Agent on Board."

The Padre, spoke up, "OK, Connor tell us what happened?'

"Father, I know you remember our driver from the airport." The Priest nodded and frowned. "Connor, we talked about before. What's so different, and what has it to do with you getting into trouble?"

I told my captive story to my friends, *I guess they were my friends.* I told them how the Samoan was caught selling drugs aboard. How the Captain refused to hold Captain's Mast because he wanted Kalama Court Martialed. "I was going to say dumb kid, but Kalama is not stupid. He is loyal to a fault. I think the word is naïve.

"He was taken to the brig. I was there when they locked the door. I'm pretty sure he did go to visit our Captain, that is when the Captain told him he was recommending a General Courts Martial. I went to his locker to get him a change of underwear. When I came back down to the brig, Al says to me that he is going to court. Then he said Ya know they gonna give me cake and champagne while I'm waiting to go to court? Anyway, when our Special Agent came down to, as he said, check on his prisoner, I questioned why he was on bread and water, especially since it had not been charged with anything at that time." Now I was rubbing the back of my neck. No fresh haircut. I did feel a headache coming on. Usually, I would have already started to pace. I didn't. I just kept rubbing my neck.

"Anyway, the Chief Master at Arms said he was asked to write me up, he didn't, but he did give me a pretty good tongue lashing."

Gunny replied, "Been around this club for more years than I sometimes care to remember. I am familiar with the Uniform Code of Military Justice, Connor if he was caught selling drugs the Captain has every right to confine him."

"But Gunny can he be put on bread and water?" I queried.

After pulling himself off the couch, rubbing his knees, Gunny remarked, "I am not sure. I think I need to find out a little more about how Petty Officer Kalama was apprehended."

Father Donahue was moving his neck in a slow circular motion he looked at me and then at Gunny. He then looked down at the blotter on his desk when he commented, "Commander Lake and I have lifted a few together." Both the Gunny just stared at the priest. With raised eyebrows, "He's the ship's JAG. Before I can enter or reply to this conversation, I need to find out what actually happened."

"You know I am not disputing the charges. I just think to put a man on bread and water, a man who has been accused of a crime, but not yet charged should not be deprived of food. I'm not even saying he did not commit a crime."

Father request, "Let's table this discussion until I talk to the ship's JAG."

"Ya know Father he doesn't have to talk to you about this. As a matter of fact, I don't think he is supposed to," added the Gunnery Sergeant.

Father Donahue abruptly, stood up and declared, "I understand that we should be at Yokosuka sometime tomorrow afternoon." Looking at me and then at the

Gunny, "If possible do you think we can meet here in the office about noon. I should have answers for you. It probably won't take long to get you guys an answer."

Chapter Fourteen

Work went well. Made a lesson plan that the sailors at the division level could use to train their people. It was getting close to noon, and I did want to hear what Father Donahue found out.

I was in the process of locking my desk when the Chief came in and requested I check the machine on the second deck that is used to fight fires on the flight deck. The chief seems to think that there is not enough foam available.

I hated when I am expected to be in two places at the same time. Chief Fairchild was turning away when I called after him. "Chief, I have another appointment. It shouldn't take more than twenty minutes. I promise I get right back to the foam machine."

"Fitzgerald, I am sure your appointment can wait."

"Chief!" When I told a little story. "The appointment is with the JAG."

Chief Fairchild filled in the blanks, "about your divorce?" I didn't answer, I just nodded.

I was winded when I reach the Chaplain's office. Gunnery Sergeant was behind me. His comment was,

"Connor you need to start working out. You are starting to sound like an old man."

The priest was just pulling his chair up to his desk when he motioned for us to sit. Taking a breath then letting it out, "I talked to my friend, Commander Lake. He mentioned something about the confidentiality of the confessional. I tried, and I think I got him to let his guard down. I told him I was trying to help Petty Officer Kalama. Which by the way is correct?"

Gunny, generally calm appeared to be getting flustered when he uttered up. "Santa Madre de Dios. I love ya, Father, but have you ever thought that your homilies might be a little long. Could you get to the point?"

"Sorry. Serious cases, commanders may need specialized, investigative assistance from military criminal investigative, that is where Special Agent Gabriele came in. The Captain then decides what action to take. As we know the Captain to pushing for a General Courts Martial.

Gunny was starting to look frustrated. Maybe frustrated may not be the right word. His face, which is usually the picture of calm was now getting red."

The priest put up his hand. "The Captain was informed that there was a drug problem on this ship and requested the Special Agent investigate. Gabriele arranged a meeting with the petty officer on the forward sponsor, a structure on the side of the ship. Kalama had no idea who Gabriele was. The information was that Gabriele approach Kalama looking to score drugs. Gabriele offered money, Petty Officer Kalama was reaching in the canvas bag that was supposed to hold his protective mask.

"Commander Lake said that they need to present evidence at an Article 32 hearing to prove that the Petty Officer was indeed selling drugs."

As usual, I did have to put my two cents in. "Can Kalama be held in the brig? I mean like he has no evidence."

Father answered, "Yes he can. That is at the commanding officer discretion."

"What about putting him on bread and water?" I queried.

"I did ask, but the JAG couldn't give me a real answer. The Jag suggested that Kalama might have resisted arrest."

Gunnery Sergeant did not say a word, he stood turned and walked out.

I stood, and said, "I've got to go too. Seems that the foam machine on the second deck might need servicing. I still have questions. I might be spending a lot of time in the library. I'm assuming I can read up on the UCMJ."

As I turned to leave Father Donahue mentioned. "There is quite a collection of books that talk about military justice?"

I stopped at the door, turned and queried if they were on the hangar deck how did Kalama wind up on the deck of the laundry with two Marines on him?"

"That is probably the spot where the Petty Officer resisted arrest."

I had a few people assist me in checking out the foam machine. There is a spout not unlike what people used to open oil cans. It was a good call has the spout needed to be cleaned. The foam machine is used to get foam to the flight deck.

Chief Fairchild had a runner great me as I descended to the second deck. I was in the process of going to the office and setting up the duty schedule for my people while in the yards. The message I received from Chief Fairchild informed me that I was to meet with a Second-Class Boatswain the name of Parks. Damage Control Striker Clark was one of the new strikers, he added to the Chief's message. "I know Parks, he's a short Korean built like a tank. Fitzgerald?"

"Yes, Clark."

"Chief wants you and me on the Special Sea and Anchor Detail." I guess I must have had something else on my mind. I looked up, and Clark was not there. I looked back, and it appeared he was running trying to catch up with me. I stopped and turned to wait up for him.

"Listen, Clark, there's nothing to it. There will probably be about half-dozen men from the First Division, they'll be handling the lines and communicating with the harbor tugs. The fleet tugs that have been with us since Okinawa will turn over the lines to the harbor tugs and drop back. Just do what the deck hands tell you to do." I started to turn away, stopped and said, "When the Bosun blows his pipe and announces for the Sea and Anchor Detail, meet me here on the hangar deck."

"No disrespect Fitzgerald, but if I wanted to play with ropes, I'd have signed up for the deck crew. Maybe I could even learn how to drive one of the liberty boats. You know be a coxswain. I think I'd really like driving one of them."

"What's your name again?"

"I'm Damage Control, Striker Clark."

"I know you're not trying to be a smart-ass."

"Sorry, Petty Officer. I was just having a little fun. I still don't think it's right to put us on the Special Sea and Anchor detail."

"Clark, you are right, but just think of it this way you get to learn more about the ship."

I headed down to the galley to get a cup of tea, and then to continue the blue funk I was in. *And then there is Al Kalama, a giant of a man who went out of his way to help me. I hardly remembered him. I had a feeling he was into something, but I wasn't sure. I knew he was following people that didn't have his best interest. Al Kalama is not using drugs. From what I know of him he is not trying to get rich.*

The few times we did talk, he would tell me about his girlfriend back on Samoa. How a retired Seaman from the United States Navy could live like a king. No someone talked him into something. It is true he probably did break the law. I just think the Navy needs to look a little harder into this. This drug problem aboard ship is a symptom of more than somebody picking up drugs and trying to sell them aboard ship.

I don't remember who reminded me that a ship was like a small city and if drugs are becoming a problem on the streets of America, they will also be a problem aboard a ship. We can't see the forest for the trees. Or we become so fixated on small details that we don't see the big picture.

I swore to Father Donahue, better yet I made a promise to myself that I would find justice for Petty Officer Kalama.

I proceeded to the galley. And for some reason walked right pass. On the second deck passageway aft of the mess decks is a soda fountain, reminded me of the old soda fountains of my youth. Only this one did not have any of those cute tables where a person could sit with his, or her special friend. No, but a person could get homemade ice cream, and the ship serviceman had a soda fountain where he would mixt the Coca-Cola or root beer syrup with carbonated water. I bought a chocolate ice cream cone.

I was just passing the ladderwell to the laundry when I literally bumped into Gunny. Of course, I lost my ice cream cone and had to find something to wipe up the mess or face the wrath of one of the deck crew. Gunny slipped back down into the laundry and came up with a rag in his hand.

After sopping up the remains of my ice cream, and wiping my mouth, I noticed Gunny just staring at me. My reply was, "I'm sorry, but you ran into me."

Not looking me directly in the face, oh, his head was up, but he was not looking straight at me. He finally spoke, "Connor, I know you think of the Samoan Petty Officer as a friend."

"Gunny he is, or he tried to be my friend. I just feel, even if he did what he is accused of that, I let him down."

It looked as if Gunny was trying to comb his hair with his finger, the problem was that he wore his hair in a crew cut. He finally said, "Your friend, Petty Officer Kalama is dead. The sergeant of the guard called me about an hour ago. It looks like he killed himself."

"How?"

"Connor, have you ever seen one of those butterfly knives. They're popular on the islands. They originated in the Philippines. For a person that knows how to use the butterfly knife, they can be faster than a switchblade, and quiet." The Gunnery Sergeant put his hand on my back and directed me off to the side of the passageway, turned me around and we started walking forward.

"OK, so now I know how he did it. What is a little hard for me is how he was able to do it?"

"Me too. I've placed the Sergeant of the Guard and the Turn-Key on report. The knife was found at his feet. His throat was slit from ear to ear. If my Marines had been doing their jobs, he should have not been able to bring a weapon into his cell."

"Gunny I was only a teacher in a juvenile correction facility, and those kids went through a body search every day before they entered my classroom."

"Sergeant Williams was the original Marine to lock the petty officer in his cell. He assured me that a cavity search was done and that there were two witnesses to the body search including the cavity search. No weapon was found. I was even told that the prisoner had hemorrhoids."

"Gunny seems like they got up and personal with Kalama. So how did he get the knife? Where is the Padre?"

"He's in Sickbay helping our doctor do an autopsy."

"We are only hours out from Yokosuka. Shouldn't we have waited until we got a real pathologist?"

"Connor, Father Donahue is a real pathologist. Gunny stopped abruptly. This time I did not run into him. "the witnesses that verified that a search of Kalama was done. Before we started the cavity search, we had a corpsman do the cavity search." Gunny made a face. I guess it was supposed to be the look of disgust.

I had trouble trying to maintain a straight face. It was just so out of character for this big bad Marine. I wanted to pace, but we were stopped in the middle of a passageway. "Listen Gunny they should be calling the Special Sea and Anchor Detail shortly. I need to be on the hangar deck.

One other question?"

"What?"

"I tried to go down to the brig and visit with Al and was told he was in isolation and was not allowed, visitors. Question. Did anyone visit with Kalama?"

"I was down there on several occasions, and of course the guards that were assigned to the brig."

We still didn't have power, but the vibrations from the engines changed. *Don't tell me that the drivers finally engaged with the screw.* "Gunny, I am expecting an announcement right about now."

Sure enough, the bosun's pipe blew, declaring, "Special Sea and Anchor Detail report to the forward elevator."

Gunny stared at me for the longest time, then said, "I suppose the next thing will be me assigned to the helm." Rubbing his crewcut, the Gunny turned back and remarked, "This ship has 80 plus boatswain mates, and they need you a snipe to handle lines. Somethun just ain't kosher."

"Gunny, I think it happened when I first came aboard. A seaman was trying to handle the lines that were attached to one of the harbor tugs, and he was fouling the lines. I gave him a hand. Now the deck apes think it's honor for me to handle lines. The second-class boats just couldn't get over how well I handled the lines. The line is usually shot over to the tug. For some reason, the seaman couldn't get the line across. I've been in this canoe club long enough to know that they now use a rocket to send the lines over. They handed this kid a Lyle Gun."

Gunny was now just staring at me. I'm pretty sure he had no idea what I was talking about. No…I'm not that old, but before 1950 the deck force used what looked a lot like a spear gun. It was called a Lyle Gun. I don't know what I was thinking, but I grabbed the gun and fired the over to the tug.

"Yeah. That second-class boatswain is still talking about that little guy that tossed the line. We were just going across the bay. I sure if I weren't already a petty officer I would now have to cross anchors under my crow."

"OK, Fitz. When you get a chance meet us in the chaplain's office. I am anxious to see what he found when he autopsied Kalama."

"Gunny I'm not sure how it will tell us how that knife showed up in his cell."

"Connor, I just find it hard to believe that two well-trained Marines and a corpsman could have missed a weapon. It wasn't like he was hiding a razor blade." "Got a go. See ya Gunny."

It was kind of eerie. The overhead lights were off. The only light was a desk lamp on Father Donahue's desk. The Priest had a manila folder opened on his desk and appeared to be concentrating on what was in it.

I was massaging my hands. Gunny reached into his pocket and gave me a small tube of lotion. I wasn't sure whether my hands were burnt or bruised. I motioned at Gunny, smiled and said, "Thanks." In addition to rubbing my hands, I was opening and closing my fist. Is it at all possible to get your hands sunburnt?" Directed at anyone who would listen.

Father Donahue raised his head, Gunny put his finger in front of his lips and whispered, "Be quiet Connor. I think the Padre has something he wants to tell us."

Running his opened fingers through his hair, he stopped. It was almost like he froze. Then he said, "My god Connor. Didn't you wear your work gloves? I know you own a pair, you were wearing them in the engine room when we had our little problem. Yeah, when are you going to stop playing Boatswain?"

"I think today was my last day, even if the Chef tells me to. Now, Father what about you? What did you find out?"

Gunny had scooted to the edge of his chair. Letting out a breath he said, "OK Father what news have you about the autopsy, what did you find. I mean we know what killed him. His throat was slit."

Looking at me and then at Gunny the Priest said, I don't think your friend committed suicide. You guys sure you want to hear this?"

Both Gunny and I nodded our heads in unison.

The Priest shut the folder that was in front of him. Father Donahue was rubbing his face. "Connor, you knew Kalama?"

"Not well, but yeah I did get to know him a little."

"Can you tell me whether he was right handed or left handed?"

"Like I said, I probably should have been a better friend, but watching him at his sewing machine, and the way he held the material, I'm pretty sure he was a lefty. I sat down at his sewing machine, and everything seemed backward." I was getting the urge to pace again. I stood and try to reenact sitting behind that his sewing machine. I wish I could remember which hand he used to write my receipt."

The Gunnery Sergeant spoke up, "What are you getting at?"

"We all knew his throat was slit from ear to ear. Now, this would never stand up in court, but if he cut his own throat, the deepest cut would have been on the left side of his face. It looked to me like someone came up behind him."

Gunny remarked, "That is not good. Especially where my men are concerned. That means it had to be one of the guards or me. Other than the guards I was the only one to see the prisoner." He looked up first at Father Donahue then at me. "I know I did not do that. Besides, I've only seen a Filipino use a butterfly knife. I tried, and almost cut my own wrist."

"Tomorrow is a holy day of obligation. I must spend a few minutes on my homily. You two hit your racks. Sleep on it."

Gunny had his hand on the door when the Priest called out, "You two need to know what I saw on my way to visit my friend Commander Lake. The door was open to the Special Agent's office. Connor, I know there isn't any love lost between you and our Agent a Float, but Gunny you might be interested in knowing that your Lieutenant was sitting in Gabriel's office with his feet up on the Special Agent's desk."

Chapter Fifteen

We were officially in the dry-dock. The Captain came over the 1MC "All division officers are to allow four section liberty where and when possible. It will be at the discretion of the division chain of command to so authorize."

My mouth tasted like somebody walked on my tongue with muddy books. I do have trouble sleeping the night we secured our ship once again in dry-dock.

Water was no longer a problem. I was standing with a towel wrapped around my skinny ass in front of a cracked mirror trying to figure out the whose face that was in the mirror. "Oh, shit!" My face looked dirty. *Don't tell me that after all these years I have a beard.*

There was a young red-headed petty officer about three sinks down, "What's that, Fitz?"

"Sorry. I must go back down to the compartment and get a razor."

The red-headed petty officer stopped in mid stroke and queried, "You don't have a razor on your kit?"

Holding the towel up around my waist with my left hand, I squinted down at the red headed petty officer. "Naw. I only use a razor for inspections."

Turning back to the mirror and continuing the downstroke of his razor blade the petty officer uttered, "Whatever."

In-port duties for the crew and officers. At least that is what we were told. I don't know if it was what I used to call busy work or all these tools, machines living spaces and the food service area really had to be cleaned. Of course, there was paperwork. Forms that had to be filled out, and requisitions that had to be completed and turned in. There was always the sheet that had to be filled with questions like, was this item lost, or damaged and if lost how was it lost.

Of course, since the ship was damaged by a torpedo, fire, and the tsunami. By claiming lost at sea, I could skip down the requisition form, sign it and turn the form in. If he were lucky, we might receive the damage and lost equipment within the next six months. Not to worry. It was now I would use my Irish. In other words, 'Cumshaw.' It is when I find the part or tool I need on another ship. I drink coffee with the sailor on the other ship and share doughnuts, see what he needs, and we exchange items.

I ran into Gunny, this time I didn't drop ice cream on his highly polished boots. Gunny was heading for the detachment compartment when I asked if the Padre had found out anything useful.

He stopped and said, "The Padre wants us to meet in the library. Can you get to the library by 1300?"

"I'm the PIC now. Yes, I'll be there."

"PIC?"

"I'm the petty officer in charge. I got my own team. So, I'll be there. You know Gunny I got a feeling, and I don't like it, but something smells.?

"Connor, you are right. Oh, I did find something out. Seems like at 0130, during the mid-shift our Lieutenant was visiting the prisoner. Sergeant Williams had been relieved, but he stuck around shooting the bull with Martin. That is when Lieutenant Rese made his presence. The Lieutenant Told Williams to leave, and he did not want to see him down in the Brig unless he had the duty. Williams confirmed that he went back to the cell. Neither one of them or the turnkey saw him enter the cell. He was gone within five minutes. Martin went back to the cell, and the prisoner was up and pacing."

"Gunny, I'll see you and the Padre about one. You know I am starting to feel paranoid." Gunny had his right eyebrow raised.

I know I am paranoid, but this feels real. How do we know who to trust? Even if we were to prove that Al." the Gunny just had a lost expression on his face. "The Samoan. I don't think he offed himself. I just don't know how he was able to get a knife past your guards."

Gunny Cortez gave Connor a hard look. Then replied, "Maybe the Good Father has an answer for us. See you at 1300.

I wasn't that hungry, so for the first time a headed to the forward mess deck and gagged down a cheeseburger. I didn't know they had fountain sodas, so I filled a Navy mug with a cola.

I told my team I had an appointment at 1300, and that they should continue changing the filters in the protective mask.

There was one comment from Tyrell, "I suppose your meeting some tall blonde."

"Naw, Tyrell. She's short with black hair, ivory colored skin and brown eyes."

"Tyrell are you trying to tell me something. I'm not leaving the ship. If you really, I mean really need me, I mean really need me. Like if we have a chemical attack or somebody fires a nuke at us."

Chambers piped up, "You know it wasn't that long ago that protesters would show up at the ship, and cause a disturbance. I think they caught a group trying to put explosive on the hull of a ship."

"I remember that. I was on the Coral Sea, we were anchored off Sasebo."

I was once again in the library watching our priest putting books on shelves. He turned to me and ask that I find a table, the Gunny just called and said he was running a little late.

Just as I found a table out of the path of traffic, not that there was any traffic, Gunny walked in with a manila folder and a stack of official looking paperwork.

Father Donahue had put the last book on the shelf when he remarked, "You know that since our episode must consist of, the books were on the deck, and I had to replace them in the proper places."

Gunny looked up, and asked, "OK Father. What kind of information do you have for us?"

Father Tim Donahue ran his fingers through his hair and replied, "I told Commander Lake about our conundrum."

I was already stumped, "Just what did you ask us legal representative?"

Sitting down across from the Gunny he said, "Well I mentioned that I thought that the prisoner, Petty Officer Aleki Kalama, and how I was having a problem figuring out how he got hold of a weapon. I did not mention your names." The Chaplain reminded me of a coach, as he put his hands on his hips. "I think we can trust him. After all, he is a lawyer."

Gunny spoke up, "See Father that's your problem."

Father Donahue looked over at the Gunny and replied, "He is a lawyer. Shouldn't we trust him?"

"Ya know Father, wouldn't an attorney do anything to get his client off?" remarked Gunny.

Father Donahue, just shrugged his shoulders and responded, "You are right. I'm just not used to someone lying to a priest. I explained to the JAG, that if an investigation were requested, I would have to use the chain of command, and I feel that someone in the chain of command may be corrupted. He told me that he would file the complaint, and no one would have to know who actually brought up the claim."

The Gunnery Sergeant looked down at the pile of papers and the manila folder, opened the folder, it was someone's Service Jacket. Gunny explained, "I talked Reynolds down at Personnel out of the Samoan's service Jacket. Rodriguez is one of the finance clerks, and I got a copy of Kalama's finance records. First, he is sending a small allotment to some girl on American Samoan. He has a savings account with Navy Federal Credit Union, couple hundred dollars. So, if he was dealing, he has to be one of the worse dealers in the world."

Father Donahue spoke up, "What in the world was he doing with drugs?"

I had to say something, "The report of the investigation that I snuck a peek at, stated that no drugs were found. Kalama supposedly threw the drugs overboard."

Gunny said, "You know he may have never had drugs on him. It is possible that someone told him to meet a sailor on the sponson." *A sponson is not part of the ship's superstructure, It's kind of like an added porch.* "Who said that Special Agent Gabriele played at being a sailor. There is no way I can picture him looking like a young seaman or even a petty officer. You can't tell me that not one sailor has noticed a man needing a haircut, wearing khakis with no markings. A person does not have to be a genius to notice that out of 5,000 sailors there is one that is different."

"You two go back to work. Our onboard JAG said he would have something for me tomorrow. Headquarters Seventh Fleet is right here at Yokosuka. There are an extensive law library and other resources that Commander Lake can use.

"Oh, by the way, Connor I think you need to go ashore. Maybe even have a couple drinks."

The Gunnery Sergeant had his reading glasses down at the tip of his nose and was looking over the frames at Connor.

Connors reply to the Priest was, "I think you and I had a long talk about this. I no longer drink anything more intoxicating than a lemon aide."

Padre's reply was, "Well go to a movie, or better yet I think Roy Clark is at the Club Alliance."

I turned to Gunny Cortez and asked, "What are you going to do Gunny?"

"I think I might write Consuela." Looking up at the Padre and me, "You remember, my wife. Maybe catch the flick on the hangar deck..."

I turned to Father Donahue and asked, "What are you going to do?"

"Nothing tonight, but I do intend to take a few guided tours while we're here in Japan."

Gunny had already walked out. I never did ask what all those other papers were about. It is not my concern. I'm acting more and more like my grandmother, *"What do you have there Sonny? Let me see what's in your hands?"*

"You know Father I used to avoid those guided tour things until on my last cruise I was out of money, I had just enough money for one of those guided tours. I had a ball. We went places, like clubs, and amusement parks. Got to see a real Japanese play, with the women wearing that white make-up. Anyway, you will enjoy yourself. You might find the tour that takes you to some of the remaining temples, and the old churches."

I was stepping out when Gunny returned with what looked like invoices and charts. I felt like a fifth wheel. I asked, and they each tried to explain what they were looking for. When I left Gunny and the Chaplain, they were huddled over some of those papers the Gunny had with him.

By the time I got to my workstation, I had seen that my crew was sitting around smoking and joking. My team didn't see me come in, so I banged one of the workbenches. All the heads popped up. I just had to say it, "All hands as you were."

It was Petty Officer Wright that spoke, "Well boss all the new protective masks now have combat filters."

Chambers interjected, "I suppose now we have to make sure all the crew and officers have fresh combat filter in their masks?"

I just couldn't let it go, "Petty Officer Chambers, you must be psychic."

I went over to what I laughingly call my desk. It was gray, and it was metal, but I'm pretty sure that John Paul Jones used this same desk. I pulled the right-hand drawer open. The drawer was deep enough to hold several folders, mostly blank forms. To be exact, they were order forms. For instance, if there were a member of the crew or an officer that needed prescriptions we would order eyeglasses for him that would fit in the protective mask.

In the drawer below that one was a ship's roster. The Roster was the most recent. I cleared my throat and announced. "Now I'm going to break these names down to divisions. I would like, that is if it is not too much trouble to call these individuals and request them to come here with their mask and we'll give them new combat filters. Let them change their own filters. It is their mask, so they need to feel confident. Works better if they must do it themselves.

Like I said it someone needs prescription eyeglasses have them get a prescription, and we will send for their glasses."

I noticed Tyrell rubbing his eyes and commented, "You woke up?" I knew he heard everything I said. I just liked to tease him because he always gave the impression that he just this minute rolled out of his rack.

Putting on my dress blues, I couldn't help but think of that giant Samoan. *He was just an islander. From what I could tell he just wanted a simple island life. He said he owned a café, and his girl was taking care of it while he was in the Navy. Do they call it a restaurant in Samoa? I think he said they served Teriyaki Steak Burger, and of course, fish squid and all those creatures of the deep.*

I have to shake this blue funk. I always enjoyed liberty in Japan. I am getting an unusual feeling. I'm looking forward to going over to Club Alliance. If my memory serves me right, the club used to serve a pretty good steak.

There was a first-class petty officer at the entrance to the club. There were several clubs, a movie theater, an exchange and a restaurant located in the building known as Club Alliance. Anyway, the petty officer asked if I wanted a ticket for the night's entertainment.

I asked, "You mean we need to buy a ticket?"

"No, the entertainment is free, but the club is only allowed to hold a certain number of people. If you get your ticket now, you can come back when the show starts. Oh yeah, tonight beer will be nickel, and liqueur will be a dime.

Wow! What a time to give up drinking? But what I said, "Put me down. What time does the show start?"

"2000 hours. You have about a two in a half hour wait."

"I'll be back."

I was not disappointed; the steak was cooked to perfection. I know this is stupid, but I sometimes ponder about the weirdest things. Two centuries ago most Japanese were Buddhist. And as Buddhist they were vegetarians. OK, they were introduced to meat. That sounds good. So instead of meat, they eat fish, but they don't cook the fish. When they do start cooking and eating meat they raise and produce some of the finest beef in the world. Now, my other question is; everybody uses chop-sticks in Japan. Forgive me I sometimes get carried away. The cook cuts the meat so that those sitting to eat will only get bite-size portions. I love the Japanese people and their culture. I have been known to go out for Sushi.

My grandmother used to always serve the strawberry shortcake with steak. I ordered another iced tea and the strawberry shortcake. I was finishing my iced tea, Mikio, the waitress, asked if I wanted an after-dinner drink. She suggested a Grass Hopper. I was thinking more like maybe an Irish Coffee. I declined and asked for the tab. Mikio, the waitress, came close to my face, so close I could smell carnations. Speaking with a voice with no trace of a Japanese replied. "No, no. This is Thursday, steak is free."

The club manager came over and asked, "Is there a problem?"

"No, I just requested the check."

"Your ship must be new in port. We have found too much money in the till. So, for the foreseeable future, Thursdays will be our steak night."

If I had pearly whites, I would have been showing them. Standing and for some reason, I put my hand out. The manager and I shook hands. "I'm going downstairs now to see Della Reese."

Turning the manager looked back at me and said, "Enjoy the rest of our night."

Other than a Coca-Cola costing more than booze, I had a great time. Miss Della was her professional self. I was sitting up near the stage, and there were a couple good-ol-boys not too far from me. One of them made a statement, which by the reaction of the audience wasn't very nice. She has such class that whatever she came back with those two good-ol-boys got up and left.

When I got back to the ship, it had to be close to eleven. I started up the after brow just as Chief Isaac's, the chief corpsman, was coming down. His tie was askew, his hat was stained and pushed back on his head, and there was some young corpsman trying to carry his sea chest down the gangplank.

I backed down the gangplank and stepped to the side. I said, "Evening Chief."

I'm not sure, but I think he mumbled something.

I stopped at the Acey-Deucy mess and saw Tyrell, Chambers, and Wright play cards. Tyrell looked up at me and said, "I guess you heard our chief corpsman is being transferred."

I was feeling pretty good. Even though I had not been drinking an intoxicating beverage, I was feeling a little light-headed. "OK. Give me the scuttlebutt."

Chambers spoke, "No scuttlebutt. He's being transferred to the Disciplinary Barracks."

"What I do not recall any chief petty officer spending time in the Disciplinary Barracks. What did he do? Did they catch him stealing the Captain's silverware?" I commented.

With a grin on his face and exposing his pearly whites, Tyrell retorted, "Seems like he was giving some kid a rectal exam. The problem being while he had this young seaman Apprentice bent over the table, he had both his hands on the Seaman's shoulders. The kid pushed him away and went directly to Chief Benedetto, who took the kid down to Chief Blood. I understand Chief Blood was having a little siesta. Anyway, Chief Blood, who is probably the only one aboard that could wake the Old-Man. Woke him. Pushed past the Marine guard at Skipper's door. The Skipper woke his yeoman and filed charges against Chief Isaacs. The Skipper informed Chief Isaac that he was going to recommend t Chief Isaac to a General Courts Martial."

I was stunned, although I had my suspicions. I thought I saw something when I was down in sickbay with Scarlet Fever. I was having all kinds of hallucinations. I guess I am still getting hallucinations, but I ain't telling anyone.

When I got down to the compartment, there was a memo taped to the foot of my rack, stating 'Please work up a lesson plan on Chemical, Biological, and Nuclear warfare. Maybe a little background, or history?'

I'm pretty sure that somewhere in the back of that square metal cubical, my locker, is my notes from 'A' School.

Almost twenty years ago I had an instructor that gave, what I thought was a fascinating history of Chemical, Biological, and Nuclear warfare. There were some descriptions of the troops that were affected by the chemicals of the First World War. I'm not sure if I brought some of the news articles that I collected over the years. There is one article that tells about a farmer in France that was digging in his field and dug into an old mustard gas canister. It showed pictures of the blisters on his hands and face.

I was feeling exhausted, but it wasn't bad. I think I should be able to sleep. That is if I am not rudely awakened. We are in the yards, not only the yards but we are parked in that giant empty cement swimming pool. So, I should have an uninterrupted sleep.

It felt as if I just shut my eyes when the lights came on and I heard the all too happy voice of Petty Officer Baily singing our favorite song. "Drop your....and grab your socks. It is time to greet the day."

Everybody was present. Although it looked to me that a few, maybe more than a few took advantage of the nickel beer and the dime shots. I found out that the dime booze was for shots and not mixed drinks. No problem, it didn't bother me. I don't think I was too condescending when I kept reminding them that I felt great. No headache, not blurry vision, and that I was ready for nice fatty pork chops with my runny eggs this morning.

I spent about an hour finding tools for the men to use. I assigned teams to check and inspect the chemical gear throughout the ship. We made sure that the foam machines were serviced and working. Nobody knew how long the repairs were going to take. Which meant the only thing that would be flying would be our helicopters. If I'm not mistaken, even our helicopters were at the airfield.

It was after lunch when I found time to gather my notes and write my lesson plan. There was too much activity in the division office for me to concentrate. I've had trouble focusing all my life, and my fellow sailors were not making it easy on me.

I finally found a table in the Acey Deucy mess. The table was all but hidden behind a pole. I had paper, my notes strewn all over the table. Started with an outline like I was taught in teacher's college. I then just decided to make a draft. I still didn't see the advantage of a draft either. I am not an organized person, so I guess the draft can't hurt.

It was then that I heard Gunny's voice. He was arguing with someone. It took me a few seconds to recognize the voice. Gunny was arguing with the Marine Lieutenant Reese. I peeked and saw that the Lieutenant was handing Gunny legal looking paper I heard, "All right Gunnery Sergeant, you need to sign this." Lieutenant Reese was not asking.

I peeked out around the pole again. I don't remember seeing Gunny's face so red. With his natural brown skin, his face looked more purple than red.

Chapter Sixteen

I almost fell off my chair trying to see what was going on. Stupid, I mean I knew who was talking. It was Gunnery Sergeant Cortez, "Sir, what is it that I am accused of doing?"

I got a peek, and I could see that the Lieutenant had his hands on his hips, and he was leaning into the Marine Gunnery Sergeant's face. I could almost hear the venom in the Marine Lieutenant's voice. "For one thing while I was on temporary duty with the Army at Fort Hunter Leggett the ship and the Marine Detachment went through an Inspector General's Inspection. The Marine detachment did not do well.

"As a matter of fact, we were written up. I just recently got a copy of the audit report. 5 material weaknesses, 3 significant deficiencies, 2 none-compliance with applicable laws. The fact is the detachment did **not** pass inspection. Did you just think that you did not have to tell me that we failed the inspection?"

"Lieutenant, all these deficiencies were corrected. What wasn't in the report was that we came up short on our weapons count. Since our Armorer is now deceased, I wrote and submitted a report that our dead failed to fill out the forms correctly."

"Gunnery Sergeant Cortez I filed the charges on you to the Captain of this ship. He informed me that I needed to send them to Marine Headquarters Seventh Fleet."

"That's excellent Lieutenant, but the one thing the Corps is right about is using the chain of command. I'm afraid that Seventh Fleet is outside our chain of command.

The Lieutenant just had to make another comment, "I'll take these charges to Commander Lake. You remember the JAG assigned to this ship."

"Since you brought up pretrial confinement. Pretrial detention can be used if the prisoner might be a flight risk. You are correct any Commissioned Officer can order am the enlisted man to imprisonment. Since the prisoner had not been charged nonjudicial punishment is not authorized. That includes bread and water. Tell me something Lieutenant, did you suggest bread and water or did our commanding officer?"

Now it appeared that the Lieutenant was getting flustered. The Lieutenant finally came back, "I do know I can add the charge of insubordination and disrespect."

"Lieutenant, the member is typically turned over to the command staff. By the way, I am part of that command staff. Since I'm the official in charge of the ship's brig, it is I that incarcerated a member of this crew. Before I leave your company. Petty Officer Kalama must have received a written form explaining what he is accused of.

"Yes, you can hold him, but no punishment can be given to him until he is officially charged. He has to go in front of an Article 32 board, and wrongdoing has to be proved, preferably with evidence. One other question, was the Commanding Officer, the Captain of this ship aware of the Petty Officer's incarceration. Did the Captain of this ship authorize this man to be put on bread and water?

"Gunnery Sergeant, what makes you an authority?"

"Lieutenant, I have been in the Marine Copse for thirty years. I was the Sergeant of the Guard at 29 Palms when your momma was still wiping your nose."

I was starting to have a problem hearing what the Lieutenant was saying, he was speaking in a whisper, "You are a cocky son-of-a-bitch. Commander Lake, our very own JAG will be filing these charges. Gunnery Sergeant Cortez, I am required to inform you of the charges and allow you an opportunity to contact your own defense. You have reminded me on several occasions how much time you have spent in the Corps."

"Buy the way Lieutenant., I have always treated you with the greatest respect."

"You are required to inspect the brig guards 4 times a day. Which you did the sign-in sheet has your handwritten name on it. Not only have you questioned me, but you indicated that putting the prisoner on bread and water was illegal."

Gunny snapped to attention, and responded, "Yes Sir!"

"Now I know you weren't planning on going ashore."

"I was not sir!"

Turning and leaving the acey Dueck mess, the Lieutenant turned abruptly and said, "Stay where I and get in touch with you."

I took a deep breath and let out a, what I thought was a quiet groan.

The Gunnery Sergeant looked back with an expression that he knew I was there all the time. "Connor, ask the Padre to get in touch with Sergeant Major Charles Wright. The last I heard he was at Iwakuni. Pass the word that I might be missing our bull sessions for a while."

I was thinking, *there was another man down in that brig. When questioned the Marine guards did not consider the OIC. After all, he had roamed of all the Marine spaces. He and the Samoan were together a lot. The Lieutenant had to know that Al always had that butterfly knife on him. The Marine guards did their job. Al did not have his knife when he was apprehended.*

I believed that the Gunnery Sergeant needed help. I'm also pretty sure that the ship's JAG is not on our side. Seems like the conversation Father Donahue, Gunny and I had gone right from Father Donahue's mouth to the JAG, and then to Lieutenant Reese.

A sailor just couldn't pick up a phone and call long-distance. At least I would think that Iwakuni was long distance. I don't know how these phones work. I do know that the few countries I visited were all different. In Australia, a person got hold of their party and then put the money in the public phone. Germany had an entirely different system. A person put money in the public telephone, and the units started ticking off immediately. I had no idea how it worked aboard ship. I do know it was much easier for an officer to use our phone system than an enlisted person. I do know I had to get help for Gunnery Sergeant Cortez.

Suddenly there was a sharp pain above my right eye, and red, blue and black are the last things I remember. The next thing was some huge blonde-haired man bent over my prostrate body. I was on my face, trying to turn my head to see his face was painful.

He spoke, "I'm Tanner. You must have cracked your head" pointing to the watertight door directly behind me. "on that door. You have one hell of a welt under your right eye. I don't know how you managed that." He helped me to my feet. I was feeling a little dizzy when he suggested going to sickbay.

"No, I'll be alright. Thanks again Tanner, I just might have become a traffic hazard if you left me there much longer."

I checked my watch. I needed to get to Father Donahue. He needs to know what's going on. Plus, I promised Gunny that I would have the Padre get hold of Gunny's friend Sergeant Major Charles Wright.

I shook my head. That was not one of my better ideas. It felt as if I had pebbles in my head. Tanner tried to stop me. Tanner gave me one serious look. It looked as if he was having a problem keeping his mouth shut. He finally commented. "What's your name?"

"I'm First Class Petty Officer Connor Fitzgerald. Listen my friend is in trouble, and I have to get hold of one of his good friends."

Tanner was a big man. He reached down and helped me get on my feet. "How can I help?"

"I have got get hold of the Gunnery Sergeant's Friend. He is the Sergeant Major at Iwakuni. I'm just a Damage Controlman, and I don't know how to use the shipboard phone,"

"Well First-Class Petty Officer Connor Fitzgerald. I'm Second Class Petty Officer Tanner. I am also an IC

Electrician. I set these phones up. Come on its almost 1600 hours. We need to get hold of the Sergeant Major before he goes home for the day."

I'd passed this room several times. I even went inside to check on fire suppression equipment. I knew the IC Electrician were the ones that showed the movies at night. I also knew they changed lightbulbs. I should have known that they even set up our phone system.

Tanner looked over at me. "This Marine must be a good friend?"

"Yeah, he and the Catholic Chaplain are just about the only ones close to my age aboard ship."

"Forgive me, Fitzgerald, but you sound a lot like me wife."

"How's that?"

She's hung up on age too. You know how it never bothers women how old the guy is their dating, well it bothers her. Fitzgerald, you're a big boy now. You can make friends with anyone. You might even learn something from the younger sailors."

We were in front of the Chaplain's office. Yancy, the Chaplain's assistant was locking up. I caught him right before he turned the key in the lock. Yancy, where's Father Donahue?"

Yancy continued to turn the lock. "He's at a conference on base."

"We need use his phone."

Scratching his head, Yancy looked at me, then at Tanner. "This is a big ship. There are phones on every deck and in every office and all the living quarters."

Tanner was just standing there staring at the door to Father Donahue's office. I glanced over at Tanner, then at Yancy. I need to make a call to Iwakuni. Gunny is in trouble, and I need to reach a friend of his. His friend is a Sergeant Major at Iwakuni.

Yancy put the key back in the lock, turned and said, "OK, You can use Father Donahue's phone, but before you make a call off to anyplace off the ship you are going to need a control number."

Tanner casually replied, "That is what I am here for. We are the guys that assign the control numbers."

Yancy stepped over to the phone, "OK, what's the phone number?"

Rubbing the back of my neck and patting the bruise under my eye, I sheepishly responded, "His name is Sergeant Major Charles Wright. I don't know his number. Ya think he's at Marine Corps Headquarters."

Yancy had to bring up the fact that there may be more than one place on a Marine Corps Base that has a billet for a Sergeant Major."

I couldn't help it, but in the most sarcastic tone I could muster, I said, "Thanks a lot, I needed that."

Tanner interrupted our little discussion, "If we are going to find this sergeant Major we need to be talking and asking now."

It seemed like it was taking forever. Looking at my watch, I mentioned, "Most of the admin and daily workers are off duty by now. I never realized that the Corpse had Regiments, Battalions, and Marines assigned to not just to Regiment, Battalion, or Company. They also have people assigned to Base personnel, and Base Finance. All these people have billets for a Sergeant Major."

"I'm just an overrated clerk, but why don't we contact the Base Locator.?" Queried Yancy.

"Tanner spoke up, "Why didn't you say something an an hour ago?"

"Never mind that. Have you ever seen Father Donahue? Lose his temper?" said Yancy

Tanner just stood there when he finally said, "I've never seen, Father Donahue."

Even though my collar was unbuttoned, I felt I had to loosen it, "No, I haven't. I don't think I want to."

Yancy said, "We better have a good story."

Yancy was on the phone, "Yes, I'm trying to get hold of Sergeant Major Charles. Do you have a listing for the Sergeant Major?"

Yancy had the phone to his ear and with the other hand was playing piano on the Padre's desk.

As usual, I was pacing, and my new friend Tanner was on the Navy issue couch with his feet up, his head back and what appeared to be his eyes closed.

Yancy moved as if he had been stung by a bee. "Can you give me the number or maybe hook me up with the Sergeant Major?

Yancy went back to playing his imaginary piano.

Yancy ran his fingers through his short hair. "Thank you. Could you pass on a message?"

Taking deep breaths, "Yes please mark this urgent. This is the Chaplain's assistant, and I would very much like the Sergeant Major to return a call to the USS Isiah Dove, at extension 715, that is the Chaplain's office. Be sure to mention that this involves his friend Gunnery Sergeant Fernando Cortez."

"Yes, Thank you very much. This office will be empty until 0730 tomorrow."

Yancy pushed the desk chair back. Looked over at us, and said, "Someone needs to be here before that phone rings tomorrow morrow morning."

I guess Tanner was not sleeping, he stood up and stretched. "Hey, guys the Chaplain does not even know me. I just supposed to him that somebody is going to be calling him from Iwakuni. Besides at 0700, I will be at formation."

Yancy spoke up. "I may be the Chaplain's assistant, but I must make a formation with the other Yeomen from the Captain's office."

Tuning the light out I motioned for the others to leave. "So, you are telling me that I am to greet the chaplain in the morning. What if he goes to the library first?"

Yancy turned and headed back to the desk. "Connor, you wait for at the library, I'll put a note on his door that you have an important message for him."

Tanner headed forward, while I headed toward the aft section of the ship. Yancy just stood there and watch us.

"OK. This is fun, but I'm going to bed. I live right under the forward mess deck. So, what are you guys doing?" Yancy commented.

I replied, "I have a nice warm rack waiting for me just under the acey deucy Mess."

Tanner countered I've got a reserved bed right below us."

Everyone started the turn, when I asked, "Can we meet right here tomorrow morning?"

"Connor, this is my duty station."

Tanner was rubbing his neck when he responded. "I can always find a phone to fix or a light bulb to change."

I couldn't sleep. I was wondering, is Gunny going to avoid us now that the Lieutenant is out to get him.

It was early, I was sitting at a table close to the chow line on the mess deck. I had my hands wrapped around a mug. Pop hides some of his special tea behind the coffee grounds. I was letting hot tea linger at the back of my throat. Pop, motioned for me to eat with the mess cooks, the kitchen help.

I was never much for grits, but over the years I found that when my stomach was a little nervous or my chest was a little wheezy a big pile of buttered grits seems to calm me down. If I ate eggs more the once in a week, I would be burping all day. I guess maybe the grits kind of snapped up the grease.

The door to the library was still locked when I arrived. So, I squatted in front of the door. I should have brought a book with me. I felt a shadow standing over me. It was, Yancy.

With a skinny hand out towards me, Yancy helped me to my feet. Considering my baby blues, Yancy stated, "Father Donahue is waiting for an explanation."

I was standing in front of Father Donahue's desk. If this were another branch of the military, I would have been at attention saluting the Padre. We do not salute inside in the Navy unless we are carrying side arms.

The priest pointed to a chair, and said, "OK, from what I heard Gunny has gotten himself in a little trouble?"

"Father I think that shave tail Lieutenant is trying his best to get Gunny in trouble. From the little bit I got out of

Gunny, this sergeant Wright is a good friend of the Gunny, plus he knows the UCMJ better than most JAG Lawyers. The Gunny told me to tell you to call the Sergeant Major."

I scooted up in the chair, when Father Donahue queried, "I don't mind you using my phone. The conference I had to attend came up suddenly. What I want to know is how you managed to use my phone. I'm given a book of the control numbers, and the phone won't even work unless I put the right control number in."

I was scratching my ear and looked up at the Priest. "The control number we used did not affect the number you were assigned."

"I have not received any call since I sat in this chair this morning. Why didn't Gunny come to me?"

I'm not sure, oh hell I am convinced. What this Lieutenant is trying is trying to get Gunny off this ship. Gunny doesn't want you to get in trouble."

The Priest slid his chair back and stood, "Connor, Track down Gunny and have him meet me in the library."

Aren't you going to wait for the call from the Sergeant Major?"

"Yancy will be here. He can take a message, although if he hasn't called my noon, I don't expect him to call."

As I turned to exit the office, the Priest stood and said apologetically, "I am so sorry Connor. I should have listened to you and the Gunny. Seems like I always had the impression that most attorneys were honorable. Oh, I'm not quite as naïve as many people think. Accurate, my head may seem locked in the clouds, which may not be a bad thing for a Priest, but I was not always a Priest, and

I should have been wary. I have a feeling we may have a monster aboard."

I would look for Gunny, but right then I had to get back to my section. Lately, I've been feeling that Baily is just waiting for me to screw up. I started out on this ship with me being a Second-Class Petty Officer and Baily being my supervisor. He is still my supervisor. I didn't see me being promoted, at least right then. It seems as if my college degree showed up, and given that I spent a very brief time teaching high school chemistry. That chemistry thing, I am sure to put me on the fast track to get my rate, rank back.

Sure enough, Bailly was waiting at the foot of the ladderwell to our section room with a little sarcasm, "Fitzgerald, I see that you could join us. I'm not even going to ask where you were, but in the future, would you give me the courtesy of letting me know that you will be late. Oh, and by the way, if you decide not to join us for formation, please let me know."

Wow! Is he pissed? "Baily, honestly I did leave word that I was checking on the arrival of a part." I don't think he bought it for a minute.

"Bull Shit! I don't know how you have managed to snow so many people, but from now on, please let me know something so I do not continually look like a jackass. Now if you wouldn't mind joining us for a little brainstorming."

It was noon when I finally caught up with the Gunnery Sergeant. I told him what Father Donahue had said and that they were to get together in the Library.

"If you run into the Padre, tell him I'll see him real soon, but I have to take care of a few things. Oh yeah, were you able to reach the Sergeant Major?"

"I called Iwakuni last night. We had to go through the Base Locator. He assured us that he would make sure that Sergeant Major Wright would get the message. He hasn't called back yet."

"So, you got Father Donahue to call Iwakuni?"

"Not exactly."

I could see the blood rising in Gunny's face.

I'd never heard Gunnery Sergeant's voice crack before, "**Not** exactly?"

"Father Donahue was not aboard the ship last night. So Yancy, his clerk, and Tanner made the call."

Gunnery Sergeant put is head down in his hands. Looked at me, "Connor, you're a sweet boy, but why didn't you just get on the 1MC and announce that the Gunnery Sergeant has been charged with not one but several violations of the UCMJ, and will probably be spending his retirement in prison? Who is this Tanner?"

"Tanner is an IC Electrician who got the control numbers for us to be able to try and get hold of the Sergeant Major."

"Go on, Connor. I'll catch up with the Padre."

I was in the chow line and heard my name. It was Baily. "Fitzgerald, it seems our Master Chief Benedetto, you remember our Master at Arms, well he would like you to stop by at your convenience. I'm pretty sure that means now."

For some reason I was hungry, but it doesn't look like I'll be eating anytime soon.

What in the world does the Chief Master at Arms want? Am I in trouble? Can that Special Agent write me up? I know he can arrest me. But for what? I deliberately tried to keep a low profile. I just came back in the Navy to finish my time, and **not** make waves. My dream was and is to get promoted to Chief and find a place to retire. Maybe someplace warm? I do not have a desire to rock this boat or any other boat. Samoa! That's it if a seaman can live like a king in America Samoa. A retired Chief?

The only thing on my tray was a peach. I grabbed the peach and handed the metal tray back to Baily. Baily did not look pleased. Not an unusual state for the way Baily reacts to me.

I trotted into the head, through cold water on my face and attempted to comb my hair. I did not feel well about my summons to see the Chief Master at Arms. It seemed to take forever to get to the hangar bay, and then cross it and then climb the ladderwell to the Master at Arms shack, it wasn't really a shack.

First Class Petty Officer Collins was a Machinist Mate when I first met him. He is now officially part of the Master at Arms force. Collins appeared to have a correspondence course open on his desk with several other study manuals. I wasn't all that comfortable with the look that Collins gave me as he pointed to Chief Benedetto's office.

This has not been one of my better days. You know it is not going to be a good day when the first thing you find out is that the Chaplain is mad at you. Your section supervisor unloads his feeling about you, you are called up to visit with the Chief of Police, or as he is called aboard the ship the Chief Master at Arms.

Chapter Seventeen

Once again I had the feeling that I should be standing in front of Chief Benedetto's desk at attention with a sharp salute. "Chief Benedetto reporting as requested."

The Chief looked up at me and replied, "As you are aware, Chief Isaac is at the Disciplinarian Barracks preparing for his Article 32 hearing. If Court Martialed and convicted, it would mean that the Chief would lose his retirement. I'm sure I do not need to go into all that. The long and short is he has suggested that you are storing, or holding illicit drugs. That you, in fact, are behind the drug problems we have been having." The Chief stood up from his desk turned his back and stretched. "Oh! I've been curious and meaning to ask this question since we left the yards in San Francisco?"

After a few minutes of silence, I asked, "OK, what did you want to know?"

"Simple. With all the space on this ship, why is it necessary to use a cargo hold as a workshop?"

"It's just easier to work on our machinery in a place where we can also store our CBR equipment. Lugging the Red Devils up and down ladders has become a problem.

We are near an elevator, so if we need to get the smoke out of a compartment on the upper decks, it just makes it more convenient."

Chief Benedetto walked over to the doorway to his office, turned back towards me and encouraged me, "Sit Fitzgerald, it will be a few minutes. One other thing? I've checked, and your expenses are not that much.

You have no wife no kids. You don't appear to be that interested in partying. You don't even care about authority or power. Why deal in drugs?"

"Chief Benedetto, I do not do drugs, hell, I don't drink or smoke. I would never hold or sell drugs. You've got my jacket." The Chief gave me a stare. "My Service Jacket. Before I returned to the Navy, I taught at a Juvenile

Correction facility. I know what drugs do to people."

The Chief scratched his head, and said, "We'll wait here until my men get back from lunch. I believe the Special Agent on Board wants to be here. Then I'm told there is a locker or a cabinet down in the number 4 cargo hold, where the drugs are supposed to be held."

"I don't have a locker in number 4. There are a workbenches and storage bins for our chemical suits and masks. That's it."

"Well, Fitzgerald you should have nothing to worry about."

"I do have one question."

What's that?"

"How would the Chief Corpsman know about illicit drugs aboard ship?"

"Good question. Would you like to be represented by? counsel?"

"Am I under arrest?"

"Not yet." Chief Benedetto unwrapped a cigar, licked it like he was licking a licorice stick plopped down in the chair behind his desk. Reaching in the top drawer of his desk he pulled out a pack of matches. Biting the end of the cigar off and striking the match then with some effort drawing in he managed to blow out smoke near my face. I do not think he meant to upset me. I've noticed that smokers, not all smokers but particularly those that smoke cigars, have no idea that there may be people that do not enjoy the smell of cigar smoke. Two things came to my mind. First, I might just be waiting a while, the second I might as well take Chief Benedetto's invitation to sit.

Scooting up near the desk I asked, "How long will we be waiting for the rest of the Master at Arms?"

Leaning back in his chair, Chief Benedetto replied, they have a few spaces that need that need to be checked out. Some of our sailors like to do a little gambling at lunch. Oh, yeah, our very own Special Agent would want to be present when we go through your personal items."

"Look I told you Chief, the only articles in the cargo hold are things used for Damage Control; no personal items."

"We don't really bust anybody for gambling, but the MA on the armband seems to get everyone's attention." Chief Benedetto looked down at his watch, pulled a Field and Streams magazine out of his desk drawer.

I've never, or at least I do not recall ever having trouble with my blood sugar, but today I skipped breakfast and was abruptly asked to get out the lunch line. I'd finished the peach and was looking in the wastebasket at the pit.

I was just a little light-headed, so I scooted closer to the desk and put my head on my folded arms. Amazing I managed to doze off. I did not eat the peach seed.

"Ouch!" It felt like my arm was about to break. I didn't know what was causing the pain in my right shoulder and elbow, but I kicked the chair I was sitting in back, pulled and turned while shoving my right elbow into a soft solar plexus. I knew it had to be that spot between an upper rib cage and a heart. I heard what sounded like a dog trying to puke. I turned and looked at the doorway where Collins was just looking down at the deck. The Chief was attempting to stub out his cigar. He looked at me and then at the deck.

Special Agent Gabriel was sitting cross-legged and bent over with his handcuffs in his lap, and his face the color of an eggplant. Gabriel was finally able to whisper/grunt, "Chief I want you to lock" with a shaky finger pointed at me, "that man up. I want him charged with assault on a Federal Agent."

Chief Benedetto looked over at Petty Officer Collins and remarked, "Petty Officer, did you see the Special Agent fall?"

Walking around his desk, Chief Benedetto looked down at the Special Agent, and with an authoritative voice, the chief remarked, "Gabriel, are you really a Federal Agent?" I'm not sure, but I think Gabriel was reaching for his tin. "You can put that badge away."

Chief Benedetto walked closer to the Special Agent. When the Agent reached up for a hand, the Chief Master at Arms turned, walked away and sat back down behind his desk. Watching as Gabriel pushed himself off the deck,

Chief Benedetto said, "If" pointing at me. "has anything incriminating it is useless."

"But he's a suspect in an on-going investigation."

"No! Gabriel, he is not even a person of interest. If Fitzgerald decides he does not want us looking at his personal items, we do not have a leg to stand on. Even if he gives us permission, and we find a meth lab we cannot use it as evidence."

Our Special Agent could not have been too bright. He asked that we go down to the cargo hold and look inside this so-called locker.

After the Chief made it clear that if we needed a witness, we would find another one.

I felt as if vultures were starting to circle. Two more of the Master at Arms team showed up and were just watching like they were planning to swoop down on a rotting carcass.

The Chief Master at Arms reached into an open desk drawer and grabbed a candy bar and handed it to me. Nodding his head toward one of his Master at Arms team,

"Johnson get this piece of shit Special Agent out of my sight."

Trying to tuck his bulging belly under his strained belt, "Now Fitzgerald, I hope I am right, but I do not feel you are selling drugs." He was mumbling something like

'Very unprofessional.'

Down in the hold with what seemed like the entire Master at Arms force and two commissioned officers watching, with apparently no clue of what they were doing. Chief Benedetto asked, "Alright Fitzgerald open the locker." He had squatted down in front of the locker, fingering the padlock "Open the cabinet."

"Chief, like I told you I do not have a key for that locker." With effort and sounds that I had not heard before the Chief stood. Looking over his shoulder, "Did someone bring the bolt cutter?"

With several tries, the padlock finally snapped. In the locker were baggies of what I could only assume were drugs. There was a white powder, a brownish powder. There were drawers on the very bottom of the cabinet with bags of loll-pops.

The Chief forced latex gloves on his hands, Collins went to reach in the locker, without thinking I brushed his hand away. Collins Snapped, "What the hell?"

The Chief raised his head and motioned for me to come closer. Staring at the baggies, he asked, "Fitzgerald you know what this is. What is it? How did you know what it was?"

"It's Fentanyl. You were here in this hold when we found Jenkins. Father Donahue had seen it before. It is so toxic that all a person has to do is touch it and it can kill." I pointed to the lolly-pops. "I'm not sure, but those lollypops are laced with Fentanyl."

The Chief had one of the Master at Arms notify the Hazmat team to come to number 4 hold with protective suits on.

"If this is not your storage locker whose is it? I'm talking to you, Fitzgerald."

"Chief, I don't know. All these months I thought it belonged to the Marines. I mean it does look like a weapons locker."

I went after the meatloaf, mashed potatoes, and glazed carrots like a drunk. I do need to check out my blood sugar.

Someone grabbed my arm. Turning I saw it was Gunnery Sergeant Cortez. "Gunny, how are you. Did your friend ever get back to you?"

"He'll be here, but in the meantime, he sent one of the JAGs from Iwakuni here. He got hold of the evidence they are holding on me. He said they have nothing. That I corrected the discrepancies. He also mentioned that a good officer commands respect.

"The Padre's going to be in the office after 2000, that is if you're up to it. I heard your day was a little hectic."

"I got to check in with my boss, but I should be there," I replied.

"Honest Gunny, I am not paranoid. I know there are people out to get me. First, my supervisor tells me I have a superiority complex. Then Chief Isaac accuses me of dealing drugs. The only conversation I ever had with our senior corpsman was about getting a nasal spray and a decongestant.

"Ya know I've always had a bad feeling about your lieutenant. He wants us out of here. He wants to throw his weight around, and I wouldn't be at all surprised if it were the Lieutenant that let the word out that I was storing drugs in a locker in the cargo hold."

Father Donahue was just watching Gunny and me. He did clear his throat once, but when we looked at him, he made no attempt to make a comment.

I watched the Gunnery sergeant as he tasted the new blend of coffee. What an expression! Gunny, after a coughing spasm finally mentioned, "Are these really coffee beans?"

Father Donahue pushed his glasses up off the tip of his nose, "Frank, I thought you might like the little bite in the coffee?"

"No Father. I'd rather have my jalapeño with my tacos."

Pointing to the counter, there was another pot. "I think you'll like that other coffee. I know you've been going through a lot. I kind of wanted to lighten the mood." Replied the Chaplain.

Quiet, nothing but peace. Even the machinery usually running was silent. There was a slight sound of a generator someplace, but most of the power that was keeping our lights and blowers running was supplied by the Yokosuka Shipyards.

Seemed like Father Donahue found something of interest in tamping tobacco into his pipe. Gunny had his hands wrapped around his coffee mug. Although like I mentioned there is a buzz of the generator running. It reminds me of life. Many years ago, I boarded one of those ships that were in what we call the Boneyard; Now that is an eerie sound. The sound of your own breathing and the beating of your own heart. No, this ship was still alive.

Father Donahue, was now looking at the overhead, better known by some as the ceiling. I guess he could have been counting the holes in the overhead tile.

Gunnery Sergeant Cortez still staring at his hands finally spoke, I am not the least bit tired. I am going to check the watch and then head down to the Chief's Quarters and try to become unconscious. I will stay still and close my eyes. I got a message just before I came here that my counsel would meet me at 0900 hours. He evidently got permission to you the old Warrant Officer Mess." Gunny stood and stretched, his joints seemed to be singing their own song.

Father Donahue tapped out the ashes of his pipe, then asked, "Gunny, An Article 32 is like a Grand Jury Hearing, right? Does a person normally get a counselor for the hearing?"

Gunny was standing in front of the Chaplain's desk when he answered, "Your right. The hearing is to show evidence and sworn statements that there, in fact, is enough to bring the charges in a Courts Marshall. I'm not even sure who my counselor is. I can only assume that when you called the Sergeant Major, that he contacted a lawyer for me."

I stood stretched and yawned. I think if someone were to take a picture it would show a beautiful portrait of my tonsils.

Father scooted his chair back and said, "Gunny, before you go and try to rest can I pray for you?" The Priest turned to me and said, "And You Connor. Would you pray with us?"

What could I say? I've never really conflicted with the belief in an omnipotent being. And it seems to me that the more people deny the existence of as a supreme being the more they keep finding answers that only make people more aware of something that is bigger and smarter than us.

Do I believe? I think of it like this. Those that don't believe might be right, but what if they're not.

"Yes, Father I would like to pray with you and the Gunnery Sergeant." I stood beside Gunny and Father

Donahue. And there we were three grown men holding hands and praying.

I kind of accidentally on purpose walked past the old Warrant Officer's Mess. The Navy did away with the Warrant officer rank. The old Warrant Officer Mess is still up and thriving. They no longer cook in the Warrant Officer's Mess, but it is kept clean and sanitary. The coffee is always fresh, and if a young officer was wandering he might even find sweet rolls

When one of Stewart's carrying in a coffee pot and fresh rolls pulled the curtain back, I peeked inside the mess. There were folders and what appeared to be law books scattered all over a large table. There was a lofty Marine in aviator greens with his back to me. He moved like an officer, and all I could see was the back of his head; his hair was a white as snow.

I was anxious to find out what the lawyer told the Gunnery Sergeant. I lingered a little on the mess deck, having some more bug juice. I looked at my watch and guessed that I wasted enough time.

The Chaplain's office was a quiet as a tomb. The Marine with white hair was pacing back and forth with a cup of the Chaplain's special coffee.

Gunny looked up and caught my eye, he motioned me to come in. "Come in Connor. We were just about to talk about the upcoming hearing. By the Way" Gunny turned to the Marine, "this is Colonel Whiteside." Lifting his hand toward the Colonel. "The Colonel was not always a lawyer.

We were in Korea together. When he showed up this morning, it made my day."

"Father you'll understand, but if you are going to talk about Gunny's upcoming hearing, I need to leave. What a client tells me or the advice I give my client I am not allowed to divulge. This Article 32 Hearing is the equivalent of a Grand Jury.one of the differences is that an Article 32 hearing is open to spectators. So, I will take my leave. And Frank I'll meet you at the Disciplinary Barracks at 0900."

"Colonel, are you staying aboard, or do you need me to walk you to the Quarterdeck?" Asked Gunnery Sergeant Cortez.

"Thanks, Gunny, but I have room at the BOQ. The O Club offers a pretty good breakfast. I'll see you in the morning."

"Colonel, if you won't let me walk you to the quarterdeck. Let me get one of my Marines to take you?" Queried Gunny.

I didn't sleep all that well. As a matter a fact for a tea drinker I am finding myself drinking more and more coffee. I felt like right then, and there I could use one of the Chaplain's unique blends of coffee.

I did not look forward to what I had to do. I had Damage Control people in most of the spaces, compartments, machines shops, of course, the food service areas. The people assigned to these spaces did most of the cleaning, but each one of these spaces had drainage area where either the moisture of the fans, blowers and in some spaces refrigeration. The drain itself was usually brass, which looked very shiny when polished. Water constantly dripping on brass causing the brass to turn green which means fungus.

I kept looking at my watch like I was in a hurry to go someplace. Gunny's hearing starts at 0900. I mean what I am doing, and the rest of the division is doing is busy work. If they see a sailor with a mop or a rag those above might think we are doing something.

Gunny's Article 32 hearing is open to the public. I know if I were up there I'd want to know my friends were close by, but then My most favorite supervisor is bound to say something smart about me getting special privileges. I looked down and noticed a rag in my hand, and I had been rubbing on one of the brass drains. It felt as if I was rubbing the same pipe forever; the fungus was shiny, but I could not get rid of it.

Hot sauce! That's what I need. Hot sauce will cut the nastiest fungus. I placed the rag and the bucket I was using out of the way and marked it. I intended to go to the galley and get some hot sauce. I pushed my cleaning material to the side stood. I was wiping my hands on my dungaree pants when another one of my favorite people stopped me.

I noticed this time that he didn't get that close to me. He did not ask very nicely, "Fitzgerald, put your hands behind your back!" Special Agent Gabriel demanded.

"What's this all about?" I grumbled.

Once he had my wrist shackled he grabbed the collar of the dungaree shirt and dragged me in front of him. His face was so close to me I could see the razor burn on his face. He finally spoke, "OK, Fitzgerald we have another dead sailor. Seems that happens a lot around you."

"What! You're charging me with murder?"

Gabriel now was putting pressure on my wrist and elbows. "Yes, how convenient. One man says that you are dealing drugs, and he conveniently winds up poisoned. The other man finds his throat cut in a secure brig. You had contact with both men. Oh yeah! I don't have to tell you this, after all, it is about you. Fitzgerald, you are kind of an expert with chemicals. You taught chemistry in high school. I bet with all the spaces you have access to, you could have your own lab." My scalp was starting to itch. I really wanted to scratch my head. The cuffs on my wrist made that problematic.

"Special Agent, am I under arrest?"

Two Marines were standing near the entrance of the machine shop where five minutes ago I was trying to get the green fungus out of the drip drains.

The Special Agent motioned with his hand for the Marines to escort me.

Gabriel was behind me, and apparently, I was not moving fast enough as my shins were now numb from tripping over the coaming, or the raised lip around the hatches. I tried to turn my head to look at Gabriel, but he just shoved me harder. I think the Marines were starting to get annoyed. "Special Agent, where are we going? There's an interrogation room up in the Master at Arms space." I queried.

The Marines were both large men. I couldn't read their name tags, but one was a large redheaded Lance Corporal, the other was built like a small tank. I noticed his eyes were a dark blue. Both Marines stopped abruptly."

Gabriel almost whined as he said, "What are you doing.

You men just keep moving. I'll tell you where to stop." The Lance Corporal stopped.

Gabriel yelled, "What are you doing?"

Responding the Lance Corporal calmly stated, "We were told to treat you as a guest, who happens to be a Federal Law Enforcement Officer. You, sir, are not part of our chain of command, and we will not move from this spot until I get direction from the Sergeant of the Guard." The Lance Corporal put his portable radio to his lips and called for the Sergeant of the Guard.

The Lance Corporal grabbed the keys to the cuffs and released my wrists. The other Marine told me to go back to my duty station.

Special Agent Gabriel's face had was becoming a bright red. Sputtering with drool running down his chin, and shaking his hand in the direction of the Marines, Special Agent Gabriel managed to utter, "You two have just interfered with a Federal Agent in the performance of his duties. Your supervisor, oh yeah, your supervisor is waiting for a Courts-Martial. Your OIC will hear about this."

"Special Agent, you do what you think you have to do. I am not going anywhere."

I made it. At least I think I did. I've loaded my tray with fresh salad. It's Thursday Steak night. The steak is grilled, but they do a pretty good job of cooking the steak to order. My stomach is a little queasy. I guess being accused of murder does that.

Almost finished my salad. Two bites of the medium ribeye. I loaded my baked potato with butter and sour cream. The baked potato was cooked to perfection; you got two bites. Chef Macintosh was standing next to the scullery. He was there because there had been a lot of waste. People were taking more than they could eat. I was sure the Chief was going to say something to me. He just glared.

Sticking my head in the Chaplain's office, I think I surprised the Priest he seemed to be concentrating on something on his desk. "Oh, Connor. Did you need to talk to me?"

"I was just wondering if you had heard anything from Gunny?"

The Priest raised his head and scratched his chin, then replied, "As a matter of fact. The hearing has been postponed until tomorrow. He called back for one of his men to pick up a clean, pressed dress uniform."

"Why couldn't they finish the hearing. There is either evidence or not." I must have had a weird look on my face.

Father Donahue pushed his chair back from his desk, stood, walked around the desk and commented, "You don't know?"

"Know what father? Did something happen to Gunny?"
"No Gunny is fine. However, Chief Isaac is dead. Apparently murdered. From what I heard the Chief's body was a bright pink, his lips were black. The Base medical examiner said it looked like cyanide poisoning. The M.E. said he would get back with Doc Miller as soon as they did the autopsy."

I plopped down in the green chair. "That explains my day."

Father Donahue was standing over me. "OK, Connor out with it?"

"Well, let me tell you about my day. My boss told me he thought I was a snob. Special Agent Gabriel Arrested me for murder."

Connor, I would have told you about Isaac. I really thought you knew. Anyway, I haven't seen you all day. I sure didn't want to get on the 1MC and announce it to the crew."

I turned to leave, stopped and asked, "So where is Gunny now?"

"He had one of his troops bring him a change of clothes and his shaving kit. He'll be spending the night at the CPO Barracks."

I turned back around to face the Priest, "I'll see you after Mass tomorrow."

"What!" Father Donahue just stare at me for what seemed like more than a few seconds, then he said, "After Mass?"

"You still say Mass in the library every morning?"

The Padre went back behind his desk and pulled out his pipe and remarked, "Sorry kiddo. Yes, I still say mass in the library every morning. That is every morning that we are not at Battle Stations. I just never thought I would hear that sentence come out of your mouth."

Chapter Eighteen

I was up and in the storage hold well before reveille.

That Special Agent called me a chemist. I'm pretty sure a chemist must be organized. Looking at the files, I've laid out on the counter, I don't think anyone would call me organized. They're mostly personnel files. The idea was to have them in alphabetic order plus by Divisions. That didn't go well.

Staring into space. I think I may have been watching the dust form on the table in front of me. I looked down at my watch, "shit!" That's all I need is to be late for formation.

I was sitting on a lab stool. I slid off the stool and kicked it out of the way. When I looked up, a Marine Staff Sergeant was standing in front of me.

"Petty Officer Fitzgerald, I'm Marine Staff Sergeant Cory, and I need you to come with me." "Am I in trouble?" I inquired.

The Staff Sergeant looked at me, and replied, "I really couldn't say, but the Captain wants you in his office."

"I'm in trouble. I didn't know the Captain had an office."

We started walking when the Staff Sergeant Commented, "If you'd ever been to Captain's Mast you would have known."

I've been all over this ship, but that walk seemed like it was taking forever. The Marine knocked on a door. The name Captain Briggs was stenciled on the door.

As we walked in, I saw the Captain's face and the backs of two chief petty officers and that windbreaker that our Special Agent Afloat was wearing. Everyone including the civilian seemed to be at attention. The Captain barked. "At ease!"

The Captain did not sit. He motioned for the Special Agent to come forward and then in a very calm voice said, "Special Agent Gabriel, I want you off my ship." He was quiet for what seemed like an eternity.

Gabriel spoke up, "Sir you cannot do that."

I don't think the Captain wanted to hear that.

The captain's face was starting to show a little color, "Special Agent Gabriel, this is my ship, and I damn well can do it. I can do most anything I want, and right now I want you off my ship."

The Special Agent started to speak. The Captain held up his hand and said, "I do not owe you an explanation, but if you feel you needed to know I will try to explain it. This may be the Navy, but my people and that includes the military have rights. Just like on the streets. We have protection against unwarranted searches. We have a right to be told of any charges against us. We do not have to answer any questions about a crime without being represented by counsel. I do not know where you got your credentials. I do hope that this new organization has better-trained people than you. Take your complaints to whoever."

The Special Agent had not moved. The Captain looked over at him and stared for about five seconds. Raising his hand, he snapped, "Now get out of my sight!"

I was still standing in front of the Captain's desk. Chief Blood was on my right, and Chief Benedetto was to my left. Benedetto spoke, "Fitzgerald, I want you to make like a mouse." Chief Benedetto must have noticed that blank stare I had. "We are going to have a little sting. I am sure we have a traitor and a murderer on board. Today we are going to get the good on him."

Chief Blood looking as usual like a man who has spent way too much time in the sun and the sea turned toward the door and motioned for the Marine Staff Sergeant to enter. "This is Staff Sergeant Cory. I want him to shadow you today. If you can use his help, that's fine. However, if he suggests you leave your workspace, please follow his instructions."

I was thinking to myself. *Maybe I should get me one of them Marine Staff Sergeants.* Cory was fast, and he seemed to have a knack for organization. We finished alphabetizing and were in the process of putting the chemical suits in order of size. I had received several pairs of glasses and was just about to look up the names of the people that needed glasses in the protective masks when the staff Sergeant suggested we leave our little hole.

It was too early for lunch, so Staff Sergeant Cory and I were having a refreshment. I can only say I am glad I was drinking tea. The coffee that Cory was drinking was so strong and so stale that a person could stand a spoon in the middle and it would not fall.

The staff Sergeant pointed at about a half-dozen men in olive drab fatigues and carrying M16s. "If you'd like and you promise to stand behind me we can follow those men and maybe see a little action?

Hanging back and trying to stay hidden we watched as the six men entered the number 4 hold. The six men fanned out and get themselves pretty much out of sight. I saw Lieutenant Reese had for what I had always assumed was a weapons cabinet. The Lieutenant reached into his pocket and pulled out a set of keys.

It looked as if the Lieutenant was trying each key to no avail. It looked like Reese was about to leave the storage area. He stopped and stared for a few minutes then went over to the Damage Control area where he grabbed a bolt cutter.

Back to the weapons cabinet, he popped the lock. We were all close enough to see a half dozen RPGs (Rocket Propelled Grenade Launcher), and a dozen m16s.

I turned to Cory and whispered "What." That is when he put his hand over my mouth.

By the time the Lieutenant turned around the entire armed team had him surrounded. He was searched, and one of the team members found a vile of what looked like powder. It looked me like that team member was about to open the vile.

That is when I yelled, and that is when the Lieutenant decided to run. He still the bolt cutter in his hand. I broke away from the Staff sergeant and was in the process of tackling the Lieutenant. Reese swung around and caught me right on the knee. It did stop the Lieutenant, and he was informed that he was under arrest. He was informed of the charges which included falsifying documents, false statements, and misappropriation of military weapons.

Lieutenant Reese was placed in the ship's brig, guarded by the Marines that once worked for him.

Gunny returned to the ship where he had the pleasure of escorting First Lieutenant Reese to the Yokosuka Brig. Charges of treason and murder were added. The powder in the vile was ground peach seeds; cyanide. It was never proven that he killed the Samoan.

Gunny was promoted to Master Sergeant. He turned down the promotion and put his papers in for retirement. Father Donahue requested an assignment with the Marines in Vietnam. Last, I heard he was with the Third Marines in Vietnam. I was offered a replacement for my left knee; I refused. I have become pretty good at using a cane. The Navy offered, and I accepted a medical retirement.

www.ingramcontent.com/pod-product-compliance
Lightning Source LLC
LaVergne TN
LVHW021046100526
838202LV00079B/4589